# UNSOLICITED CONTACT

LAURA SNIDER

SEVERN RIVER PUBLISHING

# ALSO BY LAURA SNIDER

**Ashley Montgomery Legal Thrillers**

Unsympathetic Victims

Undetermined Death

Unforgivable Acts

Unsolicited Contact

Unexpected Defense

To find out more about Laura Snider and her books, visit

severnriverbooks.com/authors/laura-snider

*For all victims of sexual violence, stalking, and other predatory behaviors.*
*You are strong.*
*You deserve peace.*
*You are not alone.*

# PROLOGUE

Monday, December 2

Amanda's feet crunched against the crushed rock as she ran along the local biking trail. Her throat stung as she sucked in large gulps of air. The cold was sharp as it sliced its way into her lungs before bursting out in a gust of carbon dioxide, visible in the frigid Iowa air. It was a typical morning in early December. That time of day when the sun was barely peeking over the horizon at the start of her run, but it would be in full shine by the time she rounded that final curve and called it quits.

Lake Goldenhead glittered off in the distance, the red light of the sun reaching across its surface. Amanda lived and worked in a town called Brine. She worked as a veterinary assistant at a small clinic. This biking trail—the one she had been running on every morning for the past week— stretched hundreds of miles throughout Iowa, coming from the east, passing through Brine and traveling west until it cut through Des Moines and on westward through the state. It was an old railroad track, converted to a trail after disuse rendered this particular track obsolete.

As she ran, she wound her way toward the lake, trying not to think of the conversation she'd had with her friend Michelle the night before. She was failing. Her mind bounced around during runs, which was often a good thing because it allowed her to work out difficult problems. But no matter how hard she tried to focus on other things—like Christmas lists and weekly meal plans—her mind kept circling back to Michelle.

It had been girls' night out last night. Two for the price of one cocktails at Mikey's Tavern, which usually resulted in a late night and a raging headache in the morning. Amanda had announced that she was leaving after only two cocktails, stating that she needed to keep to her running routine. Michelle had pleaded with her to change her mind, but Amanda had stated that she couldn't possibly stay later. She was on a diet and there were a lot of calories in every drink, even vodka. Michelle, as her best friend, should have understood. But she hadn't.

Michelle had begged her to stay, saying that the night had only begun, but Amanda hadn't budged. She had gained five pounds over the Thanksgiving holiday, and she needed to lose it before she gained another five at Christmas. Her current boyfriend was close to dropping her, and she couldn't let that happen. It wasn't because she truly *cared* about this one. It was more that she was tired of being the only single one in her friend group. These girls' nights were only once a month. The rest of the time Michelle had her husband at her side. Showing up alone was getting tiring. Girls' nights were the only time that she didn't feel like an extra unwanted, unused wheel, and that was why she'd gone at all, despite her diet.

So, after two drinks, she settled her bill and called it quits. When she'd gotten up and started threading her arms through her coat sleeves, that was when Michelle had said it.

*Suit yourself,* Michelle had said, *but you won't catch me running on those isolated trails. That's like an invitation for a serial killer to nab you. The only thing more dangerous is prostitution.*

The very thought of a serial killer sent a chill up Amanda's spine. It was Michelle's intended effect. She could be cruel like that sometimes. Especially when she didn't get what she wanted. A last-ditch effort to deter Amanda from her goals, to keep her in Michelle's orbit, doing as Michelle wanted her to do.

*That's ridiculous,* Amanda had said, waving her hand in a way she'd hoped would seem dismissive, despite the heavy beating of her heart.

*Don't you watch those crime shows?* Michelle had said.

The question was rhetorical. Michelle had known that the answer was a resounding "no." Amanda used to watch shows like *Dateline* and *Forensic Files*, but that was before her sister had been brutally murdered five years earlier. It was her sister's husband, Arnold von Reich, that had killed poor Amy. Stabbed her right through the chest multiple times. But he never served his term in prison. His attorney, Ashley Montgomery, had gotten him out of it. Ever since then, Amanda hadn't had the stomach for or the interest in crime or the sham others called justice.

*Runners are always dying*, Michelle continued. *When they aren't, they're finding the corpses.*

Amanda cringed at the word corpses. It was a strange word. A once-living thing that no longer had that spark. Life. Something that was so difficult to create, especially as a woman got older. Amanda knew people who had been trying for months and even years to get pregnant, but without luck. Once they did, there were nine months of gestation with all kinds of safety rules like avoiding deli meat and staying away from cat litter, followed by eighteen years of raising a child to adulthood, and even then, let's be honest, they weren't actually adults for another ten years.

Yes, life was hard to create. But the flip side—the destruction of a life—could occur in a flash. A distraction on an interstate. A strong undertow on a private beach. A tornado dropping from the sky. An aneurysm traveling through the arteries and to the brain. An angry husband with a knife.

*Either way*, Michelle had said, *I wouldn't want any part of that. But you go ahead*, she'd made a shooing motion, *enjoy yourself.*

The conversation had rubbed Amanda the wrong way, chafing against her sensibilities all through the night, causing her to toss and turn. She'd slept like shit, and when she finally rolled out of bed, Michelle's words continued grating against her nerves all through her run. What had she been thinking when she'd spoken to Amanda like that? She had been insensitive at best, and cruel at worst, considering that she knew what had happened to Amanda's sister.

All these nerves, this agitation, were making Amanda feel jumpy when she was meant to feel at peace, enlightened by the silence of the morning and the stillness of the water. Running had always been an escape for her. She needed this. Not only for weight loss, but for her mental health. It helped to ease the sense of fury that came from her sister's murder and her murderer's acquittal.

She resolved to ignore her thoughts of Michelle. To calm the racing in her heart caused by last night's conversation. Thinking of death only heightened her anxiety, something she was really trying not to do since her doctor had recently announced she had "better get that blood pressure under control" or she'd have to start taking medications to regulate it. She hated pills. They were unnatural. And so was Michelle's attitude. She wasn't going to let Michelle frighten her out of her running habit.

Then she saw something out in the water. An ordinary item that caught her eye. It came into view just as the path reached the edge of the lake and turned so it ran parallel to the gleaming water. Something was out there bobbing in the tree debris lining the bank. She studied it as she drew nearer, slowing her pace.

*What is it?* She wondered. Then she realized it was a box or a crate of some kind, floating in the water.

*Ignore it.* She told herself. But she found that she couldn't. The sun was striking it in just the right way so the light ricocheted off the lid and directly into Amanda's eyes. It was like driving past a car crash. She couldn't help slowing down to rubberneck. Sometimes painful to see but impossible to ignore.

She should have kept running, but Amanda had a sudden, sharp urge to investigate. It pulled her toward the shore of the lake, like a moth to a lamp. In the coming weeks and months, she would ask herself more than a thousand times why she had done it, why she hadn't just minded her own business, and she would never come up with a more satisfactory answer than curiosity. She must have been a cat in a former life, because she walked right up to the floating box, studying it from the outside.

*Why is it floating?* She'd grown up boating on this lake, and the box wasn't in one of the shallow portions.

Once she was nearer, she recognized the type of box. It was one of those tool chests that fit snugly into the back of pickup trucks. Silver with raised squiggly ledges all over it. Her boyfriend had one just like it in the back of his Ford F-150. It was a common thing for most trucks in these rural parts of Iowa because as her boyfriend always put it, *you never know when you'll need a set of tools*. And he was right. Houses in the country were spread out, and tools were there for fixing. They were no good sitting in a garage thirty miles away.

It was odd, this toolbox in the lake, but it wasn't her business. And Amanda was not nosy. Or at least not as nosy as some people. Now, Genie, the owner of Genie's Diner, she was nosy. Amanda turned on her heel, deciding to mind her own business, but she again thought about the weight of those toolboxes. They were heavy, weren't they? Yeah. They had to be. Especially when they had tools inside them. So, what was making this one float? Something had to be in it, right? But what?

Against her better judgment, she moved closer. She found a long branch that had fallen from a nearby tree and used it to guide the toolbox toward the bank. It was heavy as she maneuvered it with the branch, and she grunted under its weight until she heard the side clunk against the rocks edging the lake. Then she moved closer.

She couldn't help wondering what was inside. The hopeful little girl buried deep inside her thought that it was perhaps a hidden treasure. Something buried for safekeeping. There were other options, of course, but she didn't allow the darker side of her mind to make a conjecture. The chest was locked with a rusted-out padlock, but whether because of the elements or a faulty lock, the latch hadn't held. With a quick jerk, it came apart.

Amanda rested her hands on the top of the lid, giving herself one last moment to change her mind. Should she be doing this? Whatever the box held was not hers, even if it was valuable. Or was it? Her heart fluttered in her chest, beating wildly, like it knew something important was inside. Something that would separate her world into two, before she found the box and after.

*Maybe I should call the authorities*, Amanda thought, but she quickly decided against it.

What would she tell them when they showed up? *There's a box and it scared me*. No, that would be ridiculous. If she did something like that, it wouldn't take long for word to get out. Everyone in central Iowa would know about it by midday—little, prissy Amanda, so afraid of a box that she called the cops. She'd be the laughingstock of Brine County. She could tolerate a lot of things, but public ridicule was not one of them.

Sucking in one last breath of air, she placed her hands on top of the box and heaved. She noticed the stench the moment the lid started to rise. It struck her like a physical assault, causing her to gag. It was a strong, clinging sort of smell, like the kind that sticks to a dog after an unfortunate meeting with a skunk. But it wasn't a skunk that she was smelling. It was something far worse. A distinct smell that she would never forget. One that clawed its way into her soul.

The smell coupled with the briefest glance inside had her yelping, stumbling back and falling to the ground.

"Oh, my God. Oh, my God. Oh, my God." The words tumbled out of her unbidden. Because the contents of the box were unmistakable. It was a decomposing body. Of that, she felt certain. The person was adult sized, curled up inside the toolbox with her knees to her chin. It was a woman, judging by her long hair. Amanda didn't know whose body it was, not in the fleeting second she'd looked at it, but there was something familiar about the clothing.

She crawled backward, continuing to watch the box, like the body might burst out at any minute and come after her. Visions of the "Thriller" music video flashed through her mind, zombies bursting from the ground and dancing in the dark. She fought the urge to vomit. She stopped backing up when she felt the rough pebbles of the running trail digging into her palms. For some reason, it felt safe—or at least safer—and she fumbled in her pocket until she found her phone.

She had trouble dialing the numbers, 911. Her fingers were numb from the cold, and she was shaking with fear, but, finally, she managed it.

"911 what's your emergency," the dispatcher's bored voice said through the phone.

Amanda wanted to shake the woman. She wanted to shout, *Good God, how can you be so calm when I just found a dead body*, but, of course, the dispatcher didn't know that yet.

"I need help," Amanda finally said. "I found a toolbox."

"Okay."

"And there's a body in it."

The dispatcher paused for a long moment, then said, "Is the person breathing?"

"No."

"Did you check for a pulse?"

"Like, touch her? No. No. No. God, no." The very thought had Amanda gagging again.

"Will you check now?"

"No!"

"How do you know she's dead?"

"Because of the way she smells."

There was a long, drawn-out pause. "What's your location?"

"I don't know." Amanda looked around, desperately searching for a sign. "I'm on the running trail by Lake Goldenhead."

"You don't see any markers?"

It was full light out now. Amanda stood and turned. She didn't see anything. "No. But I was just about to finish my run. I am less than a mile from the parking lot at the trail head."

"I'll send someone out there." The dispatcher paused again. "This better not be a joke."

"Listen lady," Amanda said, her heart pounding in her chest, "I wish it were." Then she hung up and waited.

# 1

## ASHLEY

It was five o'clock when Ashley Montgomery gave up on sleep and drove into the office. She was the only public defender in a town of six thousand people. One would think that she couldn't possibly be all that busy—it was a small town, after all—but Brine was a blue-collar city with a casino, lots of methamphetamine, and a high crime rate.

As a result, she'd once again spent the night tossing and turning, her mind swirling with thoughts of open cases. There were seventy of them, all varying degrees of severity, and that was actually low for her. Unfortunately, a lower case count didn't automatically translate to low stress. She was still waking up at all hours of the night, plagued with thoughts of motions to file and arguments to make to the court.

Yet the early morning hours were Ashley's favorite time to work. The office was still. There were no phones ringing or clients stopping by, demanding to be seen even though they hadn't bothered to make an appointment. It was the only time of day that she could pull out a file and really work on it without interruptions. And that's what she did when she arrived at her office, right up until seven thirty, when she decided to turn on the police scanner.

The scanner had been Katie Mickey's idea. Implemented when she lost her job as a police officer and spent a year working with Ashley as an investigator. She'd thought it would be a way to get an early jump on cases, and she'd been right. Ashley had been shocked to find out the kinds of things Brine law enforcement said over the open radio.

Ashley was drafting a motion to suppress and only half listening to the radio chatter. Mostly it was routine calls to service. A dog missing—people actually called 911 for that—and a couple of theft complaints. Interesting, but nothing that caught her full interest. That all changed around seven forty-five when a female dispatcher's voice rang through, far more urgent than the usual chatter.

"What's the problem?" came Sheriff St. James's familiar drawl. He was the Brine County Sheriff, an elected official. A politician who spent most of his time shaking hands rather than dealing with emergencies. He was once a deputy himself, but he didn't dirty his hands out in the field anymore. He passed all that kind of work off to his deputies.

"A runner found a body," the dispatcher said.

"A human body?" said a voice all too familiar to Ashley.

This third voice belonged to George Thomanson, a former detective in the recently defunded and replaced Brine Police Department. At one time, Ashley had tolerated him, but his arrogance over the past few years had eroded her patience with him. He'd been hired by Sheriff St. James as a deputy, but the two hadn't always seen eye to eye, so despite his law enforcement experience, the sheriff had made him start over on the lowest rung of the ladder. She was no fan of the sheriff, but it was nice to see George knocked down a few pegs.

"Where at?" Sheriff St. James asked.

"In Lake Goldenhead," the dispatcher said.

"Ten-four," Sheriff St. James said. "Backup is on its way."

That was the end of the exchange. Ashley wondered how the body came to be in the lake at this time of year. It hadn't been warm enough for boating or swimming since September, and it wasn't cold enough for the lake to freeze, so nobody would have been out there ice fishing. Unless someone put the body there, which meant foul play. That, or suicide. But death by hypothermia or drowning weren't typical methods of suicide. Of course, it could be an accident—someone drunk and wandering around—

but it was the off season for the lake crowd. The hard partiers went elsewhere for the winter.

Part of her wanted to go out there and see events as they unfolded in real time, but the more reasonable portion of her brain reminded her that this paperwork wasn't going to finish itself. She always preferred *doing* something rather than writing motions and researching arguments but writing and researching were an important part of her job, one she couldn't put off.

If this had happened a year ago, Ashley would have sent Katie out to investigate, but she no longer worked for the Public Defender's Office. The funding for her position had only lasted a year, and the plan had always been for Katie to leave once the city council decided funding for a new organization called the Mental Health Response Team. Now that the MEHR team was up and running, Katie had her hands full leading the team and was no longer available to help Ashley.

*Ignore it*, Ashley told herself. It was the only responsible decision. She needed to keep focusing on her current clients. There was no guarantee that a crime had occurred anyway. Even if it had, the person charged may not qualify for court-appointed counsel. If either of those things were true, she wouldn't be involved. Sure, she was curious, and she would love to get a jump on any serious case that could possibly land on her desk, but she had to be more careful with her time these days.

Ashley looked around at the stacks of files piled up on her desk. There was nothing for it but to keep moving, working on one case after another, knocking them out one at a time. But it felt too quiet all of a sudden, the building too empty. She logged into her Pandora account on her computer and clicked on her Cage the Elephant station, cranking it up loud. She did this often when she worked early or stayed late. She appreciated the stillness of the office outside of the regular work hours, but the silence could grow deafening.

The song "Pompeii" came on and she sang along as she turned back to her files. She was working on a case for a new client charged with a drug-related offense. The person had not been held in jail, but Ashley would need to reach out sometime soon to schedule an appointment. It was too early to call now—her clients were not usually early risers—so she wrote a reminder on a sticky note and placed it next to her office phone. Then she moved on to the complaint and other charging documents in the file. She had just started reading when a movement in the doorway caught her attention.

She looked up just as someone's head popped around the doorframe.

"Shit," Ashley said, jumping up and placing a hand to her chest. "Katie! How did you get in here?" The doors had been locked, and Katie didn't have a key anymore. They were still close friends but no longer coworkers, and Ashley's office was full of sensitive files. Katie was not supposed to have free access to them anymore.

"Nice to see you, too," Katie said, "and Rachel's here with me."

Ashley lowered the volume of her music just as Rachel's head rounded the corner. She waved demurely and issued a soft "Hullo." Rachel Arkman, formerly known as Rachel Smithson, had been one of Ashley's client's two years earlier. She'd been wrongly accused of murdering her baby when she was barely an adult herself. The case was dismissed when Ashley discovered and revealed that the baby had been stillborn and that Rachel had been victimized by her mother's husband, leading to the pregnancy.

They had grown close during the case, Ashley and Rachel, but their bond was solidified when Rachel moved in with Ashley after her acquittal. Ashley had given her a key to the office back then but she couldn't bring herself to ask for it back. Even though Rachel had decided to move in with her aunt, Stephanie Arkman, Ashley wanted her to feel like she always had a key back into Ashley's life.

The move to Stephanie's was a recent change, and Ashley had to admit that it was difficult to swallow. It felt a bit like a betrayal. It was ridiculous to think like that. Rachel loved her, she knew that in her head, but it didn't stop the sting of pain in her heart. She'd been the one in Rachel's corner even when everyone thought she was a killer, not Stephanie. Yet Rachel had still chosen to abandon Ashley and live with Stephanie.

Despite the pain of that abandonment, she was still happy to see her former houseguest. Ashley had no children, but she thought this feeling must be what it was like for a parent when a grown child voluntarily returned for a visit. A smile spread across Ashley's lips, perhaps a little forced, but genuine enough.

"Come in, you two. Have a seat." She motioned to the two chairs positioned across from her desk. "It's been a while."

"I know," Rachel said, her voice quiet.

Ashley had been struggling with the changes in her relationships with these two, especially over the Thanksgiving holiday. Six months ago, she'd seen them both daily, now it was weekly, if that. In her mind, she knew that it was the way of the world. People grew up, changed, found new opportunities, and that was how it was supposed to happen. Yet she still felt like she'd been left behind. She forced the negative thoughts down and focused on less contentious things.

"Have you been listening to the scanner this morning?" Ashley asked as Katie and Rachel sat down.

"No. We haven't been into the office yet. What's going on?" Katie was immediately dialed in. Ashley could see it in the way she was leaning forward and the sparkle in her eyes. She was still technically a peace officer as the leader of the MEHR team, but she wasn't a police officer anymore. She didn't investigate crimes or solve mysteries, and Ashley knew that there was a part of Katie that missed the excitement that came with policing.

"Sir Georgie says there is a body." Ashley had started using royal-sounding nicknames for George Thomanson when his ego had stretched to imperious proportions. A habit she would continue until he finally got off his high horse, which hadn't happened yet and wasn't likely to happen anytime soon.

"Whose body?"

Ashley shrugged. "They pulled it from the lake, so I'm guessing identity isn't—" she paused, her gaze skipping to Rachel "—immediately apparent."

Rachel wrinkled her nose, but Katie wasn't fazed. Both Ashley and Katie had seen their fair share of dead bodies in pictures and in person and they had heard plenty of horror stories over the years. Enough to be desensitized to the thought of that kind of gore. Rachel was not.

"Do you think you'll get the case?"

Ashley shrugged. "I don't know if it's going to end up *being* a case. It could just be an accident. Someone falling off a fishing boat or something."

"Maybe," Katie said, but she didn't sound convinced. Her eyes traveled to the clock mounted on the side wall and she started. "Is that time right?"

Ashley followed her gaze. "Yeah."

"It's almost eight thirty," Katie said, shooting to her feet. "We've got to get our office open." She motioned for Rachel to stand.

"Before you go," Ashley said, reaching into her desk and pulling out two envelopes. "A couple letters came in the mail for you." She held them out toward Rachel. "It's been a while since you've received any letters, but the addresses on these ones are handwritten. By the handwriting and ink color, they both look to be from the same person." Ashley didn't finish the rest of her thought, because Rachel knew what would come next. The insistent letter writers never stopped until they got a response.

Most of them simply wanted acknowledgement or a thank you for their kind words—they were often letters of sympathy for the things Rachel had gone through—but they wanted something. That meant that Rachel couldn't ignore it. Otherwise, Ashley would have simply pitched them without ever giving them to her former houseguest.

It took several moments for Rachel to reach out and accept the letters, but, ultimately, she did.

"I know these are hard on you, Rachel, but you know what your therapist said about them." Ashley didn't like to remind Rachel of these things. It made her sound like a nagging mother, but that was what Rachel needed. She was permanently estranged from her mother, so who else was going to keep her moving along the right path? It certainly wasn't going to be Rachel's rich, self-indulgent aunt.

"Yes," Rachel said with a heavy sigh. "Face the problem. Avoidance will only make it worse."

"I can help you if you'd like," Ashley suggested.

"No, no," Rachel shook her head. "You don't have to do that."

Katie looked up at the clock again. "We really need to be going. Thanks for passing the letters along. Let me know if you hear anything new about that body."

"Ditto," Ashley said.

"Okay, see you later," Katie said, waving goodbye to Ashley and pulling Rachel out by her sleeve.

As they left, Ashley's mind replayed the conversation she'd overheard on the scanner. Part of her was excited about the possibility of another murder case. Big cases were challenging, and Ashley hadn't had a real challenge in quite a while. Another equally large part of her was filling with concern at the thought. She'd been involved in her fair share of murder cases, and they always made her public enemy number one in Brine. Lately, she'd been getting along with the other townspeople. She wasn't eager for them to turn against her once again.

# 2

## KATIE

The air bit at Katie's face as she stepped out the back door of Ashley's office. It was one of those days where the weather had started out mild in the early morning, but had undergone a quick, drastic change. Fall had been like that this year. Moody, with wide temperature changes, swinging from warm to cold in a matter of hours. Today was no different. The wind had picked up, blowing colder air in from the north, forcing the temperature down and the windchill up.

Katie's teeth immediately set to chattering and she pulled up her hood, ducking her head into her coat to block the wind. "I should have worn a hat," she muttered to herself.

Rachel followed, walking a few steps behind. Rachel did things like that —lagging behind—and Katie was starting to feel like it was intentional. Like Rachel wanted to be off sync with those around her. It didn't help that they'd never had a close relationship or spent one-on-one time together before Katie hired Rachel. Neither one knew how to act around the other. Ashley had always been their buffer. The bridge between the two. And they hadn't quite figured out where they stood without Ashley present.

Katie had hoped that working together would help with the awkwardness. Some of the unease was because she was technically Rachel's boss, but it didn't have to be that way. The boss versus employee positions hadn't made a difference when Ashley had been Katie's boss. Katie had hoped that she and Rachel could meld together in that same way, but so far, that hope hadn't come to fruition.

Katie could hear the slap of Rachel's shoes against the concrete behind her. Each *clomp, clomp, clomp,* grating against her nerves like a personal assault. She considered saying something to Rachel, telling her to stop following behind her like a shadow, but she dismissed the thought. She didn't want to be a snappish supervisor. She'd bite her tongue for now, even though her patience for Rachel was running low. Instead, she forced her mind to focus on something different. Something Ashley had mentioned— the body in the lake.

Her mind automatically starting piecing together what the morning had looked like as if she were still an officer. Someone would have taped the area off. Someone else would have called the medical examiner. Other deputies would be scouring the area, looking for clues. Someone would be speaking to witnesses while others would be taking photographs, documenting every inch of the area.

*Stop it,* she berated herself. She wasn't an officer anymore, and she would probably never be an officer again. Nothing good came from dwelling on the past like this, dredging up nostalgia for a job long gone, romanticizing it in a way that it had never truly deserved. These trips down memory lane weren't healthy, but they were happening more and more these days, and she'd virtually given up trying to fight them.

Judging by what Ashley had said she heard over the scanner, George Thomanson was the first one on the scene. If Katie had still been a police officer, she would have been the second. They would have taken charge of the scene, worked together to arrange the retrieval of evidence and organization of deputies.

Katie wondered what George had already found out. The things that she would perhaps never learn. An almost visceral longing to know, to be a part of it all again, struck her heavy as a blow. She needed a role. Even if it was only cursory. Maybe she could talk to George. They had been getting along better now that George was back at the bottom of the pack, and he had no power over her current position.

"Who is that?" Rachel said, pulling Katie out of her thoughts. Rachel's voice had an uncharacteristic edge to it, that was both sharp and brittle at the same time, like an icicle dangling from a roof. Dangerous, yet easily destructible.

They were almost to the Mental Health Response Team's office. It was down the street from Ashley's office. On the courthouse square, but at the opposite end from the Public Defender's Office. Katie looked over her shoulder to see Rachel pointing in front of them. Her gaze tracked where Rachel was indicating, and she saw a tall figure in dark clothing standing beside the front door of their office.

"Can I help you, sir?" Katie said, straightening her shoulders and striding toward the man. She was using her police officer voice. The "hand me your license and registration" tone that was assertive, but not quite combative.

He grunted and cleared his throat. "I doubt it, but that's why I'm here."

Katie narrowed her eyes and joined him on the sidewalk in front of the large, clear picture windows at the front of their office. The building was old, but it had been completely renovated with donations by Rachel's aunt, Stephanie. Katie hadn't wanted to spend so much money on cosmetics, but Stephanie had insisted, and it was her money, so Katie didn't have much of a choice. It still felt pretentious, having the newest, shiniest office in town.

"What do you mean? 'You doubt it.' You can't just stand out front of our building." Katie pointed to a white sign that said "No Loitering" in bright red ink. "It's illegal."

"I'm supposed to be here. These papers say so." The man pulled several crumpled documents out of his pocket.

Katie took them and smoothed them out. There were three pages, all to the same document, and all smeared with dirt and grime. There was a caption at the top of the first page that said *State of Iowa v. Ivan Volkov*. "Are you Ivan?"

"Yes."

Katie turned back to the documents, scanning the sentencing order for a specific section. She found it near the bottom of the second page. "As an added condition of your probation, you are hereby ordered to contact the Mental Health Response Team within seven days of today's date. You shall sign up as a client and complete all recommendations and treatment made by said team." It wasn't placed where the judge usually put it, but judges did strange things sometimes. The order was dated November twenty-fifth. It was now December second.

"Cutting it a little close, aren't you?" It was his last day to contact Katie's office. That fact, coupled with his earlier comment, didn't bode well for his recovery. She knew his type all too well. The ones who did the bare minimum, going through the motions of probation but never truly intending to change their ways. But he'd never dealt with the MEHR team before, so he was about to learn that slacking wasn't possible anymore.

"I'm on time," Ivan said, his lip curling into a sneer. Rachel shifted her weight behind them, and the rustling of her coat caught Ivan's attention. His eyes drifted over Katie's shoulder and his sneer disappeared, curling up into a lewd form of smile. "Hey, there, little lady."

Rachel didn't respond.

"You're awfully pretty. Are you the one giving the treatments? I'll take any treatment from you." He waggled his eyebrows. "Catch my drift? Me and you, we could have some happy endings in our future."

"If you don't stop talking to her like that, you're going to be getting your happy endings from a tattooed skinhead inside a prison cell," Katie snapped.

Ivan frowned, the loose skin on his forehead wrinkling into a line of deep trenches. "I thought you was supposed to help me."

"I'll help you with your addiction." She paused, looking down at the sentencing paperwork, searching for Ivan's conviction. "Lottery Fraud," it said, "a Class D Felony." "Which is likely gambling. Am I right?"

"Yes," he said through gritted teeth. "But I'm not addicted. The judge just thinks I am."

"The first step to recovery is admitting it," Katie said, pulling the key to the office out of her pocket and opening the door. She motioned for Rachel to enter first. "Come on in," she said, stepping in behind Rachel and motioning for him to follow.

"Will I be working with that pretty lady?" Ivan nodded toward Rachel as she retreated down the long hallway toward her office in the back.

"No. That might have been an option, but you torpedoed it with your little stunt out there." Katie nodded toward the front door. "Now, you get me."

"You seem like a ballbuster."

Katie led Ivan back to her office, flipped on the light switch, and motioned for him to sit in one of the two light pink chairs across from her desk. "I'm more of a ball destroyer than a buster."

"Didn't you used to be a cop?" Ivan sat in the chair closest to the door.

"Yes. How do you know that?" Katie had made plenty of arrests over the years. She didn't remember them all by name, but she recognized faces. Yet his was a new one.

He shrugged. "I make it my business to know things."

The comment put Katie on edge. There could be a reasonable explanation. He could be the one person she had forgotten. He could have been present when she'd arrested someone else. Yet the only thought that really stuck out in her head was that he'd been watching her.

"Isn't that, like, a conflict of interest or something?"

"How so?" Katie was already annoyed, but this irritated her further. It wasn't a conflict. Katie's current role dealt with mental health and substance abuse, which normally would fall under medical treatment, but her position held no such confidentiality. It was part of Ivan's probation, which meant that he would have to sign a release of information to the court, his attorney, probation officer, and the prosecuting attorney.

"I don't know..."

"That's what I thought. Now, let's get started."

Katie opened the top drawer of her desk, removing a stack of documents and placing them in front of her. "We are going to go through all of these," Katie said, placing her hand on top of them, "and you are going to sign at the bottom of each page to acknowledge that you read and understood its contents."

Katie slid the top document across the table so that it was facing Ivan. Then she started going through it line by line. She did this with every new client. It was to ensure that they understood expectations. Specifically, that expectations weren't low. That they would be working hard for their sobriety, and there would be no wiggle room. He signed in the places indicated, but his eyes kept traveling toward the door in the direction of Rachel's office.

She got the distinct impression that he wasn't comprehending a single word she said. His mind was elsewhere, thinking. Planning, perhaps. The question was, what was he planning? And how much did that have to do with Katie's young, vulnerable employee?

# 3

## RACHEL

Rachel hated receiving letters. All they ever contained was heartbreak. A reminder of her past. A part of her life she tried to block from her mind. These days, she could sometimes go days and even weeks without thinking about the suffocating amount of trauma roiling barely beneath her skin. But the letters, they brought it all back.

They had started when she was criminally charged for the death of her baby. Back then, they would come to Ashley's office in torrents. Her first response had been to ignore them. What was the point in reading them anyway? They wouldn't change anything about her situation. It didn't matter whether they contained kind words or the opposite. Ignoring them seemed like the only logical way to handle them.

But she hadn't considered the determination of these letter writers. If she didn't read and respond to them, the author would send another letter. And then another. And another. And another. And another. Until the dozens of letters daily had turned into fifty or more. The only way to make them stop was to respond. Thank the writer if the content was encouraging or apologize if it was the opposite.

These days, the letters had dwindled. A few letters a week had turned into almost none. She hadn't received a single one for a few months. She'd almost allowed herself to believe that there wouldn't be any more. That the public had forgotten about her and moved on to terrorize someone else. She was foolish enough to start thinking she could be at peace. That she could start living her life.

But she was wrong. The letters Ashley had given her earlier that morning were proof of it. She hadn't read them yet, but she could discern plenty from the envelopes. She had both out, studying them, as she and Katie walked from Ashley's office to the MEHR office down the street. Rachel always kept a step or two behind Katie out of deference, but her interest in the letters had caused her to fall farther behind.

Both letters were postmarked in Brine, one week apart. That meant that the writer was persistent. The kind of person who demanded a response. And it was the same person, Rachel was sure of it, despite the lack of a return address. It was obvious from the writing and the odd color of the ink.

Her name was handwritten in all caps with the first letter of her first and last name slightly larger than the rest. RACHEL SMITHSON, it said in careful, almost perfect print. The address that followed, the address for the Public Defender's Office, was written in the same way. The writing was so precise that it was almost eerie, with stick-straight lines and evenly rounded bubbles.

Then there was the color of the writing. A bright blue shade that she had never seen before. It shimmered in the light, making it difficult to read unless she had it turned to a precise angle. Nobody had ever written her in anything outside of traditional black or blue ink. She'd never even received anything in red. The precise letters meant the writer cared. The size of the font—small and compact—meant the writer was likely male. But this shimmery blue, she had no idea what it meant, if anything.

A heavy sense of dread settled in Rachel's heart. It was the not knowing. These letters did not fit with her past experiences, and that made her feel uneasy. She didn't know how to prepare herself for their contents. Messily slashed letters pressed down into deep indents were easy to discern. Those were the angry letters. The hateful ones. She could steel her emotions before breaking those ones open. But this, she had no idea what to expect.

*I'll read them later*, she thought before sighing heavily and pocketing the letters.

That was when she noticed it. Eyes on her. A dense, heavy feeling that crawled along with her as she walked. Pressing down with each step. Was it in her head? Maybe. Maybe not. Her childhood trauma had taught her to recognize the feeling. A survival tactic in a barely survivable environment. But the letters had thrown her off, got her hackles up. It could all be in her head. But then she saw him.

The man was in a heavily worn coat. Navy blue with a faded Dallas Cowboys logo. Starter Jacket, a brand from the 90's, dusted with grime. He wore a brown beanie and a scarf up over his chin, but his eyes were visible and locked on her. She met his gaze but broke it in milliseconds. He had dark brown eyes set against pale, weather-beaten skin. There was a desperation there. A hunger for something other than food.

Rachel stopped, her breath coming in tiny clouds of condensation bursting from the heat of her lungs into the frozen air. "Who is that?" Her voice was raw from the cold, and her arm rose to point at the man, moving seemingly of its own accord.

Katie turned, looked at Rachel. Her gaze traveled along the trajectory of Rachel's outstretched arm. When her eyes settled on the man, her shoulders stiffened and her hands balled into fists, but the man never looked away from Rachel. Not even as Katie stalked toward him, joining him on the pavement in front of their office. There was a heated exchange, but Rachel couldn't hear their words. Not over the blood rushing in her ears, and the screaming of her mind, warning *Danger. Danger. Danger.*

The man handed something to Katie, they exchanged a few more words, then to Rachel's horror, Katie was unlocking the door to the office. Why was she letting this guy inside? Nothing about their conversation had changed the way he was leering at Rachel, but everything had changed about Katie's reaction to him. That meant that he had to be a client. A man that would be coming back again, and again, and again.

When the door swung open, Katie turned around and motioned for Rachel to enter first. She didn't want to walk past the man, but she also didn't want to refuse a directive from her boss. So, she sucked in a deep breath and forced herself to move forward, one step at a time. She didn't look at either of them as she passed, but she felt the rustle in the air as the man leaned closer. Heard his intake of breath as he sucked in her scent.

Then she was past him, and Katie was behind her, separating the two of them. Rachel walked swiftly down the hallway, heading straight for her office at the very back of the building. She didn't turn around, but she heard Katie usher the man into her office. She felt the click of the door as it closed. And she could breathe easily again.

Once inside her office, she collapsed into her chair. She took deep steadying breaths in the way that her therapist had taught her, trying to calm her nerves. She was on edge. Overreacting. That was it. There was no danger from the man. He was a client. But hadn't Katie been on edge at first, too? Yet she had still found a way to get past it, to allow herself to be alone in a room with him. Part of Rachel wanted to have that same sense of security. The other part understood her reaction as a necessary survival instinct.

"Get out of your head," Rachel grumbled, smacking herself on the temple with the heel of her hand. It was time to focus on work. Helping others with their mental health and addictions. She'd worry about the man in Katie's office and the letters later.

# 4

## ASHLEY

Once Katie and Rachel were gone, Ashley settled back into paperwork, trying to get a jump on the day. She didn't get far before her office phone started ringing. The display bar said it was an internal call from Elena, the office manager. Ashley picked it up and brought the receiver to her ear, cradling it against her shoulder as she wrote a few additional notes in a client file.

"What's up?" Ashley said.

"Are Katie and Rachel gone?" Elena asked.

"Yeah. They left a few minutes ago. Why?"

"It's nice to see them. It's been a while," Elena said in her sing-song voice.

"Yes. So, what's up?" She knew Elena wasn't calling to ask her about Rachel and Katie. If that was her goal, she would have walked back and sat down in one of Ashley's worn but comfortable office chairs. They never chatted over the office phone.

"Someone's on the phone for you."

"Who is it?" Ashley glanced at the clock on her computer screen. Nine o'clock. Too early or too late for a client. Calls from wild nights out usually ended around four or five o'clock in the morning then there was a lull while everyone slept before starting back up around noon.

"An attorney. Says his name is David Dirkman. Do you know him?"

"Yes and no."

"Huh?"

"He's in private practice. I've crossed paths with him a time or two at the courthouse, but he hardly ever takes criminal cases. He's more of a civil litigation guy."

"Ambulance chaser?"

Ashley chuckled. People disliked her as a criminal defense attorney, but she could always count on people hating personal injury lawyers even more. "Something like that."

"Do you want to talk to him?"

"Did he say what he wanted?"

"He said he's calling for some advice."

Ashley groaned. "Of course he is."

There weren't many private criminal defense clients, but when there were, they inevitably went to people like David Dirkman. Someone who was polished with fancy clothes and an overly white smile who was also well known as a litigator. What they didn't understand was that David was skilled in civil litigation, and he knew jack shit about criminal litigation. He probably didn't even know where to find the rules of criminal procedure in his rules of court book. It was the equivalent of asking your podiatrist to perform heart surgery. Sure, they were both doctors, but they were not interchangeable.

"Do you want me to patch him through or take a message?"

Ashley massaged her temples. "Did he say what he wanted advice about?"

"He mentioned something about Lake Goldenhead, but that's it. Do you want me to get more details?"

Ashley straightened, suddenly far more intrigued. "No, no. That's not necessary. I'll take the call."

"Okay. He'll be on the line when I hang up."

There was a click, and Ashley paused before saying, "This is Ashley Montgomery," in the cold yet professional tone that she reserved for private practice attorneys that she didn't know very well.

"Ashley, so good of you to take my call." David spoke in a warm, overly genial tone that probably charmed the pants off most people, but Ashley was far more cynical than most.

"Yeah, sure." She could have said more, been more welcoming, but she kinda liked to make these guys squirm. Few people ever did.

"How is life at the Public Defender's Office? I bet you are busy."

Ashley rolled her eyes. Small talk was such a waste of time, yet all these private practice attorneys clung to it like a life raft. It became a habit to them, formed from drawing out client meetings to eke every last dime out of each and every one of them.

"Yeah. I'm busy. And that's why you'll understand when I cut right to the chase. What is it that you want from me, Mr. Dirkman?"

"Advice."

"I gathered that from my office manager. What sort of advice?"

David sighed heavily. "How much have you heard about this incident at Lake Goldenhead?"

"I know there's a body. That's it."

"Okay, well, there is reason to believe that foul play might be involved."

Ashley drummed her fingernails against her desk. "I'm a defense attorney, not a cop. I'm not sure why you are telling me this."

"I have a client. He's um . . ." he paused, thinking, then continued, ". . . he believes he may be connected to the person who died."

This was getting more intriguing. "How so?"

"The cops have been putting some pressure on him. Leaving messages asking him to go down to the station, those kinds of things."

"I see." It was typical. The body was barely at the morgue before the cops started pointing fingers. But how had they known it was a homicide instead of an accident? It was all interesting, but also not her problem. "What I don't see is how this has anything to do with me."

"I was hoping that we could meet sometime, preferably sooner rather than later, to discuss the possibility of working together if charges are filed."

"Why would I do that?" Ashley was a court-appointed attorney. A full-time state employee. She was not allowed to take payment for outside work. His client was probably some rich dude she had never met. There was literally nothing in it for her and everything in it for David.

"Because it's a former client of yours."

"Shit," Ashley grumbled. That changed things. If it was a former client, then they had at least started to get their life together. Enough to have a job and be able to pay the outrageous retainers that private practice attorneys charged. It was rare when someone crawled out of the hole in their life created by the criminal justice system, and she didn't want this person to get wrangled back into it by an unknowledgeable lawyer.

"I'm not sure what that means . . ." David said.

"It means that I'm busy with hearings all day, but I can meet you tonight. Mikey's Tavern at five o'clock. Does that work?"

"Um, yeah."

"Alright. See you then." Her eyes traveled back to the clock on her computer. It was already nine fifteen and she had to be at the courthouse at nine thirty for a sentencing hearing.

"I truly appreciate it, Ashley—"

"We'll talk later. I really have to run. I've got to be at the courthouse in a few minutes."

Ashley hung up without waiting for a response. Then she shut her laptop and packed it up, along with several pens and a couple notepads. She hustled down the hallway and past Elena, toward the front door.

"I'm headed to court," she called over her shoulder. "I'll be back before noon."

She closed the door behind her and hurried across the street. As she did, she turned to see a scruffy looking man as he came out the front door of the Mental Health Response Team building. He looked like someone who would have needed a public defender, but Ashley didn't recognize him. He lingered outside the front door of the office, like he was unsure of what to do next.

There was something about him that made Ashley want to watch, to see where he was going and what he was doing. It was a feeling that ran right alongside her almost maternal feelings toward Rachel. There was a wildness about his appearance that made him seem unpredictable, even dangerous, and she didn't like that he had been in that building with Rachel. Katie could take care of herself, but Rachel was still fragile.

The church bell started ringing, indicating the half hour. She was already late. There was no time left to linger. Ashley tore her gaze away from the man and dashed through the front door of the courthouse and up the stairs to the courtroom. She'd ask Katie about the man later.

# 5

## KATIE

When Katie's meeting with Ivan ended, she stood up and led him to the front door, opening it with a swish, and holding it for him.

"Thank you for stopping by. Start working on job applications. I will come by your house tomorrow to discuss your progress." She didn't normally do that with clients, escort them out, but his fascination with Rachel had Katie's police officer senses on high alert.

"It'll be you, then." He sounded so disappointed. "Not that other girl who works with other people downtown?"

Katie narrowed her eyes. Rachel was the only other woman in their office, and she didn't have a driver's license. She and her aunt were part of one of the richest families in Iowa. Stephanie's personal driver, Bryce, brought Rachel to work every morning and dropped her back off. How Ivan knew anything about her was something Katie was going to have to ponder, but none of that mattered for this decision. She was not letting Rachel get within ten feet of him.

"No. You probably won't see Rachel again. It might even be Tom instead of me." Ivan's creepy stock had gone up exponentially in the past few minutes. Katie didn't want to be in his house alone with him.

"A man?" Ivan said with a snort.

"Yes. Tom is a man's name. Either way, someone will be checking on you tomorrow, so you better get to it if you are going to start on that job hunt."

Katie made a shooing motion with her hand, and he stepped outside. She closed the door swiftly behind him, turning and leaning her back against it. What had she gotten herself into with this job? She'd never brought a firearm to work even though she had a conceal and carry permit. Mental health and guns didn't mix. And she didn't want to frighten her clients. Or at least that's what she used to think. But Ivan was starting to persuade her otherwise.

After a few moments, she pulled herself together, straightened, and pushed off the door with her foot. She glanced out the front window. She didn't see Ivan anywhere, which meant that he had either ducked around the side of the building or he hadn't moved, and was still standing on the other side of the door.

*What the literal fuck*, Katie thought.

This job was hard enough with regular clients. But this guy added an extra layer of difficulty. She'd have to find a way to provide him services while keeping him separate from Rachel. It wasn't going to be easy. Drop-ins were common with clients, and it was an important component of the services the MEHR team provided. Mental health breakdowns, anxiety spikes, and urges to use could not be scheduled on a calendar. So, clients had to be able to stop by any time they needed help.

As she continued looking through the window, waiting to see if Ivan appeared, she saw Ashley hurrying out of the front door of the Public Defender's Office and across the street to the courthouse. When she was almost to the front doors of the courthouse, Ashley paused, turning to look in Katie's direction. She lingered there, staring at the MEHR team office for a long time, then the church bell started chiming, and she shook her head and hurried inside.

Ivan had to be still standing on the other side of the front door. Had Ashley recognized him? His sentencing paperwork had identified Ashley as Ivan's attorney, so she knew him, but she hadn't waved. That wasn't like Ashley. She wasn't friends with her clients, but she was friendly. She was often the only person on their side and in their corner, and she took that responsibility seriously. So, why had she ignored Ivan?

*Does Ashley know he's dangerous?* Katie wondered, but it was only a fleeting thought. There was no point dwelling on a question that Ashley would never answer. That information was protected by attorney-client privilege. Just then, her office phone started ringing. Katie stepped away from the window and rushed down the hallway toward her office. There was no receptionist—Katie was trying to get everyone settled before she hired any more employees—so her clients called her direct line. She picked up on the very last ring before it went to voicemail.

"This is Katie Mickey," she said, slightly out of breath. She worked out daily, but she was more of a distance runner than a sudden burst of energy type of athlete.

"Hey, Katie, it's George."

"Oh, hey. How are you?"

It had been a while since Katie and George had last spoken, but the conversations between them had been growing more frequent. The rift in their relationship had come from working together at the police department. Now that the entire department was nonexistent, none of those issues seemed quite so important anymore.

"I'm good. Settling in at the Sheriff's Department."

"I'm glad to hear that. So, what's going on? Why'd you call the office line instead of my cell?"

"I tried that first, but you didn't answer."

"Oh. I was with a client," Katie said, casting a dark look in the direction of the front door.

"I've got a new case. This thing out at Lake Goldenhead."

"I heard," Katie said.

George sighed. "Still listening to the scanner?"

"Not me, Ashley."

"She would."

"Anyway . . ." Katie motioned with her hand for him to go on. He couldn't see her, but she used her hands when she spoke and that didn't stop just because she was on the phone.

"Anyway, I want to bounce some ideas off you."

"Isn't there someone there, someone at the Sheriff's Department that could help you out with that?"

"Not really."

Katie sighed heavily. "Picking fights a little early, aren't you? I mean, you haven't been working there that long."

"I'm not picking fights, Katie. Nobody will listen to me. It's frustrating. I have twice the experience of half these idiots over here, and they all ignore me like I'm some newbie that hasn't even been through the academy."

He was referring to the Law Enforcement Academy. It was basically school for baby cops. Officers were often hired on, started working, and then went to the academy a few months later. Those first few months were rough for everyone because the new officer didn't know anything about the job. Which made them practically useless because they didn't know what they didn't know yet.

"How am I going to help with that?" She wasn't a police officer anymore. She'd never been besties with anyone at the Sheriff's Department, but after spending a year working with Ashley Montgomery—the defense attorney that the deputies despised the most—she wasn't on very good terms with any of them anymore.

"I just want to bounce some ideas off you. These guys over here, they are making me feel like I'm crazy. But I know I'm not completely off base. I just need to talk it out with someone rational."

"And *I'm* that someone. I feel so important."

"Don't be sarcastic. That's Ashley's thing, not yours. And she can barely pull it off."

"I'm going to tell her that you said that."

"Said what?"

"That she can pull off sarcasm."

George sighed heavily, and Katie knew he was pinching the bridge of his nose. "Come on, Katie. Can we be serious?"

"Sorry, yes."

"Is that a 'yes' you will help, or a 'yes' you'll be serious."

"Both."

"Great. When are you available? We can meet at Genie's Diner like old times."

Katie looked at her watch. "That's not going to work. I've got a full day of appointments and follow-ups. I can meet you after work, though. Want to get a drink at Mikey's Tavern?"

"That works. Five o'clock?"

"See you then," Katie said, hanging up without waiting for him to say goodbye.

Then she grabbed her keys, phone, and a notepad, shoving them all into her work bag. She needed to get to the other side of town for an in-home appointment with a longer-term client who had been doing better for a while, but recently suffered a setback. As she stepped out into the bitter Iowa cold, she tried to focus her thoughts on her client. He deserved her full attention, yet she couldn't keep her mind from wandering back to the body in Lake Goldenhead and what George would have to say about it later that evening.

# 6

### RACHEL

After Rachel's last meeting of the day, she had returned to the office. Both Tom and Katie were there, but they were in their respective offices, wrapping up paperwork. She passed Katie first, who was so focused she didn't even look up. She was typing at her computer in quick, hurried strokes, like she was in a rush.

Tom's office was next. He looked up as she passed, his bright blue eyes catching on her, an even smile spreading across his lips. "Hi, Rachel," he called in his familiar and friendly manner.

Rachel paused in his doorway, waving back at him. Then she continued walking. She didn't know how to talk to men. They all made her uncomfortable. Even Tom with his kind eyes and pure heart. She was trying to work through that with the help of a therapist, but it was going to take a while. And deep in her soul, she knew she would never be completely normal. Not with a childhood like hers.

When she reached her office, she walked around the desk and sat in her rolling office chair. The scent of new leather filled her nostrils as the soft material cradled her body. The furniture was expensive, which was atypical for a government office like theirs, but it all came as donations from Rachel's aunt, Stephanie. She'd hired an interior designer and that woman had turned the MEHR team office into something Rachel would expect to find in a high-end modern living magazine.

Rachel's day had been unremarkable, which was what she had needed to get past the odd man that had appeared at their office at opening time. Her daily routines had lulled her into a sense of comfort and she had virtually forgotten about him and the two letters Ashley had given her. But the busyness was only a temporary fix. A tourniquet to staunch gushing blood. It was not a true solution.

Now that it was the end of the day, she needed to face the letters. There was no point in putting it off. It was better to know what an insistent letter-writer was saying to her than to stay in the dark. If the person was angry and threatening, she'd know to keep a lookout. If it was bad enough, she could even enlist the assistance of law enforcement, and then someone else would share her problem, and she wouldn't have to suffer with it silently on her own.

"No time like the present," she said to herself.

Both letters were in the top drawer of her desk. She reached in and pulled them out, once again studying the odd shimmering light blue ink. They looked exactly the same on the outside aside from date on the postmarks. One letter was postmarked November twenty-second, the other was a week later.

She focused on the earlier letter, pushing her finger under the flap at the corner, pausing to take several deep, calming breaths in the way her therapist had instructed. *Just do it*, she told herself, *like tearing off a Band-Aid.* Two more deep breaths, then she ran her finger along the top, ripping the envelope into jagged edges.

The paper inside was white and of a thicker card stock. There was only one piece of it, and it fit snugly into the envelope. Rachel slid it out. The front side was blank white. She flipped it over and saw words in the same light blue ink. Like the envelope, they were handwritten in all caps with the leading letter slightly larger than the rest.

OH RACHEL, MY SWEET RACHEL, WHY
DID YOU MOVE OUT OF THE ATTORNEY'S HOUSE?
WRITE BACK.

YOU CAN LEAVE YOUR ANSWER OUTSIDE THE BACK DOOR.

When the words sank in, Rachel dropped the letter like it was on fire. It fell flat on her desk, its words still staring up at her. Someone had been watching her close enough to know her movements. The letter wasn't an explicit threat—not something she could report to law enforcement and expect action—but there was a dangerous undertone.

This person had been following her. How else would he know that she had moved? Ashley lived out in the country, where there were no neighbors within a mile or two. Stephanie lived on the other side of Brine County but also out in the country. There was no reason for anyone to know about the move unless they'd been keeping tabs on Rachel.

*Maybe the person had overheard that she'd moved. Yeah, it's got to be that,* she told herself. Ashley or Katie had said something about it down at Genie's Diner and that place was a den for gossip. She turned back to the envelope, staring at the postmark. Her heart sank. November twenty-second. That was the same day Rachel had moved. There was no time for the news to get out. And Ashley and Katie were not big gossips. Genie was always trying to pry information from them, but they rarely spilled the beans.

Then there were the words "my sweet Rachel." It wasn't the last two words of that phrase that bothered her, but the first. *My.* It showed owner-ship. Like this person thought Rachel belonged to him and only him. Where had that sense of ownership come from? And how long had this person been following Rachel to feel as though he had some hold over her?

She'd never received a letter quite like it. She'd had plenty of threats of violence and even some death threats, but nothing so implicit like this. It was far more frightening, because the person's true intentions were unknown. Maybe it was nothing, but it just as easily could be something worse, far worse than even death.

She shook her head, her gaze settling on the second envelope. Should she open it? Her hands were already shaking, and her nerves shot. She didn't know if she had it in her to handle more semi-threatening words. But wasn't not knowing worse than knowing? Perhaps this letter would have something specifically violent that she could then take to law enforcement and have them open an investigation.

*Okay*, she told herself. *Just one more. You can do it.*

She picked up the second letter, jamming her finger beneath the lip. She ripped at it violently, pulling the envelope in half rather than along the seam. Part of her wanted to destroy the envelope. Tear it up into tiny little pieces and burn it in a fire. But she couldn't do that in case she needed it for evidence one day. The letter fell out of the envelope, landing face up on her desk. Unsurprisingly, the words were written in the same color ink in the same handwriting.

IT'S VERY RUDE NOT TO WRITE BACK.
I THOUGHT YOU WERE A GOOD GIRL.
MAYBE YOU ARE DIRTIER THAN I THOUGHT.


Rachel jumped out of her seat, her stomach churning.

"Are you okay?"

Rachel looked up to see Tom in her doorway missing that characteristic grin of his. Instead of joyful, he looked concerned.

"Um, yeah," Rachel said, her gaze darting down to the letters on her desk, then back up to him.

"Is there something you want to talk about?" He was looking at her desk now, too.

Tom was a kind person; she knew that from the year he spent dating Ashley. He had royally screwed up his chances with Ashley, but he'd done that out of a misguided belief that he was protecting Ashley's feelings. He'd been an idiot, but he hadn't meant to be, and that was what set him apart from other men. The intention behind a man's actions meant everything to Rachel. But still, she couldn't bring herself to talk to him even about simple things. She didn't know where to begin when the subject matter was something like these almost vulgar, not quite threatening letters.

"No, there's nothing," Rachel said, opening her drawer and sweeping her hand across her desk so that the letters and their envelopes fell into it.

"Are you sure?"

"Yes," Rachel said with a firm nod.

"Well, then." He rocked from his heels to his toes, a disbelieving expression on his face. "It's quitting time. Are you planning on leaving soon?"

Rachel glanced at the clock. It was already five thirty. The office closed at five. "I didn't realize it was so late."

"Katie's already gone. I'm leaving now, too. Do you have a ride home?"

Rachel nodded and pulled out her cell phone. "Yeah. I'll call Bryce."

Bryce had been working for Rachel's aunt Stephanie for over ten years, and Stephanie seemed to trust him completely. Rachel did not feel the same way. He had started driving Rachel to and from work when she moved in with Stephanie, and Rachel never felt comfortable in his presence. She hadn't quite figured out if that was because of her past or because of Bryce himself.

"Okay," Tom turned to go.

"Wait—"

Tom turned back to her.

"Sorry, um, do you mind waiting with me. Just until Bryce gets here?"

Tom glanced back at Rachel's desk, where the letters had been, then back up to her. This wasn't her usual behavior, and she could tell he had linked the letters to her uncharacteristic request.

"Yeah, sure," Tom said. "Whatever makes you comfortable."

"Thank you," Rachel said, a heavy sense of relief washing over her.

She called Bryce as she and Tom walked toward the front door of the office. Bryce answered after the first ring, and he said he would be there in a few minutes.

"Is it going to be a while?" Tom asked when Rachel hung up.

"Um, no."

"Oh," Tom said. There was a question and a statement in the way he said it. An *oh, that's odd.*

It was odd now that Rachel thought about it. Stephanie and Rachel lived forty minutes north of town. If Bryce was coming from home, it should take him a while to get to her. He must have been waiting for her downtown. She didn't leave work at the same time every day, so they'd agreed on a system. Rachel would call, then he'd come. Yet he'd come this time without prompting.

The question was whether he'd done that out of anticipation that she'd need a ride or if it was something far more nefarious than that. He would have known about her move. Was he her mysterious letter writer? If so, did that mean that the author hadn't intended to harm her, or did Bryce's connection make the situation more dangerous?

# 7

## KATIE

By four o'clock Katie was mentally exhausted from a full day with clients and ready for a drink. Her days as a police officer were longer—she had worked twelve-hour shifts then—but they were not quite so draining. Back then, she was always up moving around, keeping her body as busy as her mind. But now, she spent far more time at a desk in her office, which made for sleepy afternoons. And there was also a neediness that came from her clients in this job that seemed to suck what was left of her energy out of her.

This afternoon had dragged like so many others. She'd been unable to stop her mind from wandering back to that early morning phone call with George and their scheduled meeting at Mikey's Tavern. Every time she thought of their potential conversation, her heart would pound with excitement. George and Katie had agreed to meet at five o'clock, and she had another hour to kill. She tried to focus on paperwork, opening new client files using their client management software, including a file for Ivan and a few other new appointments, but she still couldn't keep her mind from drifting.

*How had that body gotten into the lake?* She kept wondering.

The local news coverage over the noon hour had dedicated a full story to the body in the lake. The reporter had said that law enforcement was calling it a "suspicious death," but they wouldn't give any further details. The identity of the body was not revealed, but Katie didn't know if that was because law enforcement didn't know who it was, or if they were still trying to notify family members, which had to be completed before they would release the name to the public.

When the clock showed four forty-five and she had barely finished setting up one new client file, she decided the best thing to do was to give up and start fresh the next day. The last forty-five minutes had been a complete waste of time. She grabbed her coat and popped her head into Tom's office to tell him that she was leaving a few minutes early, then headed out the front door toward Mikey's Tavern. George would probably be there early, and even if he wasn't, she could still grab a drink and catch up with Mikey, the owner of the pub and a friend.

The air was cold, the wind picking up and whipping at her nose and ears. The last week had been unseasonably warm, with temperatures hitting high sixties nearly every day, but that had been a blessing and a curse. The weather was turning quickly now, dipping into the thirties and below. There was no easing into it this year. Summer was meeting winter without the benefit of fall.

She pulled her hood up over her head and tugged her scarf up over her nose, picking up speed. The sooner she got to the bar, the better. She wasn't paying attention to where she was going, only that she needed to get there and warm up. When she was only a block from the bar, she ran straight into someone. She banged into the person and bounced off them, causing the person to drop something.

"I'm sorry," Katie said. "Let me help you with that."

"No." The other person said. It came out almost forceful, causing Katie to wince. It was a man, she could tell by the broadness of his shoulders, his deep voice, and his shortly cropped hair as he crouched down. He scooped the item up and tucked it in to his coat pocket in one swift movement, before straightening. The item was small and rectangular. An envelope, perhaps. "Thank you, but I've got it," he added, a smile spreading across his face.

"Noah," Katie said.

Now that she could see his face, Katie recognized the man. He was one of her first clients when the MEHR team had opened its doors. Noah had been struggling with methamphetamine for years, but he'd been doing well. All clients started out with daily appointments to deal with acute addiction issues. Then they moved to appointments twice a week. When those were going well, it moved to weekly, then bimonthly, then monthly, and after that they graduated from the program. Noah was at the monthly stage.

"How are things going?"

"Um, not so good. That's why I'm here." Noah wouldn't meet Katie's gaze. "I'm starting to, um, struggle with my sobriety."

"Have you used?" There was no point in beating around the bush. This was the crux of the issue, and he wouldn't even look at her. It was a clear sign that he was feeling guilty about something, and the only logical assumption was that he'd relapsed.

"No. Not yet." He put his hands up in a gesture of surrender. "Not yet, but there have been some things happening lately that make me want to, um, escape. I just got off work, so I was hoping I could catch you before the office closed."

"The office isn't closed, but I left a few minutes early. Tom's still there."

"Tom? Is there anyone else I can talk to?"

"What's wrong with Tom?"

"Nothing," Noah said, looking down at his feet. "I just have a hard time talking about emotional stuff with men."

There was something about Noah's demeanor that made her feel like he wasn't being entirely truthful with her. Call it police sense or simply a woman's intuition, but it was there, tugging at her thoughts. What he was being untruthful about was still up in the air, but judging by the amount of fidgeting she was seeing, she guessed he would fail his next drug test.

"If you need help right now, you should go to the office and talk to Tom. I'll call him and let him know that you are on your way. Otherwise, you can come by tomorrow morning. I have a pretty busy schedule, but I should be able to squeeze you in first thing tomorrow morning."

"I'll do that," Noah said.

"Do what? Meet with Tom or come tomorrow?"

"Come tomorrow."

"Okay," Katie said, "but don't get into any trouble in the meantime."

"I won't," Noah said, flashing what looked like a forced smile.

Katie probably should have stayed there, talking to Noah at least long enough to determine how close he was to falling off the wagon, but she was freezing cold, and if she delayed any longer, she would be late for her meeting with George. She'd been early, but this conversation had sucked up nearly fifteen minutes of her time.

"Alright, then. I'll see you early tomorrow morning."

Noah nodded and continued down the street, headed in the opposite direction. She guessed he was going to see Tom. He had said he didn't want to talk to a man, but he could have been saying that so Katie would make time for him in the morning. Either way, it was an issue she could sort out later. For now, she had a meeting to get to.

She turned and hurried toward Mikey's Tavern, pulling the door open and ducking inside. A blast of warm air and loud animated voices greeted her. She saw George right away. He was bellied up to the bar, talking to a man with a large, pockmarked, bulbous nose. Katie recognized his face from her days as a police officer, but she couldn't place his name.

As Katie made her way toward George, she noticed Ashley sitting at one of the high-top tables near the back corner of the bar, and there was a man sitting across from her. Katie knew the man was an attorney, but he didn't do a lot of criminal work, so Katie had never dealt with him in a courtroom. By their body language, Katie thought they might be on a date. They were both leaned in close to one another, speaking in low, hushed tones. Whatever they were doing, they clearly didn't want company. Katie turned her attention to George and hopped onto the empty barstool next to him.

"Hey, George," Katie said. He was in a heated conversation with the man with the bulbous nose and he hadn't noticed her yet.

He swung around, facing her. "There you are, Katie." There was relief in his voice. "Will you tell Adam here to mind his own business?"

"About what?"

"This Goldenhead Lake thing." George hooked a thumb toward the man. "Adam over here thinks he has a right to know everything."

"It's an open investigation. Nobody outside of law enforcement has a *right* to know everything." Katie understood Adam's desire to know. She'd been feeling the same way throughout the day, but that curiosity didn't afford them any rights.

"What would you know," Adam said, waving a dismissive hand toward her. He was swaying in his seat, sloppy drunk. "You're that lady cop that got fired."

Katie bristled. "I wasn't fired. I was laid off."

"Same difference."

"Actually, no, it isn't," Katie said. *And you'd know that if you'd lay off the booze for a day or two and work for honest wages.*

Before Katie had started working for the MEHR team, she would have said the last part, but she had learned some restraint over the past six months. Especially when it came to substance abusers. And Adam had an alcohol problem. It wasn't a choice for him anymore, it was a compulsion. Sure, Adam could ask for help, but denial was also part of the disease.

Adam was swaying in his chair, glaring at Katie like he had plenty more to say, but he was interrupted by the bartender. "What'll it be, Katie?"

"Just a beer. Thanks, Mikey."

Mikey was the owner of Mikey's Tavern. He usually worked in the kitchen, but just like many other small businesses, he filled in wherever he was needed. If a bartender quit or took the day off, he was there pouring pints without complaint.

Mikey nodded, then turned to Adam. "I think you've had enough for one evening. You ought to go on home now. You can come back tomorrow."

"Are you cutting me off?" Adam said, his words thick and slow.

"Yeah," Mikey grabbed a beer glass and headed to the tap. "Which one?" His gaze was set on Katie.

"The local IPA is fine," Katie said.

"You can pour me one, too," Adam said.

Mikey ignored him and filled the glass, placing it in front of Katie. "On the house."

Katie pulled out her wallet. She and Mikey had always been friendly enough over the past few years, but they had become genuine friends after she was named the leader of the MEHR team. She understood the urge to give a friend a drink for free, but this was Mikey's business. She wasn't going to take advantage of his hospitality.

"Put that away," Mikey said, nodding toward Katie's wallet. "Your money's no good here."

"What about me?" Adam groaned. "My money isn't good either."

Mikey crossed his arms. "I'm not accepting your money for a wholly different reason. Now, do as I say and get on out of here. I'm not going to have you disrupting my clientele."

"She's not even paying. She's a—"

"Whatever you are about to say, you'd do best to rethink it." Mikey gave him a hard stare. He was normally kindhearted and good-natured, but he was not someone to cross.

George patted Adam on the back. "I'll walk him to the door. Let's go, Adam." He reached beneath Adam's armpits and gently encouraged him to his feet, then led him toward the front door.

Katie watched them as they walked away, then she took a drink of beer, her eyes drifting toward Ashley and the man sitting across from her. They didn't look quite so cozy anymore. Ashley had been leaning forward with both hands on the table, but she wasn't doing that anymore. She was now leaning back with her arms crossed.

"Looks like trouble," Mikey said. Katie turned to see he was looking at Ashley, too.

"What do you mean?"

"I wouldn't want Ashley looking at me like that, would you?"

The corners of Katie's lips kicked up into a half smile. "I remember what it was like, and no, you wouldn't want that." Katie and Ashley had been enemies before they'd become friends. It felt like an eternity ago, but Katie would never forget what it was like to receive that intense look. "Do you know who that guy is?"

Mikey shrugged. "Some hot shot attorney in town. A rich country club type that doesn't associate with riffraff like me."

"I'd take you over him any day."

"You say that now, but you haven't met him. That's the type of guy could talk a tree into buying paper."

Katie watched Ashley and the other attorney, wondering why they were meeting. Was it a date? If so, Tom would be brokenhearted. He and Ashley's relationship had ended a long time ago, but they'd both remained single, so he'd been hanging on to a tiny thread of hope that Ashley would give him another chance. Not that this guy was going to be Ashley's next boyfriend. If this situation was a date, it didn't look like it was going well. But it meant Ashley was open to dating, which meant she would eventually meet someone.

With some effort, Katie swung back around in her seat and faced the bar. Ashley's love life was none of her business. Unless, of course, Ashley wanted to tell her about it. And she'd seen Ashley that morning and she hadn't said anything about a date. She ought to mind her own business until Ashley was ready to spill the beans. If she was ever ready.

# 8

## ASHLEY

It was five o'clock on the dot when Ashley left her office to head for Mikey's Tavern. She was in for a cold walk, but she had been watching the weather channel and she'd expected the turn in the temperature. She was bundled up in her dark red, down-lined winter coat. The coat was long enough to skim the tops of her knees and the hood had light brown faux fur around the trim. She had a beanie beneath the hood and had a scarf wound tightly around her neck.

When she stepped out the front door of her office, she locked the door and began walking. Out of the corner of her eye, she thought she saw a couple people stopped halfway between her office and the MEHR team office, talking, but she didn't stop to investigate. It was too fucking cold for that. She kept her head down to block the wind and pushed ahead. She couldn't really see where she was going, but she didn't need to. She was a Brine native, and she knew these streets like the back of her hand.

The bar was only a few blocks from her office, so she was walking through the side door in a matter of minutes. The place was warm and buzzing with the low murmur of conversation. She scanned the bar, looking for David Dirkman. There were several people bellied up at the bar. All were men, faces she recognized, including George Thomanson. He hadn't seen her come in, and she preferred to keep it that way. She turned her back to him and headed toward the tables at the back end of the bar. David was seated in the very corner.

"I see you chose the darkest, most secluded corner," Ashley said by way of greeting. "You better not be expecting to get lucky."

David looked up, his dark eyes wide with surprise. "I, um, no. I just wanted some privacy." He lowered his voice and looked left to right, like a teenage girl about to spill a secret. "This is sensitive information."

Ashley started taking off her cold-weather gear, slinging it over the back of her chair. It took her a few minutes to get down to her actual clothes. David kept his eyes averted, looking everywhere but at her. She must have made him uncomfortable with her innuendo. It was only a joke.

"Do you want a drink?" David nodded at his half-empty glass of beer, still unable to look at her.

"Yes, but I'll get it." Before he had a chance to respond, she turned on her heel and marched up to the bar, careful to stay away from George Thomanson. It had been a while since she'd last seen him, but they'd been at odds for the past few years, and she didn't see any reason why that would be different tonight.

Mikey was at the end of the bar, shining a wine glass with a rag. He smiled and started making his way toward her, grabbing a bottle of red wine on his way. He popped off the cork, poured the wine, and placed it in front of her in one fluid movement. Mikey was a big man. Some might even describe him as intimidating. But what stood out to Ashley was his grace. He moved in liquid, smooth movements, almost like a dancer.

"Thank you," she said. "What do I owe you?"

"You know your money's no good here."

Ashley placed a ten-dollar bill on the bar and turned to walk away.

"You must not have heard me right," Mikey said.

Ashley paused and turned half around to answer. "I heard you just fine, Mikey. I also know you've got kids at home. Accepting free drinks is taking food out of their mouths."

Mikey snorted. "Don't you worry about that, Miss Ashley. You've done plenty to help my family out."

"Call it a tip, then," Ashley said, turning and walking back toward David.

Mikey gave Ashley far too much credit. She did represent Mikey for a possession of marijuana charge when he was much younger, but that was a bullshit charge to begin with. He shouldn't have needed her help. The only other thing she had done was help to form the MEHR team. They had been working with a couple members of Mikey's extended family, getting their lives on track. Sure, the team had been her brainchild, but there were plenty of other people who had done more to bring it to fruition than she had.

"They have wine here?" David asked when she got back to the table.

"Sorta," Ashley said, sliding into her chair.

They were at a high-top table meant for four people. It ran parallel to the bar top, so Ashley could see the back of George Thomanson's head out of the corner of her eye.

"What does that mean?"

"It means that Mikey has wine, but it's not for everyone. He keeps a couple bottles for me and Forest Parker."

"The city councilman?"

"Yeah."

"Why?"

"Because he likes us." That wasn't the full answer. The truth was that they had most of their early, off-the-record discussions about the MEHR team at Mikey's Tavern. Ashley had always preferred wine, but she wasn't a picky drinker. Forest, on the other hand, only drank red wine and it had to come from a certain region in California. Ashley wasn't fancy enough to care about the region, but she did enjoy the wine.

"I'm not sure if I should take offense to that or not. Doesn't Mikey like everyone?"

"Take offense if you want," she said, shrugging one shoulder. Her words were short and slightly barbed, but she couldn't help it. There was a flirtatious gleam in his eyes that she didn't like. Maybe she'd regret that little joke earlier.

"Okay."

"So, what did you want to discuss?" There was no point in drawing out the conversation. They weren't friends, and she didn't expect them to become friends.

"Do you know Noah Scott?"

"Yes." Ashley had represented him six months earlier. It was a possession of methamphetamine charge. He'd been convicted but avoided jail
time by agreeing to join the pilot project for the MEHR team.

"He came to my office a week ago and wanted to hire me."

"Why?" Ashley hadn't heard of any new charges against Noah. But he
did have a good-paying job now that he was working for Stephanie Arkman
at the Arkman family's ethanol plant. He wouldn't qualify for court-
appointed counsel, so she wouldn't know about new charges.

"It has to do with his girlfriend."

"Erica?"

Ashley had heard that Noah and Erica Elsberry had started dating
shortly after Ashley's representation of Noah had ended. Both were hard
core into methamphetamine, and both had been ordered by the court to
complete the MEHR team program. Ashley had her doubts that two users
could get sober together, but apparently Erica and Noah were the exception
to that rule, because neither had picked up any criminal charges since then.
Or so she thought.

"Yeah. What do you know about Erica?"

Ashley snorted. "I'm not going to discuss former clients with you." In
truth, she knew a lot about Erica. Most of it was well outside the parame-
ters covered by attorney-client privilege, but she didn't gossip. Especially
when it was about someone like Erica, whose past intertwined so often
with Ashley's. They'd both been the target of plenty of town chatter
throughout the years, and Ashley wasn't going to contribute to the
nonsense.

"Did you know that she's disappeared?"

"How would I know that? My representation ended half a year ago. I'm
not sure what you do, but I don't have time to keep tabs on former clients."

"Did I say something offensive?"

Ashley took a drink of her wine, setting it down on the table with a
soft *clink*. "No," she said after a long moment. "Sorry. I'm just a little on
edge. I don't know what you want from me, and it's starting to irritate
me."

"Fair enough. I'll cut to the chase. Noah came to my office a week ago.

He said that Erica had left the night before, but she didn't take any of her things. Her bags were all there. So was her makeup and toiletries."

"Okay." Ashley's mind was listening to David's words, but she was also trying to figure out why he was telling her any of it. While her knowledge of Erica's past would not have been covered by attorney-client privilege, the rule most certainly covered this information about Noah. He met with David and told him this information in confidence. David didn't do a lot of defense work, but every attorney knew the importance of privilege. Otherwise, it wouldn't be long before they lost their license to practice.

"Noah wanted me to track her down."

"Why? Do you moonlight as a private investigator or something?"

"No," David said with a chuckle. "He thought Erica had fallen off the wagon and was on a bender. I have a private investigator that I use regularly. You know, for personal injury type stuff, and Noah knew that."

Ashley had never even dabbled in civil litigation, but she knew there were a lot of false claims in personal injury cases. People saying their arm was permanently injured who were later photographed on a tennis court, holding a racket, swinging at a ball with a full range of motion. Lawyers often used private investigators to follow people and get photographic evidence of their lies.

"But why go to you? I mean, why didn't Noah cut out the middleman and go straight to the private investigator?"

"Because Erica was supposed to meet with her probation officer a couple days ago. Apparently, the woman showed up at their house asking questions about Erica's whereabouts, claiming that Erica needed to get in touch with her or she'd move to revoke Erica's probation."

"And he wants you to represent Erica in her probation revocation. That all makes sense, but I'm not sure what you need from me."

"Yes, well, I think that Noah's focus is starting to shift."

"How so?"

"Well, you heard about the body pulled out of Lake Goldenhead, right?"

"It's all over town," Ashley gestured to the bar around her. It was quickly growing packed with people. "You'd be hard pressed to find someone who *hasn't* heard about it."

"Noah thinks it might be Erica."

Ashley had just taken a drink of wine and she had to force herself to swallow it. "Excuse me. Are you saying that Noah thinks Erica was murdered and the cops are going to blame him for it?" David was beating around the bush, delivering information slowly and delicately, but it didn't take a rocket scientist to figure out where he was headed with this twist in the conversation.

"Yes," David said, his expression solemn "He does."

"What makes him think it's Erica? I mean, they haven't identified the body yet, have they?"

"Not that I've heard, but Deputy Thomanson called him this morning."

"Jesus Christ. He didn't talk to the cops, did he?" If there was one thing she always told her clients, it was that they should never ever under any condition speak with law enforcement. She'd say, "If the cops show up and you didn't call them, then they aren't there to help you." If nothing else sank in, she tried to at least make sure they understood just how important it was to remember to keep their mouths shut.

"No, he didn't, but Deputy Thomanson left a voicemail asking Noah to call him back."

"Okay. If that's all, then it's simple. Tell Noah not to call back. It's as easy as that. Nothing requires him to respond to the voicemail, and he's good at dodging calls. I know that from my days as his attorney."

"It's not quite that simple."

"What am I missing?"

"If it is Erica, Noah is worried that there will be some damning DNA evidence."

"Like what? Semen? They are dating and living together. I don't think them finding seminal fluid in her body is all that damning."

David's face flushed. "It's not that. It's worse."

"Then what is it?"

"Noah said that he and Erica had rough sex shortly before she left. They'd apparently been in an argument, made up, and then something set her back off and she left."

"I just told you what I thought about semen. If that's it, you really shouldn't worry and this meeting is a complete waste of both of our time."

"She scratched him. He said she uses her fingernails when she's really excited. And he thinks that his skin will be under her nails."

Ashley was gearing to stand up and leave the table. So far, their conversation had gone nowhere. But this, well, it changed things. She'd heard the "rough sex" excuse from plenty of clients in the past. Sometimes to explain the presence of semen, others to explain the presence of vaginal tears. She'd never heard it as an excuse to explain skin cells under fingernails, though.

"Rough sex is a difficult argument to make to a jury," Ashley said with a heavy sigh. "Juries usually don't buy it."

"I figured that." David paused, downing the last bit of beer in his glass. "Now, do you understand why I need your help?"

"Yeah. I think so, but you are privately retained. That means Noah doesn't qualify for court-appointed counsel. If I were to file an appearance, I'd be doing it pro bono, and I really don't have time for that." Pro bono was the equivalent of free services, and Ashley's services were already discounted enough as a public defender.

"I know. I just thought you might be willing to help out here and there. On a more informal basis."

Ashley chewed on her lip, thinking. She didn't want to get tied up in something that really wasn't any of her business and would most likely suck up a good deal of time. On the other hand, Noah was a former client, and she also didn't want him getting screwed over by an inexperienced attorney.

"I want to talk to Noah before I make a decision."

"Okay. When? I'll set it up."

"Tomorrow morning. Eight o'clock sharp. And I mean sharp. Not eight fifteen or eight o' five. I mean eight. I've got an hour to spare, and that's all. This stuff is time sensitive, and I'm tied up in hearings all day tomorrow."

"Consider it done. If Noah is supposed to work, I'll tell him to call in."

"I'm not saying I will definitely help you. I want to make that clear. I'm saying it's a possibility."

"That's all I can ask. Thank you, Ashley. I truly mean that. Everyone knows you are one of the best defense attorneys in the state."

Ashley finished her glass of wine and stood. "I know." She pulled on her coat and wound her scarf around her neck. "But I should be going. I'll see you bright and early tomorrow morning."

Ashley turned and started toward the exit. As she did, she noticed George Thomanson was no longer sitting alone. Katie was next to him. They were chatting and laughing in a way she hadn't seen in years. She wondered what was going on with the two of them, and what that meant for the future of Ashley's relationship with Katie. The last time George and Katie were friendly was when Ashley and Katie were at odds. She hoped that he wouldn't drive a wedge between them, but her intuition told her she had reason for concern.

# 9

## RACHEL

Tom waited with Rachel in the lobby area of their office, both standing awkwardly side by side looking out the large picture window. The sky was spitting snowflakes, but it wasn't anything thick enough to affect travel. Rachel could tell that Tom was curious about her request for him to wait with her. She'd never done that before. Part of her wanted to explain it to him, but she couldn't find the words.

What would she say? *I got some letters that bothered me.* Then he'd just want to see the letters, and she didn't want to show them to him. The only person she wanted to discuss them with was Ashley.

"So," Tom said, breaking the dense silence, "Bryce is the guy who has been driving you around?"

"Um, yeah."

"Do you like him?"

Rachel shrugged.

Tom gave her a sidelong look. "That's not a glowing review."

"I don't have a choice."

"You don't have a choice? What do you mean by that?"

Rachel continued staring straight ahead, trying to think of a way to explain herself. She'd never been all that good with words. "I don't know him."

"Do you feel comfortable around him?"

"I don't feel comfortable around anyone."

Tom nodded. "Fair enough."

He knew her background. He'd been dating Ashley when Rachel was arrested and charged. He was also sitting in the courtroom when the truth came out and charges were dismissed.

"Do you feel safe with him?"

"As safe as I do with anyone else."

"Fair enough."

They fell back into silence, both still staring out the window. A large black SUV pulled up, coming to a stop right in front of their building.

"Is that Bryce?"

Rachel nodded. She pulled on her coat and grabbed her work bag. All their work files were computerized, accessible from a shared server on their work laptops. Rachel was bringing her laptop home to see what she could learn about that strange man that had appeared at their office that morning. Katie had called him Ivan, and said she was assigning him to Tom. He gave Rachel the creeps in the same way the letters did, and they'd both turned up on the same day. It made her wonder if he had some connection to the letters.

"I'll walk you out," Tom said.

He shut the lights off while Rachel was still looking out the window. As darkness descended around her, she realized with a start that she and Tom hadn't been alone. The dark gave her a clearer view outside, and what she saw had her stomach twisting. A man stood in the shadows across the street. He wasn't looking at her. He didn't seem to be looking at anything. He was just, lingering. She couldn't see his face clearly, only that he was a man of average size and build. She only saw a glimpse of his face before he turned away, but there was something familiar in his features that she couldn't quite place.

"Ready?" Tom asked.

"Do you see that?" Rachel pointed across the street. The man had turned his back and was starting to walk away.

"Who is that?"

"I don't know."

Tom ran outside and Rachel followed. "Excuse me," Tom said to the man's retreating form. "Are you looking for assistance?"

The man picked up speed, disappearing down a nearby alleyway headed in the direction of the Public Defender's Office. Rachel's heart was beating wildly, pounding against her chest. It was working too hard, like it might break into two.

"Is everything alright, miss?" Bryce had gotten out of the SUV and come up beside her and Tom.

Rachel didn't answer. She could feel Bryce's intense gaze crawling along her skin. It felt like he wanted something from her. All men, except for maybe Tom, wanted something from her.

"It's fine," Tom said. "It was probably just a client that got spooked when you pulled up."

Bryce tore his gaze from Rachel, allowing it to settle on Tom. "Who are you?" His words were sharp, accusing.

"Tom Archie," Tom extended his hand to shake. "I work with Rachel."

Bryce eyed Tom's hand like it was something poisonous. "Let's go, Rachel. We'd better hurry if you plan to dine with Miss Stephanie this evening."

"Okay."

Bryce opened the door for Rachel. She stepped inside without looking at him. There was a possessiveness in the way he leaned close to her, separating her and Tom with his body.

"See you tomorrow, Tom," Rachel called as Bryce slammed the door shut. She couldn't hear his response, but his hand was raised in a wave.

Bryce got into the driver's seat and the engine roared to life. He was watching her even now, using the rearview mirror. It had been this way every day for the past few weeks since she'd moved in with Aunt Stephanie. It bothered Rachel, yet she couldn't bring it up to her aunt. Stephanie trusted Bryce, and Rachel didn't have anything tangible to point to other than the fact that he made her uncomfortable. But as she'd told Tom earlier, everyone made her uncomfortable, so that wasn't much of an argument.

The letters popped back into the forefront of her mind. They'd started when she had moved out of Ashley's house and in with Stephanie. She'd wondered how the person could know such intimate details, but Bryce—Stephanie's confidant and driver—would have access to that information. At first she'd thought that her letter writer was a client of the MEHR team, but now, faced with Bryce's possessiveness, she was starting to wonder if it was someone a whole lot closer to home. If it was the man who was always watching her through the rearview mirror.

# 10

## ASHLEY

As Ashley was making her way toward the exit, George stood up and grabbed the man next to him by the arm, pulling him to his feet. The other man stumbled, but George had a tight grip on him, preventing him from falling. Then he began pulling the man toward the door, like a bouncer in a club.

Ashley's gaze darted from the door to the now empty barstool next to Katie. She didn't want to be a part of whatever was happening between George and the man. At first, she'd thought George was planning on having the man charged with public intoxication—which in Ashley's opinion was fucking ridiculous. Iowa law allowed such nonsense—bars were public places and people did get intoxicated inside them—but Ashley felt like it was entrapment.

But once they were near the door, George's demeanor changed. He was patting the man on the back and talking to him in hushed tones. If Ashley didn't know George better, she would have thought he was comforting the man. Whatever was happening, it wasn't Ashley's business, and the man didn't need her help, so she switched directions and headed toward Katie.

"What's going on with you and Boy George?" Ashley said, dropping into the barstool next to Katie.

"Oh," Katie's eyes widened, like she was shocked to see Ashley, then she flashed a tentative smile. "Hey there."

Ashley raised her eyebrows. An indication that there was still a question pending.

"Nothing. We just met up for a drink."

"That's how it starts."

"What starts?"

"Open the door a crack, and he'll kick it down."

"I'm not following. Do you want a drink?" Katie gestured to Mikey. "I think I'm going to need another."

"My mother used to say 'a tiger doesn't change its stripes.'"

Mikey came over. "Two more?"

"None for me," Ashley said. "I'm on my way out in a few minutes." Her gaze lingered on George, who was still talking to the man, but she didn't expect the conversation to last much longer.

"Yes, please," Katie said, sliding her empty glass toward Mikey.

Mikey grabbed it and returned with a full glass within seconds. Then he turned back to his customers, likely catching the tension and realizing that they needed some privacy.

"I take it that George is the tiger in your tiger stripe scenario," Katie said.

"He hurt you badly. Don't you remember? I just don't want to see it happening again. You can't trust him. You know he will throw you under the bus if there is any benefit in it for him."

"I'm not sure how he could. I mean, we don't even work together."

"Where there's a will, there's a way. And King George will find a way."

"You're full of platitudes tonight, aren't you?"

Ashley flashed a brief smile. "I guess I'm channeling my mother. She's the one who gave me all the advice I needed when it came to men."

"Speaking of men," Katie nodded toward David, who was putting on his coat. "What's the deal with that guy?"

"There's no deal."

"You looked awfully cozy back there."

"We are not cozy. He's a lawyer. He wanted some advice. That's it. You know I've sworn off dating. Life is easier that way. And you've changed the subject, you jerk." She bumped Katie's shoulder with her own.

Katie shrugged. "You fell for it."

"Touché." Ashley clapped her hand down on the bar top and stood. "On that note, I think it's time for me to go. I've delivered my dire warnings for the night." She was watching the door. George had finished his conversation with the man and sent him out right behind David. "I'll talk to you soon."

"Okay, bye," Katie said.

Ashley passed George halfway between the door and Katie. He made a gesture of tipping a nonexistent hat at her, and she ignored him. Katie might be hoodwinked, but he wasn't going to fool her with his prince charming act. She walked out the door and was greeted by a blast of arctic air. Snow had started falling while she was inside the tavern. At first, the snowflakes were small and wet, but they had transformed into large white flakes by the time she reached her office.

The employee parking lot for the Public Defender's Office was behind the building. Ashley could either go down a dark alleyway or through the office to reach her car. Rather than tracking wet snow inside, she decided to take the alley. It wasn't well lit—the only lights were at the front and the back of the building—but Ashley could see well enough to avoid running into anything.

She slowly made her way through the alley, stepping around the large, industrial sized trash can. It smelled, but not too bad during the winter. The cold tempered its stench. When she reached the back of the building, she realized that she was not alone.

Someone was standing at the back edge of the parking lot. The lighting was better back there, but she still couldn't make out the person's face. The person was wearing a heavy coat with the hood pulled up, casting a deeper shadow over their facial features. It was a man, Ashley felt sure of it. It was a physique of someone that felt vaguely familiar, but the poor lighting and heavy clothing made identification impossible.

She was still in the darkness of the alleyway, so the man had not noticed her. He wasn't looking at her anyway. His focus was intense, and it was directed at the back door of her office. A shiver ran up Ashley's spine, and the lyrics from Rockwell's song "Somebody's Watching Me" sprang to her mind. Was this person waiting for her? If so, then why? It could be a disgruntled client, here to threaten her or worse. She didn't have a lot of those, but every defense attorney had a few. It was impossible to make everyone happy.

It was for this exact reason that Ashley carried bear mace in her purse. She reached for it now, feeling the familiar weight of it in her hand. She pulled it out, holding it in her right hand as she pressed herself up against the wall of the Public Defender's Office, melting into the shadows. If this guy thought he was going to get the better of her, he had another thing coming.

Ashley slowly crept toward the man, placing her thumb firmly on the trigger of the mace and holding it out in front of her, ready to shoot at a moment's notice. The man didn't move. At least not until Ashley's toe caught on an uneven spot in the pavement and she stumbled. Then his head darted toward her.

"Shit," Ashley hissed through her teeth.

She tensed, raising her bear mace higher. It was a warning to stay back, but if he had a gun, she now realized, her little can of pepper spray wouldn't be much of a threat. Regardless, she wasn't going down without a fight. She would defend herself if it came to a struggle. Luckily, she didn't have to. The moment the man saw her, he turned and ran.

"Hey," Ashley yelled, shocked by his sudden departure. She'd been gearing up for a fight, not a chase. "Stop!"

The man didn't stop. He raced down the street and disappeared around a dark corner. Ashley stared after him in stunned silence.

"What the hell was that?" Ashley said to herself after a few beats of silence.

She turned to look at the back door of her office, the place where the man had been staring. A flash of white caught her eye, and she marched up to the back door. As she drew nearer, she realized what it was. It was a letter, jammed beneath the door. She turned to look back over her shoulder, but the man had not returned. Then she leaned down and picked it up. There were words written on the back, but it was hard to read in the poor lighting, so she headed to her Tahoe, pulled out her keys, opened the door, and hopped inside.

She started the car and flipped on the dome light. The words FOR RACHEL were written in all caps in a familiar, shimmery light blue ink. She also recognized the handwriting. She was no expert, but it had the same characteristics as the handwriting on the two letters that had previously come in the mail for Rachel. The ones she'd handed over to her young friend earlier today. Both words were in all caps, but the first letter of each word was slightly larger than the rest.

She wondered if the man she'd seen in the parking lot had left the letter, or if the letter's presence and the man's presence had been coincidence. It didn't seem likely, especially with the way the man was staring at the back door, but she couldn't rule it out as a possibility. After all, she hadn't seen him place it there. It was possible that he was staring at it because he didn't know what it was. But if that were true, then why was the man there at all? Leaving the letter would be strange, but there was nothing nefarious about that action alone.

She shook her head, casting the thought from her mind, and put her old Tahoe in gear. But once she was safely on the highway, headed back to her acreage south of town, her mind wandered back to the incident. *What the hell was that man doing?* She felt sure now that he'd taken pains to keep her from seeing his face. But why? She guessed that if she had seen him, she would recognize him, and he knew it. But why had he been hiding behind her office?

She told herself that it could have been a client, waiting to see her the next morning, but deep down she knew that explanation didn't hold water. The man's actions had been inconsistent with that conclusion. If it had been a client there for legitimate reasons, he would have approached her when he saw her in the alleyway. The man had acted like a stalker wishing to remain in the shadows, not a client who needed help.

No, the man's behavior meant something more. He was there for a reason, and Ashley had thwarted it. Whatever his motives, she didn't get the sense that this man was the type to give up easily, and Ashley wondered what he—whoever he was—would do next.

# 11

## KATIE

"Ready to talk about this mess?" George asked when he returned to his barstool.

"Yes," Katie said, her stomach flipping. On the surface, she had discarded Ashley's warnings, but Ashley's words were starting to sink in. George could have ulterior motives.

"Let's go find a more private place to sit." George motioned to Mikey. Mikey was at the other end of the bar, pouring a drink for another customer. When the bar owner looked up, George pointed at his beer and then at the tap, mouthing the word *more*.

Katie stood up. She still had a full beer. "I'll go find a table."

"Okay," George said without looking at her.

Katie grabbed her coat and made her way to the back corner, choosing the table where Ashley and that other attorney had been sitting earlier in the evening. She placed her beer on the table and her coat over the back of the chair before sitting so her back was to the wall and she faced the door.

"Alrighty," George said when he reached the table. He had two full beers, one in each hand. They were both a dark color. Stout beer. The type of drink he enjoyed, and she hated. He set the beer down and slid into his chair.

"Need some liquid courage?" Katie said, nodding at his hands.

"Something like that."

"I guess this is important."

If she was honest with herself, she'd admit it was important to her, too. The phone call from George that morning had lit a fire somewhere inside Katie. A flame that had been extinguished years ago when she'd been passed up for the detective and later laid off as a police officer. Police work had once been the center of her life. Every day was an adventure. Sure, she saw plenty of horrible things throughout the years, but she had also made a difference. And there was a rush that came with the work. One that was exclusive to the crime control arm of law enforcement. She was out of that now, and a big part of her missed it.

"I don't know any easy way to say this, so I'm just going to blurt it out," George said, taking a drink.

Katie gestured for him to go on.

"The body in Lake Goldenhead, we have an identity. We had a warm snap a few days ago, remember?"

"Yeah." It had been unseasonably warm earlier that week. In the sixties and even seventies for four days straight.

"That caused some decomposition, but we were able to identify her by her clothing. She also had a few tattoos, unique to her."

*Her.* That was the primary word Katie had heard. The body was female. Before that moment, she hadn't known any details, but for some reason she'd thought it was a man.

"Who was it?" For someone who had said he was just going to blurt it out, George sure was holding back.

"We are still working on contacting her son. Until then, we can't reveal the identity."

Katie sat back, her spine colliding painfully with the unupholstered chair. "So, you want advice, but you aren't going to tell me anything." Ashley's earlier warning flashed through her mind. Was he gloating? Had he brought her here to remind her that he was in the know and she was an outsider?

"No, no," George said, raising his hands in a gesture of surrender. "I was just saying that you need to keep it quiet. You can't tell anyone. Not even the world's worst defense attorney."

"I think you have that backward. Ashley is definitely not the worst."

"She's the worst in my book. The worst to deal with," he flashed a smile.

"Dad joke," Katie said, but she couldn't help grinning. Ashley would see it as a compliment. She liked pissing off cops, especially George.

"But that's not my point. I know you are still close friends with Ashley, and you have to promise not to tell her or anyone else."

"Fine, fine." Katie said. She didn't like the idea of keeping things from her best friend—especially at George's direction—but her desire to know the body's identity outshined that notion. Besides, it would likely become common knowledge within a few days. "Who was it?"

"Erica Elsberry."

Katie gasped.

"I know. It's bad."

Erica and Katie had not been on friendly terms maybe ever, but they'd been downright hostile for years now. That resentment was one-directional, coming from Erica, but Katie didn't blame her. Several years earlier, when Katie was an officer, she had screwed up a search warrant that pertained to Erica's son's sexual assault. It resulted in the perpetrator's acquittal, and Erica had never forgiven Katie. Katie hadn't forgiven herself either.

"What happened?" Lots of Brine locals frequented Lake Goldenhead to fish, but Katie had never known Erica to be among them. "Did she fall off the wagon?"

Erica had gotten into the methamphetamine scene after the acquittal of her son's abuser. She'd been working with the MEHR team for close to six months, but she'd been clean, so she was now under the most lenient version of supervision. Tom was her assigned team member, and he only checked in with her once a month. Tom hadn't mentioned that Erica was at risk of relapse, but these things could happen quickly, and they had a snowballing effect.

George shrugged. "I don't know. It will be a while before we get the toxicology results. We don't have a rush on that information because it isn't important at this stage of the game. I will say that there weren't any drugs or drug paraphernalia inside the toolbox, and I didn't see any evidence of track marks on her. Not that I looked all that close, because honestly, she was not in good condition."

"Wait, what? Toolbox? What kind of toolbox?" Her mind automatically drifted to the kind found in garages with lots of drawers. There was no way anyone was fitting inside one of those unless they'd been dismembered. The thought of something like that happening to one of the MEHR team's clients turned Katie's stomach.

George sighed heavily. "It was one of those toolboxes that fit into the back of truck beds. A runner saw it floating in Lake Goldenhead and fished it out."

"Floating? How was a toolbox floating? Aren't those things heavy?"

"Pretty heavy. It was made heavier by the sandbag, but yeah. It shouldn't have floated."

"How many sandbags?" She wasn't sure why she'd asked this question. It didn't really matter. The presence of one meant foul play. Someone was trying to hide evidence at the bottom of a murky lake bed."

"There was one."

"So, how was it floating if there was a sandbag plus Erica's body and they were both inside a heavy toolbox? That doesn't make sense."

"That's what I thought, but then I talked to the medical examiner. He had a long, convoluted way of explaining it, but I'll simplify it, because I can't repeat all the medical mumbo jumbo he told me if my life depended on it."

"Okay," Katie didn't smile at this attempt at humor.

"The medical examiner said that Erica's body had released gas during the decomposition process, which was faster than usual at this time of year, thanks to the heat. Since the toolbox was airtight, those gasses were trapped inside the box with nowhere to go. And the gases caused the whole thing to float."

George had used a couple of concerning words during his explanation, but Katie's mind had snagged on the word *airtight*. It was the investigator in her waking up. A body had been found in suspicious conditions. Cause of death was naturally the next question on her mind.

"She didn't suffocate, did she?"

"Don't know yet, but all signs are pointing to yes. There was no other obvious cause, at least. No stab wounds, bullet holes, or blunt force trauma."

"That's bad." It was all Katie could manage to say. She couldn't help thinking about what it must have felt like to be Erica in her final moments. Locked inside a box in complete and total darkness while her air supply slowly dwindled. It would have felt like being buried alive.

"Yeah. A horrible way to die."

"Do you know if the toolbox was in the lake before she died or tossed in afterward?"

George shrugged. "I don't know that it matters. The inside of the toolbox was completely dry aside from the wet parts of the decomposition process, of course."

Katie could have done without that bit of information. "So, she definitely didn't drown."

"I can't say with absolute certainty. At least not until we get the ME's report, but no, she didn't drown."

"Are there any suspects?"

"Sheriff St. James and one of the other deputies, Frankie Pitch, are hellbent on making Noah their target."

"Noah Scott?"

It didn't surprise her. Noah was Erica's boyfriend, and he had a criminal history a mile long. But his crimes had all been centered around methamphetamine, and he'd been working with Katie and the MEHR team. He'd been clean. But when Katie had just bumped into him, he had said that he needed to meet with her. There had been an urgency to him that Katie hadn't seen for quite some time. It was a potential indicator of use. She'd told him to try and catch Tom before he left, but now she wondered if he had.

"Hold on a minute. I need to check on something," Katie said, digging out her phone. She quickly typed out a group text, sending it to both Rachel and Tom. *Did Noah Scott stop by after I left today?*

Rachel's answer was almost instantaneous. *No. Why?*

*I saw him when I was walking to Mikey's Tavern. I'm worried about him.*

*Do you want me to call him?* Rachel asked.

Katie was the MEHR team member assigned to Noah's case, so she should be the one making the call, but she didn't want to step away from her conversation with George. There was no telling when he'd decide to hit the off switch on the tap of free-flowing knowledge.

*Yeah.* Katie typed back. *Would you? I've just received some information that makes me worry that he is imminently likely to relapse.*

*I'll call him,* Rachel typed back.

With that resolved, Katie set her phone down and turned back to George. "Is there any evidence that points to Noah as the killer?"

"Yes, and no."

"Okay." That was a nonanswer if Katie had ever heard one.

"He is the significant other, so naturally he's the first one they wanted to look at. But there are also several witnesses that say that the last time they saw Erica was, well, here."

Katie tsked. She couldn't help it. Erica's prime addiction was methamphetamine, but she was supposed to stay away from all mood-altering substances, including alcohol. Once an addict, always an addict. Trading one addiction for another was not a solution.

"Noah was with her."

*Another sign pointing to relapse,* Katie thought.

"Apparently, they had a major argument. Witnesses weren't sure of the basis of the fight, but they thought it centered around cheating allegations. They weren't certain on whose end the alleged cheating had occurred— Erica or Noah—but it was definitely a very public and very volatile verbal altercation."

"Who are these 'witnesses?'"

"They wanted to remain confidential."

Confidential informants could be reliable, but they were far more suspect than those who were willing to go on the record about the information.

"We are executing a search warrant on Noah's house tomorrow," George said. "I was, um, hoping you would come along."

Katie arched an eyebrow. "Me? Why?"

"Because we work well together." He scratched at the tabletop with a fingernail. "And none of these guys at the Sheriff's Department listen to me. I told them I thought they were barking up the wrong tree. I mean, you know Noah," he looked up, his eyes meeting Katie's. There was a desperation there that she hadn't seen before. "He wouldn't do this."

Over the years, Katie had learned that everyone was capable of murder. The real questions were how they might commit that murder—quick or cruel—and what it would take to tip the scales for them to decide that murder was the answer. She didn't know Noah well enough to know his tipping point, but in all her years in dealing with him as a police officer and later through the MEHR team, she had never seen any cruelty in him.

"I agree."

"We are executing the search warrant first thing tomorrow morning. Eight o'clock sharp. Can you be there?"

Katie's office didn't officially open until eight thirty, and it probably wouldn't hurt to pay Noah a house call after all the things she'd seen and heard about him tonight. Ashley's warning about George making Katie his scapegoat still stuck in the back of Katie's mind, but it was less important when she rationalized it as showing up for Noah, not George. Yet she couldn't shake Ashley's words. She didn't know how George could be setting her up to take the fall for him, or what that fall might be, but it wouldn't be the first time he had used her in that way. Ashley was right. She needed to be vigilant, but she also needed to check up on her struggling client.

"Yes, I'll go."

"Thank you, thank you."

"Don't get too excited. I'm agreeing to this primarily because I want to be there for Noah. I'm not agreeing to assist you in your investigation. Noah is still one of my clients, and I don't think he should face a bunch of deputies bursting through his front door on his own."

"I'll take whatever I can get," he said with a wink.

# 12

## RACHEL

It had been fifteen long minutes since Bryce had picked Rachel up at her office, but there were still another thirty minutes to go until they were back at Aunt Stephanie's house. The silence was heavy, every second drawn out so it felt like minutes. She'd checked the time on her phone more times than she could count.

She looked at her phone one more time, and as she did, it buzzed with a new text message. She could have wept with joy. She clicked on the messaging icon and saw it was from Katie. A group text to her and Tom. Katie was asking about Noah Scott. If he'd stopped in at the end of the day.

Rachel had replied in the negative, but part of her wondered if that was a lie. Someone had been standing outside the MEHR team office when Rachel and Tom were leaving. It could have been Noah. She'd been nervous and frightened by the person's presence, but now she was starting to wonder if that was an overreaction. That those new letters coupled with her past had put her so far on edge that it was causing problems for their clients. She hoped not, but she couldn't completely dismiss the possibility. So, when Katie had asked Rachel to call and check up on Noah, she'd jumped at the opportunity.

"Who was that?" Bryce asked, gazing at Rachel in the rearview mirror.

Rachel ignored him and pulled her laptop out of her backpack. She was working on building up her backbone, and she felt certain that none of the stronger women in her life—Ashley, Katie, Aunt Stephanie—would answer a question like that. They'd tell her that her business was hers alone unless she chose to share it.

She powered up her laptop and opened the MEHR team client management software, searching for *Scott, Noah*. When the file appeared, she clicked on his name, opening it. There were multiple tabs that she could choose to click on including *case notes*, *underlying offense*, and *medical diagnoses*, but she ignored them all and chose the *contact information* page.

A picture of Noah appeared in the upper left corner. He stared out at her with an even yet blank expression. He had dark hair and dark brown eyes that were not kind or unkind. He wasn't smiling, but few did in these pictures. It was the ones who smiled in their mug shots who caused a shiver of fear to run up Rachel's spine. Those that smiled did not seem happy, they looked deranged.

Next to Noah's picture was a list of contact information. It contained his phone number, email, home address, and work address. She picked up her phone and dialed his number, ignoring Bryce, who had continued stealing glances at her in the rearview mirror since her text conversation with Katie.

"Hello?" A deep male voice picked up after two rings.

"Is this Noah?"

"Depends on who's asking."

"Um, this is Rachel Arkman. I work for the MEHR team."

"Oh, Rachel," Noah said, his tone taking on a softer edge. "Sorry. I didn't mean to be rude. I thought you were someone else."

"Okay." She wasn't sure what to say after that. If she were Katie, she would probably have followed with *who did you think I was?* But Rachel was not Katie. She'd love to have Katie's ability to confront people with impunity, but that was never going to be part of Rachel's personality, no matter how hard she tried.

"Arkman? As in Stephanie Arkman, I assume. I work for her."

"I know."

"You know?"

"Well, I mean, that's what your file says. I assume that it's correct, but if it isn't, please let me know and I'll update your information."

"Nope. It's correct. I thought your last name was Smithson. When did you change it?"

Rachel winced at the mention of her childhood surname. It was given to her by her abuser, her mother's husband, who would remain in prison for the rest of his life. The change in her name had been an attempt to shed the beat-down, violated version of herself, and inspire the growth into someone new, someone stronger, better. It wasn't an overnight transformation as she had foolishly hoped, but she was working on it.

"A couple months ago."

"I didn't realize that."

"Yeah, well, I didn't advertise it. I'm a private person." His comment had struck a nerve with her. Why would he care about her last name?

"I'm sorry, I'm being nosy, aren't I?" Noah said. "I do that sometimes. I'll back off."

He had settled into their conversation with a comfort Rachel hadn't expected. It was almost like the two of them had been lifelong friends, rather than two people who had never spoken in their lives. She, on the other hand, was struggling. At a loss for words more often than not.

"Um, okay."

"What is the reason for your call? Not that you have to have a reason."

"Yes, that. Katie asked me to check on you. She was worried. There is concern that you may be struggling with your sobriety."

"That . . ." his voice trailed off. "There are some," he paused, swallowing audibly, "difficult things going on in my life right now. I, uh, thought my life was going in one direction, but now it seems like everything is shifting. It was in my control, but it's not anymore."

"Oh."

Rachel could feel the intensity of Bryce's heavy gaze on her as he continued driving. It had somehow grown more concentrated, more severe, since she'd started her conversation with Noah. She wondered if the phone was loud enough for Bryce to hear the tone of Noah's voice, its deepness. Not what he was saying, but the pitch, which would easily indicate that she was speaking to a man.

"Do you want to schedule a meeting?" She pressed on, trying to ignore Bryce. This was her job, and it was none of his business. She couldn't let him affect her treatment of clients who were in need. "I'm sure Katie has time tomorrow. Let me pull up her schedule."

"Can't I meet with you?"

"No. You are Katie's client. You should meet with her."

"What if I want to be your client?"

This was not the first time Rachel had heard these words, and she knew that it wouldn't be the last. It was her beauty, or perhaps it was her weakness. She didn't have the strength to stand up to people in the same way that Tom and Katie could. But more likely, at least in her mind, it was the way she looked. Others saw it as an asset, but it was a curse to her. Everything bad that had ever happened in her life was tied to the way she looked. She knew she was objectively beautiful, stunning even. *A face carved by angels*, as many had said to her throughout the years. But it also caused men to grow attached, possessive even, when she had no intention of cultivating even a platonic friendship with them. And she didn't have to look far for examples of that behavior. She was faced with two of them right then— Bryce and Noah.

"It's not possible." Her instincts told her to start her response with *I'm sorry*, but she bit back those words. She was not sorry. Once this conversation ended, she didn't intend to have any more to do with Noah aside from telling Katie about the hastily added-in appointment. "Katie is available for an eleven o'clock tomorrow, or she can squeeze you in at noon. Will either of those times work?"

"No." The word held an edge that had not previously been there.

"Well, then, I'll have Katie reach out to you tomorrow. Have a nice evening," Rachel said, ending the call and dropping her phone next to her on the leather seat. She hastily shut her laptop and shoved it back into her bag.

"You were talking to someone named Noah," Bryce said.

Rachel jumped at the sound of his voice, her already fraying nerves unraveling further. "Yes." There was no point lying. Rachel had used Noah's name when he'd picked up.

"If that was Noah Scott, you should know that he is no good."

"No good. Why?" Rachel picked up her phone, remembering that she needed to inform Katie of her conversation with Noah. She typed out a quick text with the barest details of the call and sent it.

"Noah is dating my ex-girlfriend, Erica Elsberry."

"You dated Erica?" Rachel said, shocked. She didn't know Erica well, but she did know that she'd been working with the MEHR team. She was assigned to Tom. Apparently, there was some bad blood between her and Katie from before Rachel's day.

"I haven't heard anything from Erica in a week," Bryce continued. "It's not like her."

"I don't understand. If she's your ex, why do you talk to her?"

"We stayed friends. There was something off about her and that Noah guy. I'm telling you, he's no good." He said the last few words with such force that Rachel winced. Everyone knew about her past—it was a highly publicized trial—and that kept them from addressing her in the same manner they might someone else. It bothered her that everyone tended to handle her with kid gloves, but she would prefer that over the newfound harshness in Bryce's tone.

"Oh."

She decided not to say anything more. Not that she had anything to say. She'd spent enough time around Ashley and the criminal justice system to know that anytime a woman goes missing, the likely suspects were the significant other and the ex. She'd heard grumblings around town about Erica's disappearance, including a few stories about her ex-boyfriend. Bryce's name wasn't mentioned, but she was even more uneasy now that she knew there was a connection. What had happened to Erica? If it was foul play, was Bryce or Noah involved?

# 13

ASHLEY

Tuesday, December 3

Ashley spent the night tossing and turning. Her mind wouldn't shut off. She tried to steady her breathing, counting her inhales and exhales, in and out, focusing on clearing her mind, but her thoughts kept wandering. Back to the letter left for Rachel. Back to the man standing in the parking lot behind the Public Defender's Office. *Stop thinking, keep your mind blank,* she reminded herself, and it would work, but only for a few minutes. Then she'd start thinking of David and his request for assistance with Noah. For what, exactly, she still didn't really know.

By the time her bedside clock read four o'clock, she'd given up on sleep. Tossing the covers aside, she got out of bed and dressed for the day. If her mind was going to continue spinning, she might as well put it to use working on cases. She'd been letting her dogs sleep in the bed with her since Tom had vacated that spot, but neither one got up with her. They lay there, watching her through half-open eyes.

She pulled her hair back and applied a dab of makeup before heading downstairs, filling a to-go cup with coffee, and heading out the door. There was a fresh layer of snow on the ground, sparkling in the moonlight. She had always loved the image of undisturbed snow. It made her think of Christmas, which was quickly approaching.

Her old Tahoe roared to life when she stuck the key into the ignition and turned. She flipped the wiper blades on to swish the snow off the windshield. Her acreage property had outbuildings she could park inside to keep her car out of the weather, but she never did. Her Tahoe was old. It didn't need special treatment.

The temperature had dropped even further overnight, and she could see her breath coming out in puffs inside the SUV as she put it in gear and headed toward town. It took a good ten minutes before the vehicle was warm enough for heat. When it was, she turned it on full blast.

Rachel's letter was still in her car. Ashley had tossed it on the passenger seat the night before. She still didn't know what to do with it, whether to give it to Rachel or toss it out, but she knew it would have been ruined if she'd left it out in the snow. Rachel didn't seem happy about the first two letters, but she also hadn't called Ashley distressed about them. Now that she thought about it, she probably should have left the letter where it was; that would have been an easy answer to her dilemma.

She pulled into the parking lot behind the Public Defender's Office. It was empty this time of morning, no sign of the man who had been lurking the night before. Again, she looked at the letter, wondering what to do with it. *Better bring it in*, she thought, grabbing the letter. She could give it to Rachel if she stopped by or discuss it with Katie if she had a free moment.

The snow crunched beneath Ashley's feet as she made her way toward the back door, leaving a trail of footsteps in her wake.

Inside, the air was warm and stuffy, but it was peaceful, quiet. Ashley headed straight to her office, careful not to turn on many lights. If her clients saw that someone was there, they sometimes appeared unannounced, pounding on the door, demanding to meet with her. This was the time of the day that many of them were still up partying. Piss drunk and buzzing from a meth high. She might have the time to deal with that nonsense, but she didn't have the energy, so her office light was the only one she turned on.

She sat down at her desk and grabbed a file, flipping it open. For the next several hours, she focused on case after case, reading reports, writing notes, and drafting motions. She moved almost methodically, her mind clicking off possible defenses and potential holes in the state's cases. In times like these, she envisioned herself as a machine, going and going, a bit like the energizer bunny. Except that she would be made of steel, with cold corners and sharp edges, rather than a fluffy pink bunny.

An alarm went off on her phone, startling her. She'd set a reminder for ten minutes before eight o'clock. *Time to get going*, she thought, hopping to her feet and grabbing her coat. She swung her coat around her shoulders, shoved her laptop in her bag, and headed out the back door. A tractor was in the parking lot, pushing snow. She recognized the driver as a former client, and she waved. He returned the gesture, then gave her a thumbs up. She smiled and hurried on her way. She couldn't remember the tractor driver's name or what he had been charged with—there were so many clients in and out of her door—but it was nice to see that he was working. It was an important step to staying out of trouble.

Noah and Erica lived in a small bungalow a quarter mile from her office. It was a cold day, but Ashley needed exercise, so she walked. At a few minutes past eight o'clock she knocked on the door. She shifted her weight as she waited for someone to answer, regretting the choice to walk. She couldn't feel her nose or the tips of her fingers anymore.

David answered the door. He was smiling, a warm, broad smile that had Ashley immediately distrusting him. His wavy, chestnut hair was perfectly styled, and there wasn't a hint of exhaustion in his light grey eyes. Ashley kinda hated him for that. They were near the same age, in their mid- to late thirties. An age when everyone looked just a little tired, even after a decent night's sleep.

"Come on in," David said, stepping aside and motioning for Ashley to enter.

She walked around David, giving him a wide berth, and avoiding a proper greeting. The home was small but cozy, with the entryway opening into a living room. The furniture was out of style, faded, but well maintained. The overall feel was masculine, but there were a few feminine touches here and there. A pastel-colored throw draped over the dark plaid couch. Pictures of a smiling young James Elsberry, Erica's son, in gaudy faux gold frames.

The home had been renovated to create an open-concept feel, with the living room spilling directly into the dining area and kitchen. Noah was seated at the scuffed dining room table, looking as tired as Ashley felt. His brown hair was disheveled, his dark eyes blank as he drank a cup of coffee.

"Hey, Noah. How you holding up?" Ashley said.

The ghost of a smile formed on his lips, then disappeared. "I'm hanging in there, I guess."

"How long has Erica been gone?" Ashley said, walking over to the table. The dining table was small and rectangular with four chairs around it. She chose the seat directly opposite Noah and sat down.

"A week, I guess."

"Did you report her disappearance to law enforcement?"

"No."

Ashley had represented Noah many times in the past, but there was an edge to his voice now, a defensiveness that had never been there before. "That's going to be a problem."

"What? Why? I thought I wasn't supposed to talk to law enforcement. That's what you've always told us. 'They aren't there to help you.' Isn't that what you say?" Noah spat her words back at her.

"That's if they show up unannounced. You're forgetting the first part of that mantra. 'If you didn't call them, they aren't there to help you.' Now, cool it and stop trying to blame me, or I'm going to get up right now and leave. I am not here as appointed counsel. I do not have to stay, and I do not have to help you."

Noah glared at her for a long moment, then all the energy seemed to seep out of him. His shoulders rolled forward and he dropped his head into his hand. "I know. I'm sorry. I'm just so goddamn stressed out."

"I bet." He was dodging the difficult part of the conversation. First by shifting blame onto her, and then by making excuses. "I know you don't want to but let's focus on the issues at hand."

Noah nodded.

"Erica has been gone for a week, and you didn't say a word to law enforcement. You see why that could be a problem, right?"

"Yes. I just thought she was using again. You know how people can go on benders. They can disappear for days at a time."

"But it usually isn't more than a couple days. You obviously thought something was wrong, because you hired David," she gestured to the other attorney who was standing between the kitchen and the dining room, where he could listen to their conversation but wouldn't be required to participate.

"I know. I got scared. I thought she was in trouble. And then, when I heard about the body in the lake, I thought I might be in trouble."

"Where is James? Where is Erica's son?" Nobody knew the identity of James's father, so his absence in addition to Erica's was troubling.

"He's at the youth shelter. He's been acting out, so a social worker suggested that we take him there."

"How long has he been there?" Ashley didn't do juvenile work, but she knew that shelters weren't a wonderful environment for children. They usually housed kids who were violent but hadn't yet committed any major crimes.

"A month."

"That's a long time."

"Yeah, well, he's been a handful. Spitting at his teachers, flipping desks, hitting his mother, you name it and he's done it. I blame you since you represented the bastard that raped him."

"That's bullshit and you know it." She had represented Victor Petrovsky, James's abuser, but it wasn't her representation that had harmed James. His damage had come from a sadistic psychopath with a taste for children, and a mother who willingly left him with that sadistic psychopath so she could play house with her boyfriend at the time.

"Whatever."

"There's nothing about what's happening here," she gestured toward Noah, "that makes me want to help you right now. You're defensive, accusatory, and quite frankly, you're acting like an asshole."

"I'm sorry. I'm sorry. I don't mean to be like this."

"Then stop." She took a deep breath, then focused back on the issues at hand. "So, what happened the last time you saw Erica?"

"We fought."

"Like, fought," Ashley raised her fists in the air in a boxing stance, "or you argued?"

"A little of both."

"What was the argument about?"

Noah shrugged. "I can't remember."

Ashley didn't believe him. It had been the last time he would maybe ever see Erica. If he'd forgotten, then he either didn't care about her or he'd been pretty sauced.

"Where were you when you had this argument?"

"Mikey's Tavern."

Apparently, the answer was sauced. "You realize you are both addicts and neither of you should be at a bar."

"Yes. I don't know why we did it. We hadn't been out in so long. Then we started drinking and one thing led to another and—"

"Stop!" Ashley shouted. This conversation was getting too detailed. As a defense attorney, she didn't want to hear it. She hadn't agreed to represent him yet, but she also hadn't completely ruled out the possibility. If she did file an appearance, she and David were going to have to develop a defense strategy. Details outside of what the prosecutor knew could cut off some potential arguments.

"What?" Noah looked confused.

Ashley was about to explain herself even though she didn't feel like she should have to. After all, this wasn't Noah's first rodeo, so he should have understood. But just then, there was a knock at the door. It was three sharp bangs, knuckles rapping hard against the wood.

"Expecting company?" Ashley asked, looking from Noah to David. Both men shook their heads.

The banging came again, this time hard enough to shake the door in its frame. "Open up, Noah," a familiar voice called from outside. It was George Thomanson. Ashley would recognize the sound of that snake anywhere.

Noah froze. He looked as though he might piss his pants.

"We have a search warrant," George continued. "Open up or we are going to break this door down."

It didn't look like either Noah or David was eager to confront their new houseguests. Ashley, on the other hand, was gearing up for a fight. She stood and started walking toward the door. It had been a while since the last time she stood toe-to-toe with law enforcement. If Sir-George-a-lot wanted to play, she was happy to oblige.

# 14

## KATIE

Several deputies separated Katie, who was at the back of the group that was serving the search warrant on Noah's house, and George, who was at the front, knocking on the door. She was already starting to regret agreeing to come along. Yes, it was a convenient time to pop in for a visit, and yes, she could help to keep any overzealous deputies in line, but arriving along with them was probably not the best way to maintain a positive rapport with her client.

When George had first floated the idea, she'd been completely on board. But that was after a long day and a couple drinks. In the clarity that inevitably came with morning and a good night's sleep, she now realized just how flawed her thinking had been. She'd been too excited to be a part of law enforcement activities again. To be back in the field and in the action.

The door swung open just as George was lifting his hand to knock for a third time.

"Hello, King George," Ashley said, a smug smile playing on her lips.

There was a shift in the energy of the men surrounding Katie. Ashley was not a traditional beauty. She was built a bit like a teenage boy, rail thin with only slight curves, but there was something striking about her appearance. It was in the way she held herself, like she'd accepted her flaws, even loved them. That kind of confidence shone brighter than any traditional beauty, even unblemished beauties like Rachel. Or at least that was what Katie thought, and her senses told her that at least a few of the men around her felt the same way.

"Don't call me that," George said.

Ashley ignored him. "To what do we owe the pleasure of his majesty's company?"

A man joined Ashley in the doorway. It was the same man Ashley had met at Mikey's Tavern the night before. Today, he was in a charcoal, neatly tailored suit, with a white shirt and blue tie. His grey eyes scanned the crowd of law enforcement, skipping over Katie as though she wasn't even there.

"I'm David Dirkman," he said, projecting his voice like he was giving a speech. Katie noticed that he was looking at them, but he was careful not to meet anyone's gaze. A future politician if Katie had ever seen one. "I am representing Noah Scott."

Ashley gave David a look that Katie easily recognized. An, *are you fucking kidding me; I've got this*, kind of look, and it almost caused Katie to burst out laughing. Then Ashley's gaze flickered to her, and Ashley's mocking smile dropped for a moment before she regained her composure.

"We're here to execute a search warrant," a younger, heavily muscled deputy said, joining George on the top step of the small front porch. The guy's name was Frankie Pitch. He was a good ten years younger than George, but he started his law enforcement career with the Brine County Sheriff's Department, so he was higher ranking than George, who was a new hire.

"Are you now?" Ashley said, her gaze darting back to Deputy Pitch. "Well, let's see this warrant."

Deputy Pitch thrust a stack of documents into Ashley's hands and shoved past her. She stumbled when his shoulder struck hers, but she regained her composure quickly, and started reading the documents.

"I need to search you," Deputy Pitch said, turning back to Ashley.

"No. You need to go fuck yourself," Ashley said without looking away from the documents.

"I *am* going to search you." The deputy was doubling down, which was never a good sign when it came to Ashley.

"Suit yourself," Ashley said, lowering the search warrant documents to her side. "But then I *am* going to sue you."

"What? Why?" Deputy Pitch spluttered.

Ashley held up the search warrant. "Have you even read this?" She stared at him for a long moment, waiting for a response. "I'll take that as a 'no.' Okay, well, you are authorized by this warrant to search the residence, Noah's vehicle," she gestured to a beat-up car parked in the driveway, "the detached garage, and Noah himself. Do I look like any of those things? I mean, I'm obviously not a house, a garage, or a car, and I'm a woman, so I can't possibly be Noah. I know you and I haven't worked together," Ashley said gesturing from Deputy Pitch to herself, "but you at least know who I am. So, go ahead, fucking search me, see what happens."

Deputy Pitch glared at Ashley, and Katie could practically see the wheels in his head turning. He wasn't sure what to do in that moment. They had both drawn lines in the sand, and Ashley was right, but the deputy did not want to admit it. He took a step forward, clearly deciding that he was going to search her, but George intercepted him.

"Not worth it, man," George said, patting him on the shoulder. "Noah, why don't you and your attorneys step on out so we can have a look around." George was inside the threshold of the house, and motioning to someone farther inside the residence, presumably Noah.

A few moments later, Noah and David were shuffling past the officers and into the front yard. Ashley had not budged. A fact that didn't surprise Katie. She was going to follow the deputies around through the entire search, discovering evidence alongside them while demanding that they return every item to its proper place.

"Hey, there, Noah," Katie said, once Noah and David reached the front lawn, where she was standing.

"Katie," Noah said. "What are you doing here?"

Katie cast a dark look at the deputies who were starting to funnel into Noah's residence. "I'm starting to wonder the same thing. I heard about the search warrant, and I knew you were already struggling with Erica's disappearance."

"How did you know about the warrant?" Noah asked.

"We can talk about it later," Katie said. "But for now, I'm going to help Ashley keep those boys in line while they rifle through your things. But you hang in there." Katie gave Noah's shoulder a squeeze and followed the last deputy into Noah's residence.

Ashley was at her side within seconds.

"A little early to be making house calls, don't you think?" Ashley asked.

"I could say the same thing to you. Noah hasn't been charged with any crimes, so what's the public defender doing here?"

"Touché," Ashley said, a smile flickering across her lips. "But now that we are here, we might as well keep these bullies in line. Yeah?"

Katie nodded and fought the urge to smile. It felt like old times, Ashley and her against the world. She wasn't for or against law enforcement anymore, but Noah was her client. She had to make sure that he was treated fairly. Ashley was firmly against law enforcement, but ultimately, she was there for the same reason: fairness.

"We might as well," Katie said, once again standing shoulder to shoulder with her best friend.

# 15

## ASHLEY

There were only six deputies in the house, but it felt like people were everywhere. They funneled in like a pack of hungry wolves, then split, prowling off in different directions to start sniffing around for evidence. Logically, she knew they were just doing their jobs, but she couldn't help the intense sense of violation and hate welling within her. And this wasn't even *her* home.

It was the helplessness that came with the situation. A search warrant gave the cops the absolute right to do what they wanted with the property. And this one, the warrant she held in her hand, was a problem for Noah. She flipped to the affidavit for search warrant, drafted and signed by Deputy Frankie Pitch, rereading some of the more important lines.

*On Monday, December 2, the body of Erica Jene Elsberry was pulled out of Lake Goldenhead, Brine, Iowa. Deputy George Thomanson was the first to respond, finding one witness, Amanda Stone, at the scene. Amanda had been on a run when she noticed a toolbox floating in the lake. She fished the toolbox out of the water and opened it. It had been locked from the outside, but the lock was defective. Erica's body was curled up in the fetal position inside, fully clothed. There were no signs of outward trauma, there were fingernail scratch marks on the inside lid of the toolbox, indicating that Erica had been alive when she was placed inside. There was one other item inside the toolbox with her, a large sandbag.*

Noah had been right. Erica was dead, locked inside a weighted toolbox and tossed into the lake. Ashley's relationship with Erica had been complicated. They were more enemies than friends, but Erica was a mother, and she didn't deserve to die at all, let alone in such a horrible manner.

*The toolbox is the type that is designed to fit into a truck bed. Serial numbers match a toolbox sold from a local hardware store two weeks ago. Noah Scott does not have a truck, but inquiries at the local hardware store indicated that a man of similar build to Noah Scott had purchased the toolbox, paying cash. Grainy surveillance footage was provided by the store and reviewed by this officer. The man in the footage wore a white shirt and jeans.*

The officers would be searching for the clothing. They already were. Ashley could hear the scrape of drawers being ripped open by the deputy who was in what Ashley presumed was Noah's bedroom. They were bound to find both items of clothing. Every man in the Midwest owned a white undershirt and jeans. It was a cornerstone of their wardrobe. Like all the men had gotten together and decided that this was going to be their uniform, no matter where they worked, what they did, rich or poor, a white shirt and blue jeans would be a closet staple.

*Erica's body was examined by the Brine County medical examiner late Monday morning. Scrapings were taken from beneath her fingernails. Noah Scott has a criminal history, including a felony conviction that required him to provide a sample of his DNA for profiling. Due to the violent nature of this crime, a rush order was placed on the scrapings from Erica's fingernails. This officer personally transported the DNA samples to the criminalistics laboratory in Ankeny, Iowa. Results were received late Monday night. DNA from the skin cells found beneath Erica's fingernails matched the known profile for Noah Scott.*

"Shit," Ashley said, shaking her head. This was expected. David had told her as much the night before. She'd known even then that it would be problematic, but it felt damning, almost insurmountable, written down like this.

"What?" Katie asked, looking over Ashley's shoulder.

"It's bad, that's all," Ashley said.

"Yeah," Katie agreed.

She didn't seem as shocked as Ashley. George must have told her the night before. Because the facts about the toolbox would normally send Katie into a rage or a depression. The very thought of a woman locked inside a box like that, it was heartbreaking, and this was someone that they'd both known. But Katie wasn't reacting as she read over Ashley's shoulder, so she must have already had some time to let it sink in.

"Should we go see what they are finding?" Katie asked, gently tugging on Ashley's arm.

Ashley nodded and followed Katie into the bedroom where George Thomanson was searching. There was one other deputy in the room, a young guy who looked like he couldn't be a day older than twenty. He had a drawer open, and he was shoving an entire stack of jeans and white under-shirts into an evidence bag.

"Do you plan on leaving any clothes for Noah to wear?" Ashley said.

The young deputy looked up, his eyes widening in a manner that would have been comical if circumstances were different. She knew about her reputation among law enforcement, but she hadn't realized the young ones were physically frightened of her. "It's not my fault that this is all he wears."

Ashley rolled her eyes and walked over to the nightstand beside the bed. A framed photograph of James Elsberry sat next to a sleep mask with a floral pattern and a tube of Softlips brand lip balm. It was definitely Erica's side of the bed. There were three drawers to the nightstand, and they were all undisturbed. Nobody had bothered to look inside yet, even though it would be the perfect place for Erica to keep a diary if she had one. They were all so focused on convicting Noah that they were missing some of the more important things—like what Erica was thinking at the end of her life.

She pulled open the drawer, and sure enough, a journal stared up at her. It was black with no other adornments, but Erica might have used it to jot down her innermost thoughts and secrets. She took it out and flipped it open, expecting to see Erica's bubbly handwriting. The same handwriting Erica had used in high school when she would push notes through the slots in Ashley's locker, saying things like *nobody likes you*. But Ashley was wrong. There was no writing in the journal at all, only a stack of letters.

There were ten letters in total, all written in the same light blue ink as the letters addressed to Rachel and sent to the Public Defender's Office.

She'd never seen that color of ink before Rachel's letters, and now here she was with a whole stack of them. Was that color of ink really all that popular? It wasn't very easy to read. It shimmered when it caught the light in a way that hurt her eyes to read it. So why would anyone use a color like that?

There were no envelopes, but the letter writer had dated each one. The top letter was dated November 20, and the bottom dated October 28. The other eight were dated somewhere between. Erica must have received the November letter shortly before her death. Ashley started scanning the most recent letter. Lines like, *I can't be without you*, and, *In such a short time, you have become the most important thing to me.*

"What's that?" Katie asked, causing Ashley to jump. She hadn't realized that Katie had come up next to her.

"Love letters. And they're recent. You know what this means, don't you?"

"There's another potential suspect."

Love could be a balancing act, especially when that love formed into a triangle. Then the edge left for balancing could be as thin as the blade of a knife.

"I'll take that," came a man's voice just before the journal and letters were ripped out of Ashley's hands.

"What the fuck," Ashley said, looking up and glaring at Deputy Pitch. "I was reading those."

"You shouldn't even be in here. If you haven't noticed, we are in the process of executing a search warrant."

"If I weren't here, you probably wouldn't have even found those."

"What are they?" Deputy Pitch looked down at the documents, squinting as he read the light blue handwriting.

"What? You can't read?" Ashley said. Sarcasm probably wasn't the best way to ease the tension, but she couldn't help herself.

He ignored her and continued looking at the letters. A few moments passed, then he let out a long, low whistle. "This is the smoking gun."

"What? No, it's not," Ashley said, trying to grab the letters, but he was tall, and he held them out of her reach. She hadn't had time to scan them all, let alone read them carefully. He'd taken them from her before she had the chance. "Give them to me."

"Um, no. That would be dumb, and despite your earlier insinuations, I'm no idiot."

"The jury is still out on that one."

Deputy Pitch turned on his heel and marched out of the room, down the hallway, and out the front door. Ashley followed close behind.

"Noah," Deputy Pitch said, waving the letters in the air. "I've got some questions for you."

"That's too bad," Ashley said, running out in front of the deputy, and stopping at Noah's side. David stood at his other side, looking from Ashley to Deputy Pitch like he was frightened. "Noah's not saying anything."

"Can't he speak for himself?" Deputy Pitch was not looking at Ashley as he spoke, he was directing his words at Noah. "Or does he let his women speak for him?"

"*His* women?" Ashley was seeing red now. "His attorney, maybe. But I'm not *his* woman. You're disgusting, you know that? A chauvinistic pig with the intelligence of a squirrel with a head injury."

"You don't want to talk?" Deputy Pitch said, leaning closer to Noah.

"Are you deaf and dumb? No. He's not talking to you."

"In that case," Deputy Pitch removed a pair of handcuffs. "You're under arrest, Noah Scott, for the murder of Erica Elsberry."

"What?" Noah's gaze darted from Ashley to Deputy Pitch.

"You have the right to remain silent. Although, look how far that's gotten you," Deputy Pitch said with a smirk.

*Keep up the commentary, dickbag*, Ashley thought. It was bound to lead to a suppression issue.

"Anything you say or do could be used against you in the court of law. You have the right to an attorney. Judging by the presence of these two bloodsuckers," he nodded to David and then Ashley, "you were well aware of that. If you cannot afford an attorney, one will be appointed to represent you."

Deputy Pitch led Noah toward his police cruiser, opening the back door for him.

"I don't understand," Noah said. "You're arresting me because I wouldn't talk to you?"

"I'm arresting you because I have probable cause to believe you murdered your girlfriend."

"David and I will meet you at the police station. Do not say anything before we get there," Ashley said just before Deputy Pitch closed the door.

She stood there, watching as Deputy Pitch got into the driver's seat of his cruiser and started his car.

"That got out of hand quickly," David said. His words weren't exactly accusatory, but they had an edge.

"That was always going to get out of hand quickly. Don't you see that?" Ashley said, turning to glare at him. "Deputy Pitch had every intention of arresting Noah today. It didn't matter what anyone said or did."

David shrugged, and it made Ashley want to punch him in his smug little face. He was the one who had asked for her assistance. Not the other way around. And he better start remembering that, or she was going to be out that door, leaving him to represent Noah on his own. If that happened, she'd be sitting front and center during the entire trial, watching David make a complete fool of himself in a case he had no business handling on his own.

# 16

## RACHEL

When Rachel woke up that morning, she did something she almost never did. She watched the news. Her conversations with Bryce and Noah on the drive home from work had her on edge, and there had been so many whispers around town about the body in the lake. Was it Erica? If it was, what did that mean for Rachel? Erica Elsberry had been involved with Noah and Bryce, and so was Rachel, albeit in a far different way, but that didn't completely alleviate her concerns.

She planned to turn on the news while she got ready for the day, half listening until the morning anchors mentioned Lake Goldenhead, but she didn't have to wait for long. It was the first story of the day.

"The body pulled from Lake Goldenhead early Monday morning has now been identified as a local Brine woman, Erica Elsberry," the male anchor said, his tone deliberately grave. "The Brine County Sheriff's Department has not released the manner of death, but they have classified it as a homicide."

Rachel sucked in a sharp breath. It was Erica, and someone had killed her. That had been her suspicion, but none of it seemed real until now, when it was confirmed.

"If you have any information that could lead to an arrest, contact the Sheriff's Department."

Rachel flipped the television off, tossing her remote on her nightstand. She had nothing to report. They'd know Bryce and Noah's ties to Erica without her input. So, she tried to force it out of her mind and got ready quickly, heading downstairs. Bryce was waiting for her by the front door.

"What time would you like to leave, ma'am?" He said as she descended the stairs. He didn't look at her, which was uncommon. Usually, his eyes followed her like the eyes on a portrait in a haunted house.

"Now is fine," Rachel said.

"Would you like to eat breakfast first?"

"No, thanks."

"Are you sure?" Bryce allowed his gaze to settle on her, roaming up and down her body in his characteristically fervent way. "You're awfully thin."

Rachel grabbed her largest, puffiest coat from the nearby coat rack, pulling it over her shoulders and zipping it up to hide her figure. "I'm fine," she said as she headed out the front door and up to Bryce's black SUV. She wrenched the door open and got into the back seat before Bryce had a chance to offer her a hand. She didn't want to touch him.

"I apologize if I offended you, miss," Bryce said as he got into the driver's seat and brought the engine to life. "I want us to be friends, good friends."

*You would*, Rachel thought, but she kept her mouth shut, reminding herself that someone had murdered Erica, and Bryce was a potential suspect. He was her ex-boyfriend, but he had admitted the night before that they'd recently been in contact.

She wondered if she should comment on Erica's death, express some sympathy for Bryce. But then she'd have to talk to him, which she didn't like to do. It was probably easier to feign ignorance. He knew she made a point to avoid local news, so he wouldn't know the difference. They drove the entire way in a tense silence. When Bryce pulled up outside Rachel's office, he put the vehicle in park and turned around to look at her.

"I mean what I said. I want us to be friends."

There was fire in his gaze and a passion to his words that alarmed Rachel. And he continued staring at her. He wanted, no needed her to say something, and he wouldn't stop looking at her like that until she did. But she wasn't going to lie. She didn't want them to be anything other than driver and passenger.

"Thank you," she said, opening the back door and getting out.

She slammed the car door shut before he could respond, then turned and walked up the sidewalk to the front door of the MEHR team office. The two large picture windows were still dark, and the door was still locked.

*That's weird,* she thought. Katie always beat her to the office. She shrugged, used her keys to unlock the door, and stepped inside. She flipped on the light switch, then locked the door again before heading to her office at the very back of the building. It was still before official office hours, and she was alone. Tom or Katie would unlock the door when they arrived.

Once she was back in her office, she powered up her laptop and settled into her office chair. She opened the client management software and ran a calendar report. After a few moments, a PDF document popped open, populated with all MEHR team member schedules for the day. Rachel's first appointment was scheduled for nine o'clock with a man named Jackson Weatherspoon.

Rachel opened Jackson's electronic file, re-familiarizing herself with his background. The MEHR team had been working with him for close to a month now, but Katie had handled the first several weeks of intensive meetings, then she'd handed the case file off to Rachel a week earlier. This would be her second meeting with Jackson.

She studied his diagnosis and medication schedule. *Obsessive compulsive disorder, adult onset. Antisocial personality disorder.* His medications included mood stabilizers, antianxiety medications, and an antidepressant. When she arrived at his residence, she was going to have to count to see if he had the proper number of pills remaining.

At eight thirty, she heard the back door open and close with a loud *bang.*

Tom appeared in her doorway a few moments later, waving and smiling broadly. "Is the front door unlocked?"

Rachel shook her head. "I didn't want to unlock it when I was here alone."

"Makes sense. I'll get it now." Tom began whistling as he made his way down the hallway. He was gone for a few minutes, then his head popped back into her doorframe. "Someone's here for you, Rachel."

"Who?"

He didn't answer. Instead, he motioned with his hand for her to follow, and then he was gone. She grabbed her laptop, shoving it into her bag along with a notepad and a couple pens. It was nearing time for her to leave anyway. She followed Tom down the hallway, pulling her coat on while she walked. There was a middle-aged woman standing at the front entrance, holding a large bunch of roses.

"What's this?"

"Delivery for Rachel Arkman."

Rachel stared at the flowers "From who?"

The woman shrugged. "I didn't read the card. I could lose my job for that. But a man dropped in just before closing last night. Purchased them in cash and paid extra for them to be delivered this morning."

"Right." Rachel didn't know what to say. Nobody had ever given her flowers before, and she wasn't sure she wanted that to change.

"Where should I set them down?"

"Um..."

The woman looked around, her gaze settling on the built-in reception desk. Katie hadn't hired a receptionist yet, but there were plans to do so in the future. "How about there," she nodded at the empty desk. "Your clients will probably appreciate a fresh bunch of flowers. They always lift my mood."

"What a good idea," Tom said, smiling brightly. He accepted the flowers from the woman and set them down in the center of the reception desk. "Thank you for delivering them."

Rachel nodded; her mouth was dry. It was a good thing that Tom was there to handle the situation, because she had no idea what to say or do. Her mind couldn't get past wondering who had sent them. Ashley wouldn't, and neither would Rachel's aunt. She wasn't close with anyone else.

When the delivery woman left, Tom turned to Rachel. "Are you going to read the card?"

"Yes," Rachel said, and she plucked the card off the plastic placard, moving almost as though she was in a daze.

She ripped the tiny envelope open and pulled out the card. In light blue ink and a now familiar all uppercase script were the words I WILL BE SEEING YOU TODAY. Rachel dropped the card and stepped back, horrified. Once again, there was no obvious threat in its content, but it contained an ominous undercurrent. A proclamation that whoever had sent this would see her, and there was nothing she could do to stop it.

"What is it?" Tom asked.

Before she could answer, the front door opened, and a man shuffled inside. He was in his late fifties or early sixties with lines darting from the corners of his eyes like cracks in the shell of a hard-boiled egg. His hair was a deep brown and thinning at the crown. A long scraggly beard clung to his chin, curling and twisting down, stopping at his chest.

"Girlie," the man said, his sharp, aggressive eyes settling on Rachel. "There you are."

It was the same man who had been waiting at the front door the day before. "Who are you?" Rachel demanded.

"Ivan Volkov." He didn't ask her name, probably because he already knew it. "Nice flowers."

Rachel repeated his name in her head several times. *Ivan Volkov, Ivan Volkov, Ivan Volkov*, intending to look him up and go through his file the second she had a free moment. She had meant to do that the night before, but the business with Noah, Bryce, and Erica had sidetracked her.

"Do you have an appointment?" Tom said. "I believe Rachel was just on her way out to meet with another client."

"Are you the boss around here?" Ivan asked. "That woman yesterday told me that I couldn't work with Rachel. I want to work with her."

"Katie is the boss, but she isn't here right now. I can meet with you in a few minutes, but Rachel really must be on her way," Tom nodded toward the door and made a shooing gesture.

Rachel hurried out the door without looking back. When she stepped outside, she was just in time to see Ashley hurrying up to the front door of the jail. A well-dressed man followed close behind her, and there was something familiar about him that Rachel couldn't quite pinpoint. The expression on Ashley's face was one of complete and total fury. Something was happening. Rachel wanted to follow Ashley and find out, but she had an appointment in a few minutes.

As she hurried on her way, she decided she would stop by Ashley's office later that day. She wanted to talk to her about the letters and the roses. Rachel had been hypersensitive all her life, especially when it came to anything that could be perceived as a threat. Ashley was her closest confidante, and the person who would hopefully set her straight if she was blowing it all out of proportion.

# 17

## ASHLEY

The jail was in the courthouse square—connected to the courthouse—so Ashley walked rather than accepting a ride from David. She was far too furious to take anything he offered, especially if he was going to continue insinuating it was somehow her fault that Deputy Pitch had arrested Noah. The exercise helped ease her fury, so she was practically calm by the time she got to the courthouse. Then she saw David again, and it flared right back up. She'd expected to find him inside with Noah, but he wasn't. He was waiting in his car, and he hopped out when he saw her.

"I can't catch a break," Ashley muttered as he jogged up to her.

"I didn't mean to offend you earlier," David said by way of greeting.

"Is that an apology?" She picked up her speed. She had no intention of rehashing his passive aggressive bullshit. He could either apologize or he could fuck off. She didn't want half-hearted explanations or justifications.

"Um, yes. I guess."

"Apology accepted," she said, but she didn't slow down. When she reached the door to the Law Enforcement Center, she wrenched it open and walked inside without holding it for David.

He was undeterred, and followed hot on her heels, catching the door before it closed. She walked past the Sheriff's Department and straight to the jail division. A woman stood behind the counter, watching Ashley approach through wary eyes.

"Hello. I need to see Noah Scott." The jail staff had a high turnover rate. She recognized this woman, she'd seen her a few times over the past few weeks, but she hadn't gotten to know her yet.

The woman turned to her computer and clicked a few buttons. "Are you sure he's here? We don't have record of him."

"That sneaky mother fucker," Ashley said under her breath.

"I'm sorry. I don't understand . . ." the woman said. Her words sounded apologetic, almost scared. Apparently, the deputies had already filled her head with tales of Ashley's misbehavior.

"Nothing," Ashley shook her head. "Sorry. Not you. Deputy Pitch."

A half-smile formed on her lips. Perhaps this woman hadn't been easily charmed by the heavily muscled deputy either. "I can buzz you back to the interview rooms if you'd like."

"Yes, please. I would like that immensely."

The woman pressed a button and motioned for Ashley to enter through a glass door to her right. Ashley thanked the woman and then hurried through the door, David still following close behind. She jogged down a long hallway until she reached a series of three rooms. They were identical, each with a door with a small glass window. Ashley peered through the first window. She could see Noah seated at a flimsy plastic table. One arm was free while the other was handcuffed to a metal pole connected to the wall. Deputy Pitch sat across from him, his mouth moving quickly in conversation.

"Stop!" Ashley said as she burst through the door.

The deputy looked up. His expression was annoyed at first, but it quickly melted into one of horrified surprise when he saw that it was her. He had apparently thought that she wouldn't follow Noah to the police station. That, or he thought he could be in and out before she arrived.

"I don't know what the hell you think you are doing, but Noah is exercising his right to remain silent. We were pretty damn clear about that back at his house."

"Well, he's changed his mind," Deputy Pitch sounded like a petulant child. "Haven't you, Noah?"

"I, um," Noah's eyes darted from the deputy to Ashley.

"We want to speak to our client," Ashley said.

Deputy Pitch motioned toward Noah as if to say *he's right here, go ahead.* "Alone, you dipshit."

Deputy Pitch glared at Ashley, but he got up and left the room.

Ashley motioned for David to sit down while she paced along the back wall. "Do you see that," she said, pointing at a camera mounted in the corner of the room. "This conversation is supposed to be privileged, but thanks to that little guy up there, we can't say a lot."

"Why not? I mean, it's not like the information can be used against Noah," David said.

"Really? Is that so. Okay, so let's just say we start discussing strategy right now. Who's to say that the prosecutor doesn't listen to this tape, learn our strategy, and then prepare his counterargument."

"He can't do that."

"What will stop him?"

"The rules of ethics," David said.

"So, the rules themselves are going to pop out of their little rule book and tell him, *I'm sorry prosecutor, but that's cheating.* Wrong! He'll get away with it because nobody will catch him, and everyone cheats to win."

"Okay, so what are we here to talk about?"

"You're going to shut your mouth. You got that?" Ashley said, turning her attention to Noah. "I'm sure you've noticed I described you as my client. Which means that I'm going to help you two idiots out, but you're going to have to listen to me." She paused, looking from one to the other. "Both of you."

"Okay," they said in unison.

"Now, I'm going to go out into that hallway and see if I can get copies of those letters seized from Erica's nightstand. David, you stay in here with him and make sure he keeps his mouth shut. I don't want to hear any more of this 'he's changed his mind' nonsense. You are exercising your right to remain silent, and that's final, got it?"

"Yes," they again said in unison.

Ashley looked from Noah to David. They seemed so in sync with one another. It made her wonder if they'd been honest about the amount of time they'd been working together. But she disregarded the thought almost immediately. It didn't matter. And even if it did, it was a problem best left for another day.

"Noah, your preliminary hearing has to be within ten days. Bond is going to be astronomical, but there's probably nothing we can do about that for now."

"I have to stay in jail?"

"At least until the preliminary hearing."

"And that could be ten whole days from now?"

Ashley fought the urge to roll her eyes. If this case went sideways—and to be honest, she saw every indication that it would—Noah was going to spend the rest of his life behind bars. Ten days was small potatoes in the grand scheme of things.

"Yes." She turned and left the interview room without elaborating. David was the private pay attorney; he could coddle Noah. Ashley didn't have the time or the patience for it.

Once in the hallway, she found Deputies Pitch and Thomanson arguing in hushed voices. Katie stood a few paces behind George, glaring at the younger deputy.

"Deputy Pitch," Ashley said, a deliberately fake smile forming on her lips as she made her way toward them. "We need to talk."

Deputy Pitch crossed his bulky arms. His muscles were unnaturally large, like he spent every waking moment inside a gym. "About what?"

"Those letters you took from Noah's house. I want copies of them."

"No."

"They are going to be part of discovery, so you might as well hand them over now."

Discovery was an important part of the criminal litigation process. All evidence that the state expected to use at trial had to be given to defense or the judge would likely exclude it from use at trial.

"No, thanks."

"What do you mean, 'no thanks?' Hand them over."

"Um, no. I don't have to. You haven't even filed an appearance. Are you really going to be his attorney?"

"Would you like me to walk over to my office, file my appearance and come back? Because I will."

"No. I'd like you to walk over to your office and then never come back."

"Fat chance. I'm a permanent fixture in this place. I'll be here to haunt you for the rest of your damn career."

"Haunt all you'd like, but I'm not giving you copies of those letters until a judge tells me that I have to."

"Fine," Ashley spat, turning on her heel and marching back into the interview room.

She told Noah and David that she was leaving, and then left the building, ignoring the deputy's arrogant glare as she walked past him. If this idiot wanted to play dirty, then she'd take it well past dirty into filthy zones. She was the dirtiest damn player out there, and he would soon find that out. It was about time that someone knocked Deputy Pitch down a peg or two, and she was just the woman to do it.

# 18

## KATIE

After Deputy Pitch left with Noah, Katie hopped into George's cruiser, and they followed the trail of law enforcement vehicles back to the Law Enforcement Center. They were the last in line. They passed Ashley along the way, walking with her hands balled into fists.

"Should I stop and ask if she wants a ride?"

George said it as a joke. A failed attempt to cut through the tension hanging all around them. She knew he expected her to refuse immediately, but it was cold outside.

"Maybe . . ."

"Are you serious?" George said, slowing his cruiser. "If she willingly gets in this car, hell has officially frozen over."

"No," Katie changed her mind when she saw the expression on Ashley's face. "She's pissed."

"I don't blame her," George said. "I'm pissed, too."

Katie turned to look at him, curious as to why he cared so much. From the information she'd heard so far, it sounded like Noah was the most likely suspect. All the cards were stacked against him. DNA under nails. Drunk. Public argument at a bar. Missing for a week and never reporting it. Noah was an MEHR team client, but Katie wasn't naïve. George wasn't either. So, what was so different about this case that had George questioning Noah's guilt? In the past, he'd have been the one slapping on the handcuffs.

When they got to the Law Enforcement Center, George turned off the engine and ripped the key out of the ignition. His agitation had seemed to grow the closer they got to the station. Katie followed a few steps behind him as they got out of the car. She was curious about what would happen next between George and Deputy Pitch, but she was also growing increasingly concerned about Noah's future sobriety. If he'd been teetering on the edge of relapse, the recent turn of events could easily send him careening over the edge. Sure, he was in jail now, but that wouldn't last forever. Bond would be high, but he had a house, and he could use it as collateral.

"I can't believe this. I cannot believe this," George repeated like a mantra as he marched inside the back door to the building, waving a key card to unlock it.

Katie followed a step behind, remaining close while also creating some distance. There was something happening here that she didn't quite understand.

George led the way down several winding hallways, familiar yet foreign to Katie. The bones of the building were the same as they had always been, but there were subtle differences. A desk where there used to be an old weather-beaten couch. A white coffee pot instead of a black one. Little changes that reminded her that she was now an outsider.

They stopped in an area with several interview rooms lined up in a row. Each room had a small window in the door, allowing Katie to see inside. The first two were empty, but Noah was in the third, along with Ashley and that other attorney, David. Katie was surprised to see that Ashley was already inside after passing her on their way. But Ashley had been angry, and she'd been moving quickly. Katie, on the other hand, had been lingering, following George's lead.

Katie watched through the window, studying the other attorney that was with Ashley and Noah. He had been soft-spoken and polite, but there was something about the man that Katie didn't like. It was in his calculating silence. Ashley had always been an open book—explaining her thought process aloud and instigating arguments—even when she and Katie were at odds. But this guy, he was blank, devoid of emotion.

"This is bullshit, and you know it," George said, his voice a low rumble.

Katie looked away from the interview room to see George and Deputy Pitch, standing near a window, face-to-face and toe-to-toe like they were about to get into an old-fashioned rumble.

"I'm not seeing the problem," Frankie Pitch said. He, too, was speaking quietly but forcefully.

It was almost comical to see these two macho men engaged in a whisper fight. The restraint was because of Ashley, who was close enough to hear shouting. If Ashley even caught a whiff of strife between the deputies, she'd be out in a millisecond, fanning that fire, turning it into an inferno. It would be an easy distraction, and from Katie's year of working with Ashley, she had learned that distraction was a key tool in a defense attorney's arsenal. *Look over here, people. Look at this instead of my extremely guilty client.*

"*You* are the problem," George said. "You think you have a slam dunk case, and that's going to bite you in the ass."

"I think I know what I'm doing."

"You *think*. You don't know. That's the problem. There's a defense attorney in there," George pointed to the interview room, "who is going to tear this case apart. Mark my words. You don't *think* you have problems, but you do."

"What attorney? That guy?"

"No. Ashley Montgomery."

"That woman? Pssh," he waved his hand like he was swatting at a fly.

Just then Ashley emerged from the interview room. She looked around the hallway and her eyes locked on Deputy Pitch.

"Don't worry. I can handle her," Deputy Pitch said as Ashley drew near.

"Deputy Pitch," Ashley said. "We need to talk."

George stepped away from the other deputy, moving in slow deliberate steps, like he was backing away from a rabid animal. If Deputy Pitch didn't watch his words, he was going to learn just how wild Ashley could be. They were at the front door, ready to step outside when Ashley started shouting. Katie didn't wait to see the fireworks. She didn't like to be anywhere near Ashley when she was in this kind of mood. She pushed the door open, motioning for George to leave first. She followed without looking back.

"He's going to be sorry," George said once they were outside. "She's going to rip this case limb from limb and eat it while forcing him to watch."

"That's an oddly visual way to put it."

George shrugged as though he didn't care, but his nostrils were still flaring with anger. "Pitch keeps focusing on the DNA under Erica's fingernails, like it's a smoking gun. And it would be if Erica and Noah hadn't known one another because there would be no reason for the DNA to be there. But Erica and Noah were dating. They were living together. There are other explanations. Pitch just refuses to see it."

"Like what?" Katie asked. They were walking back to her office, side by side in a slow stroll. It felt comfortable, like it had been back in the old days. Back before he had screwed her over and she lost her job.

"Maybe they got into a spat, and Erica scratched him. You know how emotional she could be. And then she ran off and was abducted and killed by someone else."

"That's possible." She gave him a sidelong glance. "You're sounding a lot like Ashley these days."

"Sometimes she's right. But don't tell her I said that. She'd never let me live it down."

They fell into silence for a moment, both thinking in separate directions while they walked along the same path. The question that kept coming back to Katie was *why?* George had a point, just as Ashley's arguments were valid, but those two had never been on the same side of anything.

"Why do you care so much? I mean, isn't it good for your career if Deputy Pitch screws this up? You'll move up the ladder and he'll fall to the bottom. If he's insisting on wading into turbulent waters, why not let him drown?"

That was what George would have done back in Katie's day. If it was Katie in this scenario, George wouldn't have even brought it up to her. He wouldn't have argued or warned her about Ashley's ability to find holes in cases. It didn't seem to fit with his personality. At least not what she knew of it. So, had George changed or was he treating Frankie better because Frankie was a man?

"Noah is my cousin."

Katie stopped walking. "Your what?"

"We're related. And I know he didn't do this. I don't want him to go down for something he didn't do."

Katie stared at George for a long moment, disbelieving. Nobody knew about the familial connection between George and Noah. He had somehow been able to keep that quiet, despite Noah's long history of arrests for drug-related crimes over the years. But that wasn't what bothered Katie so much. Katie's father was a criminal; he'd been incarcerated for money laundering when she was still in high school. It had been a secret that she'd disclosed to George. Then, when City Council slashed the police department's budget and jobs were getting cut, George had used that information to argue that he should keep his job over Katie. He'd used it against her when he, too, had at least one skeleton in his closet.

"What's wrong?" George said after several beats of intense silent.

Part of Katie wanted to scream and rage at him. Because how the hell was he so dense that he didn't draw the connection between their shared past and his present revelation. But there was another part of her, a larger part, that forced the fury to remain at bay. None of that mattered anymore. It was in the past. A time when her life was tumultuous, but she'd made it through it and was in a far more stable position as the lead of the MEHR team, rather than listening to piss ant baby deputies like Frankie Pitch.

"Nothing is wrong," Katie said. "But I do need to get back to work." They were right out front of the MEHR team office.

"Okay. We can talk later."

Katie wasn't sure that she wanted to talk anytime soon, but she agreed, said goodbye, and they parted ways.

# 19

## RACHEL

Rachel didn't wait around to see how Tom's conversation with Ivan ended. When Tom gave her the cue to leave, she was out the door and headed down the street toward her morning appointment with Jackson Weatherspoon.

Jackson lived a few blocks north of the courthouse square. It was a cold day, but she preferred walking. Exercise helped contain her anxiety, and there was the added bonus that she wouldn't have to call Bryce for a ride. She preferred to keep her interactions with him at a minimum, especially after the news about Erica.

Jackson's front porch was dilapidated. The paint had chipped, leaving the wooden boards exposed to the elements. Several of them were bowing under their own weight. Broken furniture and trash lay across the porch in a haphazard way. She stepped around the junk, careful to use the strongest-looking floorboards to reach the front door. She lifted a door knocker shaped like a lion's head holding a ring, but the door swung open before she could bang it against the wood.

Jackson stood in the doorway, staring at her with sharp, intelligent eyes. "Come in," Jackson said, motioning for her to enter. "I was watching you through the peephole. Saw you walk up. I can see all the way to the street."

Rachel's gaze darted to the small, round hole in the door. "Do you often use your peephole to watch others?"

"Nope. Only when I know you are coming."

Rachel wasn't sure how to interpret that. Was he doing it because he wanted to be on time for his meeting, or was it something more than that? Once inside, Rachel's gaze traveled around the poorly lit home. It was a small one-bedroom house with a living room in the entryway and a kitchenette along the back wall. She could see all parts of the living space from where she stood aside from the bathroom and the bedroom. It wasn't much larger than an apartment.

Rachel reached into her laptop bag and pulled out a checklist. For consistency, all MEHR team members used the same checklist for all clients. They went through it every visit, giving each item a one through ten rating, with one being the worst score and ten the best.

The first item on the list was *cleanliness*. Dirty dishes filled the small sink and covered the counter in the kitchenette area. There was caked-on food, some of which was molding. More dishes sat on the living room coffee table, and there were even a few on the floor.

"I thought you were going to start washing your dishes after you eat," Rachel said. The discussion and ultimate agreement at their last meeting included Jackson using the same plate and cutlery and washing it immediately after use.

"I got tired of it."

"Okay. Well, you're never going to graduate from the program if you keep living in such filth."

"What makes you think I want to graduate?" Jackson smiled, flashing an uneven row of yellowing teeth.

Rachel ignored his comment and wrote the number four on the line for cleanliness. She moved on to the next item on the list, which was *medications*. Rachel walked into the small bathroom at the back of the home. Jackson kept his medicines in a small cabinet behind the mirror. The front of the mirror swung open, and Rachel found the two prescriptions that Jackson was supposed to be taking.

She brought both prescription bottles into the living room. She pointed to the dishes on the coffee table. "Pick those up and wash them. I need to count these medications and I have to do it on a clean surface."

"She's a bossy one, isn't she," Jackson said. Then he lowered his voice and said, "I like 'em bossy."

"Who are you talking to?"

"Myself."

"You aren't hearing voices again, are you?"

"No," Jackson answered a little too quickly to be believable.

"Okay," Rachel wrote *may need mental health reevaluation* at the bottom of her checklist in the *comment* section.

Once Jackson cleared the coffee table, she poured the prescriptions out and counted each of the pills, comparing them to the fill date and number of pills Jackson was supposed to consume daily. The number for both prescriptions checked out. She wrote a ten on the line for *medications*.

"How are you doing on food?" Rachel said, walking into the kitchenette area, opening and closing cabinet after cabinet. They were all empty aside from one bag of Raman noodles. "Not good." She wrote the number one beside *groceries*.

"I'm going to get some today."

"Are you? How are you doing for money? You don't have a job yet, do you?"

"My disability check comes next week."

"That wasn't an answer to my question. How are you doing for money right now?"

"Not good. But like I said, I get money next week."

Rachel gestured to the empty cabinets. "How do you plan to feed yourself until then?"

"Food bank."

"That's the second time this month, Jackson. You are supposed to be working toward self-sufficiency. And what about your job prospects? Have you picked up any applications in the last week?"

"No."

"I picked up a couple yesterday," Rachel said, pulling two job applications from her pocket. One was a housecleaning position at a nearby motel, the other was for a job stocking shelves at the local grocery store.

"I don't want to work."

Rachel shook her head. Jackson wasn't improving. It made her wonder if he was taking his medications properly. Sure, he had the right number of pills, but that didn't mean he was actually taking them. There was only one way to test for that. "I'm going to need a urine sample from you this time, Jackson."

"Okay." He seemed to perk up at the thought, which was odd. Nobody ever wanted to provide a urine sample. "You're going to watch me while I do it, aren't you?"

"No. I'm going to stand outside the door."

She left the job applications on the now clean coffee table and walked into the bathroom, opening all the cabinets and sifting through their contents, looking for evidence that Jackson intended to use someone else's pee. It was the only logical explanation for his excitement; that he was gaming the system. She checked behind the toilet and inside the bathtub, finding nothing out of the ordinary.

Rachel went back into the living room, removing the testing kit from her bag. She broke it open and handed the collection device to Jackson. "Go in there and bring me a sample."

Jackson accepted the device, his smile widening. "You coming with me? You can hold it for me." He wound his hips in a circle like he was hula hooping.

"No," Rachel said, wrinkling her nose. And if you do that again, you're going to end up working with Tom, and you can ask him to do that."

Jackson grunted and disappeared into the bathroom, closing the door behind him with a loud *bang*. He reemerged a few minutes later, holding a half-full collection device. Rachel took it and sealed it inside a large, clear plastic bag with a hazard symbol on the side.

"I'm going to have this processed. Your medications better show up in this sample."

"What if they don't?"

"Then I'm telling your probation officer and you're looking at a violation of probation."

Jackson shrugged.

"I'll be back tomorrow," Rachel said, heading toward the door.

"Tomorrow?"

"Obviously you need to be bumped back up to a more intense level of supervision," Rachel said, gesturing to the messy apartment. "And I expect all of this to be clean."

"But—"

"Have it done by tomorrow," Rachel said before opening the door and stepping back out into the cold.

She could feel the weight of Jackson's gaze as he observed her pick her way across his treacherous front porch, watching her through the peephole. Picking up her pace, she headed down the sidewalk and across the street. Turning the corner, she headed back toward her office. As she did, she saw Ashley hurrying across the street, back to her office. The man that she had seen entering the courthouse was still with her. They were headed in her general direction, so Rachel was able to get a better look at him this time.

As she did, she sucked in a deep breath. She had thought he seemed familiar, but now she knew for certain that she knew the man. He had represented her stepfather, Isaac Smithson. It was years ago, back before Isaac had gone to prison for violating Rachel, but she would never forget that attorney. He'd been helping her stepfather with some civil issues, and he was around often, turning a blind eye to Isaac's victimization of his daughter.

She stood rooted to the spot, watching Ashley and that vile attorney disappear into the Public Defender's Office. This man, this attorney, felt like a ghost from her past, returned to haunt her.

# 20

## ASHLEY

Elena was at her desk in the front reception area when Ashley and David returned to the Public Defender's Office. Her long mane of wavy hair flowed down her back, hanging over the back of the chair.

"Be with you in a sec," Elena called when the bell above the front door chimed. There was no pause in her typing, and she didn't look away from the computer screen.

"Don't worry," Ashley said. "It's just me."

"Oh," Elena hopped up. "Hey. What's going on?"

Elena's gaze cut away from Ashley and settled on David, reminding Ashley that Elena and David hadn't met. "This is David," Ashley said. "I'm going to be working with him on Noah Scott's case."

Elena's wide, dark eyes grew even wider. "I heard about Noah's arrest on the scanner, but I didn't realize we were appointed to his case."

"We aren't. At least, we aren't yet. I'm going to file an appearance."

Elena cocked her head, which was to be expected. Their office had an overflowing client list with appointments alone. There was no need to add to an already suffocating case load.

"I know, I know. We're busy enough, but I can't stand Deputy Pitch. I've never had to deal with him like this, and he's a real asshat."

"I'll take your word for it," Elena said. "And I'll open a case file for Noah."

"Thanks. Can you also start working on subpoenas to the preliminary hearing? It hasn't been set yet, but I expect the order to come through in the next thirty minutes or so. I want to subpoena everyone in the Sheriff's Department, and make sure that they are all issued as subpoenas duces tecum."

A subpoena duces tecum was a court order that not only required the witness to appear to provide testimony, but also forced them to bring a specific item along with them.

Elena's dark eyebrows lifted. "What do you want them to bring?"

"Copies of letters seized from Noah Scott's house."

"Is that going to piss them off?"

Ashley shrugged. "Don't know, don't care."

"Consider it done," Elena said, giving Ashley a mock salute before turning back to her computer.

"What now?" David asked.

"Nothing," Ashley said.

"Nothing?"

"Yes. Nothing. You go back to your office and do whatever it is you do during the day, and I've got to be back over at the courthouse for a sentencing hearing in a couple minutes. Actually," she glanced at her watch, "I better get going. See you later."

"Okay . . ." David said.

Ashley left David behind as she burst back out the door and across the street to the courthouse. She opened the front door and rushed up the stairs to the second floor, where the courtrooms were located. The hallway was empty except for a young woman seated on a bench closest to the double doors of the district court courtroom.

"Trixie," Ashley said, making her way toward the woman. "Sorry I'm late. An issue came up with another client."

"It's fine." Trixie didn't look up as she spoke. She clutched her cell phone with two hands, her thumbs flying across the screen, punching in letters.

"Your sentencing hearing is going to start in a few minutes." Trixie had originally been charged with delivery of methamphetamine, a felony, but Ashley had gotten a plea deal for a simple possession charge. It was still an indictable offense, which meant it was a more serious misdemeanor, but a misdemeanor all the same.

"Yeah." She still didn't look up. Her long, straggly, bleached blonde hair hung down over the sides of her face, making it impossible for Ashley to read her expression.

"We will be arguing sentencing. The state is asking for jail time, we are asking for probation."

"Okay."

Another one-word answer. "Have you done any of the things we discussed at our last meeting?"

"Like what?" She popped her gum.

*That's a resounding "no,"* Ashley thought, but she went through her suggestions one by one anyway. Just in case Trixie happened to surprise her.

"Did you get a substance abuse evaluation?" Ashley asked.

"No."

"Did you find a job?"

"No."

"Are you enrolled in school?"

"No."

"Have you gotten your driver's license?"

"No."

"Have you done any community service?"

"Like what?"

"I don't know," Ashley said, sighing and rubbing her temples. "Volunteering. Anywhere."

"Um, no."

Ashley wanted to ask what she did with her days. She was twenty-six years old. She didn't have children and she didn't care for her parents. If she kept up her current lifestyle, there was no chance she'd make it through probation. Idle minds and all that.

"It's time for your hearing," Ashley said, glancing at her watch.

She stood and Trixie followed suit, shoving her cell phone in her back pocket.

"Turn your phone off."

Trixie looked mutinous for a long moment, but she complied, then Ashley led her into the courtroom. It was empty aside from the prosecutor, Charles Hanson, who was sitting alone at the prosecution bench. He looked up at Ashley as she and Trixie made their way to the defense table, giving them an, *it's about time* look. Ashley returned it with a look of her own. One that said *go fuck yourself.*

"All rise," the court reporter said as she bustled into the room holding her black steno machine. "The honorable Judge Ahrenson presiding."

Ashley shot to her feet and gestured for Trixie to do the same. Charles Hanson lumbered up, but he wasn't in any rush. Judge Ahrenson followed the court reporter. His back was starting to stoop but he stood tall as he stepped up to the bench.

"Please be seated," Judge Ahrenson said as he lowered himself onto the bench.

The hearing proceeded as usual, Ashley and Charles fighting like stepsiblings forced together during their teenage years. She'd say something and he'd pick at it, and she'd snap back. After thirty minutes of sneering, Judge Ahrenson was ready to render his decision.

"Mr. Hanson is asking for jail time," Judge Ahrenson said, his ice blue eyes darting to the prosecutor. "Ms. Montgomery argues for straight probation." His gaze cut to Ashley. I'm not going to leave you in suspense, but I'm also not going to do what either of you want. Not exactly. I'm going to split the difference."

Trixie opened her mouth to respond, but Ashley placed a hand on her shoulder, silencing her. "Just listen," Ashley whispered.

"I'm ordering probation, but I am also going to require that you successfully complete the program designed by the Mental Health Response Team."

"But—"

"Shut up," Ashley said through gritted teeth. "Unless you want him to change his mind and send you to jail."

Trixie stopped talking, and the remainder of the hearing continued as expected. Then the judge bustled out of the courtroom and it was over. Ashley wrote the address and phone number for the MEHR team on a piece of paper and handed it to Trixie, who had been whining about the added term to her probation since the judge announced it. When Ashley was about to snap—to tell her client that it was really her fault since she'd done absolutely nothing that Ashley had told her to do—the court reporter returned.

"Ms. Montgomery," she said.

"Yes?"

"Judge Ahrenson would like to see you."

Charles Hanson started to walk toward her, but she put up a hand. "Just Ms. Montgomery." He lifted an eyebrow, in an almost accusatory way. "It's not about any cases, Mr. Hanson, so your presence is not required."

*That's not good*, Ashley thought.

She whispered to Trixie that she would call her later and urged her to go to the MEHR team office right away, then followed the court reporter back into chambers keeping her shoulders hunched and her head slightly down. She had no idea what Judge Ahrenson wanted, but she felt a bit like a kid being called to the principal's office.

The Judge was in his office, seated at his desk with his black robe hanging on a nearby coatrack. "Come on in," he said, gesturing for Ashley to sit in one of the chairs across from him.

Ashley's shoulders relaxed at his genial tone, and she dropped into one of the chairs. "You wanted to talk to me?"

"Yeah. I did. You know I'm a few months shy of seventy-two."

Ashley could have tried to flatter him. She could have said something like, *no, you don't look a day over sixty*, but she wasn't a bullshitter, so she kept her mouth shut.

"That's the forced retirement age for us district court judges."

"True." She paused for a moment. "You haven't called me back here to invite me to a retirement party, I'm assuming."

"No," he waved a dismissive hand. "I mean, you will get an invitation, but my wife's worrying about all that—I'm no party planner, you see—and I have no idea when invitations will go out."

"Okay . . ." She had no clue where this was going.

"I want you to apply for my position.

"Me?"

"Yes, you. Charles Hanson is applying. He's already going around telling everyone he's got it in the bag."

Ashley snorted. She couldn't think of a single worse person for the job. "I've ruffled too many feathers over the years. I'll never get it."

Judge Ahrenson crossed his arms. "I wouldn't tell you to apply if I didn't think you had a chance. But it wouldn't hurt for you to at least try to get along with some folks on the other side of the aisle. At least during the application process and until a decision is made."

"By 'across the aisle' you mean law enforcement?"

"Exactly."

Ashley's mind immediately went to Noah's case and the subpoenas that were going out to every sheriff's deputy in the county at that very moment. There were going to be a lot of pissed off cops by the end of the day, and that was only going to get worse when Noah's preliminary hearing started.

"Can you do that?" Judge Ahrenson asked.

"I can try."

Even as she agreed, she wondered, *at what expense*? But of course, she knew the answer to that question. It would come at her client's expense. Noah's expense. At the expense of her ethical responsibility to zealously represent each and every one of her clients. But if she could find a way to pull it off, if she could behave herself for the next few months, she very easily could find herself donning a black robe. Was it worth it?

# 21

## RACHEL

Katie was at the reception desk when Rachel returned to the office.

"Beautiful flowers," Katie said, nodding to the roses. "Tom said they were yours."

Rachel's palms grew slick. It felt an awful lot like the opening lines to an interrogation. "Yeah."

"Who sent them?"

"I don't know."

"It wasn't a client, was it?"

"I don't know."

"Do you think it could have been from a client? We can't accept gifts from them. We are a government agency."

"I said I didn't know."

"The card wasn't signed?"

"No. You can look at it if you want." Rachel almost wished Katie would demand to see it, so she could start the conversation about the letters. Then at least someone else would know her fear and could either calm her down or share in the burden.

"I don't need to. I trust you."

For once in her life, Rachel wished that it was the other way around. "You can throw the flowers out if you want to. Just to be safe."

Katie stared at the beautiful bouquet of blooms, her expression soften-ing. "We might as well leave them here."

"Okay," Rachel said, disappointed.

"I've got a new client for you," Katie said as she shifted through a stack of documents on the reception desk. She looked like she was cleaning the area up. Perhaps she was going to fill the position soon. They needed someone there. A gatekeeper to decide who was allowed back to the offices and who needed turning away.

"Who is it?"

"A woman named Trixie. She's close to your age, and she lives nearby."

"What is her struggle?"

Katie shrugged. "Her conviction is for possession of meth. It could be addiction alone, or she could be self-medicating to mask another condition. You'll have to help her set up a mental health evaluation. That way we will know for sure."

"Okay."

"Here's her address," Katie handed a slip of paper to Rachel. "I told her you'd pop over there today. Do you have time?"

"Yeah. I can go over there now." Rachel had hoped to stop by Ashley's office and discuss the mysterious letters with light blue ink, but that could wait. Besides, she didn't know how long that other attorney would be there and she did not want to come face-to-face with him again.

Trixie lived less than a block away, in one of the apartments above Genie's Diner. The address said Apartment 2, which meant the upstairs floor. There was no staircase inside the diner, unless it was back in the kitchen, but she doubted that was the case, so she walked around back to find a rickety metal staircase leading up to a landing. She didn't like the look of the staircase, but she forced herself to ascend.

The landing split at the top, leading to two separate apartments, Apart-ment 2A and Apartment 2B. She looked down at the slip of paper Katie had handed her. The handwriting was long, thin, and heavily angled, completely unlike the small, careful letters Katie used, so she assumed that Trixie had written it down. It was possible that she'd simply forgotten to include the letter behind the number, but it was more likely that the omis-sion had been intentional. A roadblock.

She looked from one door to the other, trying to decide which belonged to Trixie. The doors looked exactly the same. Cold numbers with no adornments. Neither had a welcome mat or wreath. Not that either of those items would help much. She didn't know anything about Trixie other than a partial address and a meth conviction. She decided to knock on apartment 2B and see who answered. There was a 50 percent shot that she'd be right. They weren't great odds, but it could be worse.

A young blonde woman answered the door. She didn't say a word. Her eyes darted left, then right, before she ushered Rachel inside the apartment. When the door was safely closed behind her, she turned to Rachel.

"Who are you?" There was an emptiness in Trixie's eyes that Rachel recognized. She'd had it in her childhood, back before Ashley had saved her.

"Rachel Arkman. I'm with the MEHR team."

"Oh," Trixie's demeanor changed almost instantly, the anxiety melting away. "I thought you were someone else."

"Who?"

"A guy moved in across the hall. I think it was, like, last month or something. It used to be this old lady, but now he's there and he creeps me out."

"How does he creep you out?" Paranoia was a side effect of many drugs, including methamphetamine, so Rachel wasn't sure if Trixie's concern was legitimate or a sign of active use.

"He's always hanging around, knocking on the door to ask for little things like sugar or eggs. Who the fuck keeps that crap around?"

Ashley had kept her kitchen fully stocked, especially with items used to make cookies.

"I told him the first time he did it, I said, 'There's like a goddamn diner right under your feet. Literally. And you come here asking for eggs? That's not the reason you're here.'"

"Why was he here?"

Trixie shrugged. "I still don't know. But he keeps coming back with the same old bullshit. So, obviously, I was right."

"What's his name?"

"Bryce."

Rachel froze. She only knew one Bryce, and that was her driver. But

Bryce was living in one of the smaller houses at the back of Aunt Stephanie's property. Or was he? Now that she thought about it, Bryce hadn't been around quite so much lately. He used to be everywhere, seemingly lingering around every corner she turned. He was still around lots—too much in Rachel's opinion—but it was more like he was around every other corner now.

"What does this guy look like?"

"He's old with brown hair. There's a bald spot at the top."

"How old is 'old'?"

"I don't know. Fifties-ish. I never asked his age. I don't even want to talk to him. He's always staring without blinking, like he's fucking me with his eyes."

That sounded like the Bryce that Rachel knew, but it was also a pretty generic description. There were countless middle-aged men in Brine County with brown hair and a receding hairline. "Is he tall or short? How does he dress?"

"He dresses like he's going to a funeral. He's always in a suit and tie, but he's at home during the day so he's not, like, a lawyer or a banker or something. He's just some weirdo who wears suits to get off. He's probably over there now jacking off into one of them."

That was a visual Rachel didn't need or want. "Let me know if he does anything else to unsettle you, but in the meantime, let's get started. Why don't you show me around your apartment?"

"There's not much to see." Trixie gestured around her. "It's pretty big, but it's still a studio. You can see everything except the bathroom from here."

Rachel looked around. The apartment was abnormally clean for an addict. There were no dirty dishes in the sink or on the nearby dining table. A row of tall windows lined one wall, lending a nice view of the courthouse and the rest of downtown, but they were old and drafty, and Rachel had to cross her arms to keep from shivering. A bed sat near the windows, unmade, with the sheets and blanket lying next to it on the floor. It did have sheets, which was more than Rachel could say for most of her first appointments.

A table with four chairs sat near the kitchen, but it was covered in documents. She wasn't sure if it was pure curiosity or intuition, but something had Rachel walking toward the table, intent on inspecting the documents. She didn't have to do anything but look down before her mouth went completely dry. There, on the top of the pile, was a letter written in the same blue ink and the same script as her own letters. She didn't read it, even though she wanted to more than anything, because even clients were allowed to have some privacy. But nothing could keep her from asking about it.

With shaking hands, she picked it up and held it out to Trixie. "What's this?"

"Oh, that. I don't even know why I kept it. They were weird. None of them were signed and they were all love letters of a sort. At first, they started coming in the mail. That freaked me out. I never get anything in the mail other than bills, and those I don't pay."

Rachel made a mental note to discuss budgeting with Trixie.

"Then whoever wrote the letters started leaving them wedged into my front door. I was really freaked out then. I wanted to call the cops, but you know what Ashley says, 'don't ever talk to the cops.'" She mimicked Ashley's cadence of speech so well that Rachel almost laughed. "So, I didn't tell anyone. They bothered me, for sure, but it didn't last that long."

"Why? What happened?"

"They just stopped coming a couple weeks ago."

"That's weird. I wonder what happened to make him stop."

"I don't know, but I'm happy to be done with it. Maybe he got arrested for something. Maybe that weirdo across the hall scared him off. Or maybe he's found someone else to bother." Trixie shrugged. "Doesn't matter to me, so long as I don't have to deal with it anymore."

All three suggestions were possible, but Rachel guessed it was the last one that held the most truth. The guy had found someone else to fixate on, and that someone else was Rachel.

# 22

## ASHLEY

Friday, December 6

Noah's preliminary hearing was set for nine o'clock in the morning. Ashley and David had spent the past few days preparing for it. He'd been meeting her at her office first thing every morning and leaving after it closed. She hadn't seen Rachel aside from a few hellos in passing, which was abnormal, but she assumed Rachel noticed the uptick in activity at her office and decided to stay away until things cooled down.

She was treating the preliminary hearing like a trial. It wasn't how she normally handled cases because these hearings were rarely held. They were cancelled the moment the prosecutor filed the formal charging documents, which was usually how it happened, but the magistrate had set this hearing earlier than most because the defendant had been held in jail.

Any spare moment was spent studying the application requirements for Judge Ahrenson's position. It had recently posted, and there was not a large window for applications. The application process was closing quickly, and there were a lot of requirements. She still wasn't sure she even wanted to apply.

At times, she thought it would be nice to be the decision maker, but she also wasn't sure how she'd fit in the role. She wouldn't be a perpetual underdog anymore, and she liked the challenge that came with having the odds stacked against her. By Friday morning, she hadn't decided yet, so she set the thoughts aside so she could focus on Noah.

David appeared at eight o'clock on the dot. His timing was so predictable that Ashley had taken to unlocking the front door a few minutes before eight and working from the empty receptionist's desk so she would see him when he came in.

"Good morning," David said as he came through the front door. "Are you ready for today?"

Ashley glanced at the stacks of paperwork in front of her. "As ready as I'll ever be."

"Do you want to go over anything?"

"No."

Ashley and David had hashed out their trial strategy, and they'd agreed —well, Ashley had demanded, and he had reluctantly acquiesced—that she would do all the talking. It was only the preliminary hearing, so the bar was extremely low. The state didn't have to prove evidence beyond a reasonable doubt at this stage of the game. They only had to prove prob- able cause. It was a far lower standard, and the cards were majorly stacked against them. Ashley didn't need some idiot civil attorney getting underfoot and mucking up her defense.

"Okay."

David shoved his hands in his pockets, looking around the entryway to the office. It was nothing fancy, not by a long shot, but there were some old couches for seating and a beat-up coffee table covered in yellowing magazines.

Ashley was poring over all the evidence she had, trying to pick out any unanticipated flaws in her defense, but she could see David from the corner of her eye, and his nervous hovering was getting on her last nerve. "Sit down," Ashley said, motioning toward the couch, "before I lose my cool."

"Sorry." David meandered over to the couch and sat, sinking into the faded upholstery. He was silent for a few moments, then he asked, "Where is that young lady who is always hanging around here?"

"Elena? She doesn't come in until eight thirty. Our office isn't even open until then. Why?" Ashley didn't look up from her documents, but his interest in her office manager struck a nerve. Was he trying to poach her? If he was, he could go fuck himself. He was not stealing Elena.

"No. Not her. The pretty girl with soft skin."

This time Ashley did look away from the documents. "Rachel?" She asked, raising an eyebrow. He shifted in his seat, but she didn't know if his nervousness could be attributed to the weight of her accusatory stare or if it was something else.

"Yeah."

"How the hell do you know if her skin is soft?"

"I mean," he swallowed hard. "It looks soft."

"That's a weird choice of words."

"Sorry," he looked down at his intertwined hands and she went back to her work until he spoke again. "But you didn't answer my question."

"I didn't answer your question because it's none of your damn business."

"Okay, okay, I'm sorry."

Ashley stood, suddenly unable to spend a single moment longer alone with this asshole. "It's nearing eight thirty. We might as well head over to the courthouse."

"Now?"

"Was I mumbling or something?" She bundled her notes together and shoved them into her laptop bag along with her computer, a power cord, two legal notepads, and several pens. "Yes, now."

"Okay."

Ashley pulled on her coat and walked past him. She opened the door and motioned with her hand. "After you."

David scrambled to his feet, heading out the door. Ashley followed him, locking the door behind her. The streets were deserted this early in the morning, and there was the oppressive stillness that came with a fresh blanket of snow. They crossed the street in silence. The courthouse was empty except for a local journalist who was sitting quietly in the hallway. Ashley waved to him, and he waved back. They weren't friends, but they were friendly.

*He's in for a show today,* Ashley thought as she opened the door to the magistrate courtroom and strode inside.

There were no people in the room yet. Ashley walked up to the defense table and started unpacking her things. There were two seats, and she chose the one closest to the prosecutor and the witness stand. "Get another chair," Ashley said, motioning to a row of chairs along the side wall, "and put it between mine and yours."

"Why?"

"Noah." Was all Ashley said.

As David maneuvered one of the heavy chairs over to their table, Ashley moved over to the prosecution table. She sat in the first chair and pressed the lever beneath it, causing it to lower all the way to the ground. She did the same with the second chair.

"What are you doing?"

"Making the prosecutor small."

"Why?"

"Because he sucks, and first impressions are everything."

David shook his head. "It sounds petty."

"Yeah, well, it is. But I don't care. Sometimes you have to stick it to the man wherever you can."

Ashley returned to their table as David was unpacking his things from his high-end leather laptop bag. She could smell it from where she stood, that new leather scent lingering in the air, a scent that screamed *money*. He removed two notepads and two pens, both clear so she could see the color of the ink inside them. An aqua blue. The same color as Erica and Rachel's letters.

At the sight, Ashley's heart started beating wildly as her mind tried to connect the dots between David, Erica, and Rachel, but she couldn't. There was no connection, was there?

"What's with the color?" Ashley said, nodding to the pens.

"Oh, these," David held them up to show her. "It's specially ordered. I use it in all my trials and with all my clients. It's hard to read, which means that opposing counsel can't walk behind me and read my notes."

"Oh," Ashley said, but she wasn't convinced.

It wasn't that his explanation hadn't made sense. She wrote in cursive for that very same reason, but it had more to do with his delivery of the answer. It seemed almost nervous, like he'd been caught with his hand in the cookie jar. And maybe he had. She intended to press him on the issue, but she was interrupted by the back doors swinging open. She turned to see who was coming, and in walked Noah, flanked by two disgruntled looking deputies.

# 23

## RACHEL

Ashley had asked both Rachel and Katie to attend Noah's preliminary hearing. As members of the MEHR team, they were potential witnesses. They arrived together at eight forty-five. Katie opened the back door to the magistrate courtroom, allowing Rachel to enter first. There weren't a lot of people present, but all eyes turned to look at them as they stepped inside.

A smattering of people occupied the gallery benches. A local reporter that Rachel recognized from her days as part of the news cycle rather than as an onlooker, and a handful of people Rachel didn't know. Ashley was up at the defense table. Noah was sandwiched between Ashley and the attorney who had represented Rachel's stepfather.

The prosecutor was alone at his table, sitting in a seat that was extremely short for his large frame. A trick by Ashley, Rachel felt sure of it. She watched the prosecutor for a moment, wondering if he had even noticed. He had to, right? Then he reached below his chair, fiddling with the lever to raise it, but lost his balance and barely caught himself on the edge of the table.

Rachel shook her head and moved further inside. Her legs seemed to proceed of their own volition as her gaze locked on the other attorney that was with Ashley. She wished she could remember his name. It was something biblical, naturally, since Rachel's father had been a Bible beater, but she couldn't remember which name. Was it Matthew? Or Simon? Maybe it was Luke? There were quite a few options, but none of them sounded quite right.

Katie chose a bench at the back of the small courtroom, and Rachel was relieved that she had, sliding in next to her and waiting for everyone to forget about them and refocus on the front of the room. They had just started to do that when the other defense attorney leaned across the table and wrote something on Ashley's notepad. Ashley read it, then looked up, her gaze meeting Rachel's, before standing and making her way back toward them.

All eyes followed Ashley as she walked down the aisle, but they settled on Rachel when Ashley stopped at their little corner. Ashley still had the notepad in her hands. "Hey," she said, her voice barely above a whisper.

"Hey," Rachel whispered back.

Ashley dropped down to one knee next to them. She held her notepad flat for a moment before flipping it over, but not before Rachel caught a glimpse of it. There were several notes written in black ink in Ashley's familiar courtroom cursive, but it was the final note, the one at the bottom of the page, that caught Rachel's attention. She couldn't read the handwriting, but she would recognize that ink color anywhere.

"We need to sequester witnesses," Ashley said, pulling Rachel out of her thoughts.

Sequestering in trial was a word Rachel had picked up from her time around Ashley. It meant that witnesses needed to be outside the courtroom in a place where they couldn't hear the testimony that came before theirs. In their situation, it meant that Rachel and Katie needed to leave.

Rachel rose to her feet, relieved to be getting out of there, and Katie did the same. The weight of collective gazes clung to Rachel as she made her way out of the courtroom, but it was gone the second they were out in the hallway and the doors closed behind the three of them.

"I'm actually only going to need one of you to testify," Ashley said, her gaze shifting from one to the other before settling on Katie.

"I can do it. I've been working with Noah for far longer. Rachel hasn't had much to do with him aside from their conversation the night before his arrest." Katie paused, then added, "And there was nothing significant about that conversation, right Rachel?"

Rachel nodded. "Right." She didn't think she'd heard anything important, and she'd say or do just about anything to get out of spending the day face-to-face with Noah's other attorney.

"You don't need to waste your time hanging around, then," Ashley said, flashing a warm smile that she reserved only for Rachel. "You're free to go."

"Thank you," Rachel said, her gaze returning to Ashley's notepad. It had shifted and it was facing her now. It was upside down, but the familiar blue ink flashed in the fluorescent lighting. Rachel nodded at the notebook. "That's an odd color of ink."

"Yeah," Ashley said. "David uses it. He says he chose the color so opposing counsel couldn't read his notes." She glanced down at it. "I guess it does a pretty good job. I can barely read it close up."

*David*. That was his name. That may have been the reason for the ink color, but David wasn't using it only for court hearings. Rachel's guess was that he'd penned a couple letters of his own. That, or he'd given a pen to her father, and he'd been visiting him in prison, delivering the psychopath's letters for him.

"Is something wrong?" Ashley asked.

"No," Rachel said, shaking her head.

She wanted to tell Ashley everything, but now wasn't the time. Ashley was moments away from the start of an important hearing. She didn't need to be sidetracked with Rachel's worries. Besides, Trixie had received the letters, too, and she was just fine. Her conversation with Ashley could wait a day.

"Are you sure?"

"Yes, I mean, no." Ashley knew Rachel too well for her to continue lying and expect to get away with it. "But it's nothing big. I can talk to you about it later."

"Okay," Ashley said, but her lips were dipped into a faint scowl.

"I'll stop by your office later today. We can talk about it then."

Ashley studied Rachel for a long moment, then nodded. "I was going to ask you to stop by anyway. It's been forever since we've hung out."

They said their goodbyes, and Rachel didn't stick around any longer. She was ready to get out of that courthouse and away from the attorney who wrote in sky blue ink.

## 24

### ASHLEY

Ten minutes before nine, the courtroom fell into a tense silence. There was a crackle of what felt like electricity in the air. An energy. The kind a runner feels just before the starting shot or a soccer player experiences moments before the whistle blows. This was Ashley's game, her war. And these moments, they always had her hands sweating.

At nine o'clock, the magistrate entered the courtroom through a door behind the bench. She wore a black robe like any other judge, but she was young, barely older than Ashley, with stick straight hair shorn into a shoulder-length bob. Ashley's first thought was, *I wonder if she's going for Judge Ahrenson's position*, but she immediately pushed it away. Today's hearing was about Noah.

"Good morning," the magistrate said, "I'm Magistrate Mikala Mirko. We are convened today for a preliminary hearing in *State of Iowa versus Noah Scott*. Are the parties ready to proceed?" Her dark eyes shifted to Ashley.

"Yes, your honor." Ashley rarely appeared in magistrate court, so she wasn't quite sure what to expect with this magistrate.

Magistrate court was for early hearings and minor cases like traffic offenses and the very lowest of misdemeanors. Ashley didn't take misdemeanor cases, and most preliminary hearings were cancelled by the prosecutor filing an indictment.

"What about you, Mr. Hanson?" Magistrate Mirko said, her voice hardening as her gaze shifted. "Are you prepared *this time*?" Her almond-shaped eyes flashed with the words *this time*.

"I am always prepared," Charles Hanson responded.

"In that case, go ahead," she gestured in front of her as if to say *you have the floor*. "Start presenting your case."

Ashley turned to glance behind her. The gallery was virtually empty aside from a handful of people. The local reporter smiled at Ashley, and she returned the gesture. She would have preferred to have a camera or two available to capture the action—especially if things went well for her—but some media coverage was better than none.

"The state calls Deputy Frankie Pitch to the stand," Charles Hanson said, rising to his feet and motioning to Deputy Pitch, who was seated at the very back of the courtroom. He was the only witness allowed to remain in the courtroom, because no other witnesses had testified before him.

The deputy stood. As he did, he shot a smug look in Ashley's direction. It was the kind of look witnesses gave when they expected the hearing to go well for them. Ashley was dead set on proving Deputy Pitch wrong. Even if the hearing ended badly for Noah, Ashley was still going to expend every ounce of energy making Frankie squirm.

"Good morning, Deputy," Charles said in his overconfident, slow, but not quite southern drawl.

"Good morning."

There were a few questions about the deputy's background, training, and experience, but it wasn't long before Charles launched into the meat of the case.

"Have you been leading the investigation into the death of Erica Elsberry?"

"Yes. It didn't start that way. It started as an investigation into her disappearance."

"When did she disappear?"

"We got a call about it a few days ago. The caller had said she'd been missing for close to a week."

"Who called?"

"A coworker of Erica's."

"Not the defendant?"

Deputy Pitch's grey eyes settled on Noah. "No."

"How do you know the defendant, Noah Scott?"

"Objection," Ashley said. The word was uttered with force, but it wasn't shouted like lawyers did in television and movies. She used almost a conversational tone. "Relevance."

Magistrate Mirko turned to the prosecutor. "Yes, Mr. Hanson. How is your question relevant? What does it matter how this deputy knows the defendant?"

"To establish identity, your honor."

"Well, then ask the witness to identify the defendant. Don't ask him *how* he can identify the defendant. That isn't relevant to this matter. I will sustain the objection."

The prosecutor's face flushed red. A small smile quirked into the corner of Ashley's mouth, but she forced it back. Most judges were pro prosecution, especially when the case was as serious as Noah's, but Magistrate Mirko was clearly not one of those judges. Ashley liked her already.

"Do you know Noah Scott?" Charles Hanson said.

"Yes."

"Is he here in the courtroom?"

"Yes."

"Please identify him for the record."

"He's right there." The deputy pointed a meaty finger at Noah. "Between the two defense attorneys."

"Let the record reflect the witness has identified the defendant," Charles said.

"And so it does." The magistrate sounded almost bored.

"Where was Erica Elsberry last seen?"

"At Mikey's Tavern."

"That bar down the street here?" Charles motioned in the direction of the Tavern.

"Yes."

"Did you speak with anyone who had been at the bar that night?"

"Yes."

"Who did you speak to?"

"Amanda Stone."

Ashley jotted the name down on her notepad. She'd subpoenaed the woman, as the runner who found Erica's body, but she hadn't known this tidbit of information. It was likely a coincidence. In small towns there were only a few places to run and drink, but that didn't mean Ashley couldn't use it to cast doubt on the state's case against Noah.

"What did Amanda tell you about that night?"

David's gaze locked on Ashley's, and he mouthed the word *object.* She shook her head, a barely perceptible flick back and forth. In a normal trial, Ashley would object to this question as hearsay and that objection would be sustained. However, this was a preliminary hearing, and the rules of evidence—which included hearsay rules—didn't apply in preliminary hearings. Every defense attorney worth their salt knew that, and a quick review of the Iowa Rules of Criminal Procedure would have informed everyone else. Apparently, David hadn't done his homework.

"Amanda told me that she saw Noah and Erica there at Mikey's Tavern. It was late and they were all drinking. I think it was the night before Thanksgiving, which is a big night at the bars."

"Did she mention an argument?"

"Yes. Amanda stated that Erica and Noah were arguing. She said it got heated."

"How did the argument end?"

"Erica left the bar."

"Was Noah with her?"

"No. He stayed behind and continued drinking."

"When was the next time that Amanda saw Erica?"

"Amanda found Erica's body inside a sealed and latched toolbox floating in Lake Goldenhead. She was on a run, and she saw the toolbox. She thought it was odd that it was floating, so she went to check it out. I think she regretted it."

"Curiosity and cats and all that," Charles said with a deprecating chuckle.

"Yeah," Deputy Pitch said with a smile.

"Did Amanda recognize Erica when she opened the toolbox?"

"No. The call came in as a Jane Doe. Deputy Thomanson was the first on the scene, and I was second. The body was in the decomposition process, and her head was turned, so Amanda couldn't see Erica's face unless she physically touched the body. She was hysterical at the sight of any dead body, so there was no way she was touching it."

Ashley hated that word, *hysterical*. It was only used when referring to women, and it insinuated that the woman was overly emotional. But given the situation, Amanda Stone had every right to be upset, even extremely upset.

"Who identified the body?"

"The defendant, Noah Scott. Erica didn't have any family left in the area aside from her minor son, and we weren't going to have him do it."

Ashley glanced at David. His expression didn't change. He didn't seem surprised by the statement. Yet he'd told Ashley that first night they'd discussed Noah's case that Erica was missing. Not that she was dead. And certainly not that Noah was the one to identify her body. If Deputy Pitch's testimony was truthful, then David had lied to her.

"Were there any signs of violence on Erica's body?"

"No. We believe she suffocated in the airtight container."

"Why do you believe this?"

"There was no water inside the toolbox even though it was found floating in the lake. We also found scratch marks inside the top of the toolbox."

"Like Erica was trying to claw her way out?"

"Exactly."

"Was there anything else interesting about her fingernails?"

"Yes. We found skin, like she'd recently scratched someone hard enough to break their skin and get it up under her nails."

"Were you able to determine whose skin it was?"

"Yes. The defendant has prior felony convictions, so we have his DNA on record. The DNA under Erica's fingernails matched Noah's DNA."

Charles Hanson paused for emphasis, then he said, "I'm going to show you some pictures. They are labeled State's Exhibits One through Five."

"Okay."

"May I approach the witness your honor?"

The Magistrate nodded at Ashley. "Have you shown those to defense counsel yet?"

"Um, no."

"Then do it. This isn't a damn circus, Mr. Hanson. There are rules and decorum that you must follow. The standard protocol is for you to provide copies of your exhibits to opposing counsel *before* the hearing begins. You clearly haven't done that, because I don't see Ms. Montgomery looking at anything over there. So, the very least you could do, and I mean the *very* least, is to show them to her before you start discussing them with your witness."

"Okay," Charles said.

He marched over to the defense table, his teeth gritted tightly, and handed the stack of photographs to Ashley. She accepted them, smiling in a sweet, exaggerated way that she knew would irk Charles. She flipped through the five exhibits. All were photographs of Erica's body curled inside the toolbox.

"Are you done?" Charles growled.

Ashley looked up, making eye contact with him and maintaining it as she passed the exhibits to Noah. "No."

Noah glanced at the top exhibit, then flipped them over, unable to see his once lovely girlfriend in such a horrible condition. David picked the pictures up. He looked at each one, but his expression was one of disgust, his nose slightly wrinkled like he had smelled something rotten. David handed the exhibits back to Charles, and Charles stomped up to the witness stand, handing the pictures to Deputy Pitch.

"Can you tell me what State's Exhibits One through Five are?"

"Yes. They are photographs of Erica's body shortly after the toolbox was removed from the water."

"Who took these pictures?"

"I did."

"Are they clear and accurate depictions of Erica's body as you remember it?"

"Yes."

"I offer State's Exhibits One through Five into evidence," Charles said, turning to sneer at Ashley.

"Any objection?" The magistrate asked.

"No objection."

The prosecution was using the pictures for emotional and shock value. That was their only true purpose since the defense wasn't contesting that Erica had, in fact, died, or that she'd been inside the toolbox.

"Where was this toolbox found?"

"In Lake Goldenhead."

"Is that in Brine County?"

"Yes."

"Now, this toolbox, the one in exhibits One through Five, do you know where it came from?"

"We know that the defendant bought a similar toolbox at a local hardware store a few weeks before Thanksgiving."

"Did you search the defendant's home?"

"Yes. We executed a search warrant on the defendant's home a few days ago."

"Was the toolbox there?"

"No. We did not find the toolbox."

Charles Hanson paused again, casting a dark look in Noah's direction.

*This is bad*, David mouthed to Ashley.

Ashley shrugged. It did sound bad. All of it. And a lesser attorney would have given up, but Ashley was an expert at getting her clients out of tight spots. Sure, this one was tighter than most, but she was going to try to turn it around. Because soon it would be her turn, and she was going to rip Deputy Pitch and his investigation apart.

# 25

## KATIE

"Rachel, wait," Katie said, rising from her seat outside the courtroom and catching her assistant before she made her way down the stairs.

Rachel stopped and slowly turned to face Katie.

"Is something going on with you?"

"What do you mean?"

"You've been, I don't know, jumpy lately."

Rachel had always been quiet and hypersensitive to her surroundings, but those personality traits had amplified over the past few days.

To Katie's astonishment, Rachel's eyes flooded with tears.

"Oh, Rachel." Katie wrapped an arm around her assistant's shoulders and led her to a nearby bench. Luckily, the hallway was empty with every onlooker already inside the courtroom watching whatever show Ashley was undoubtedly presenting. "What is going on?"

"Do you remember the letters," a sob erupted from somewhere deep in her chest. "The letters that Ashley gave me the last time we were at her office?"

"Vaguely."

"Well, they were creepy. And they keep coming. I don't know who they are from, they aren't signed, but they are always written in this weird light blue ink. Those flowers at our office, those were the same."

Rachel had reacted strangely to the flowers. Katie had assumed that was from guilt. That she'd known they were from a client, but she didn't want to get rid of them. She should have known better. That was a normal reaction for a teenage girl, but Rachel was an old soul, aged by years of abuse.

"Then Ashley comes out here," Rachel waved an arm toward the closed courtroom door, "and there's a note on her notepad with that same color of ink. I don't know," Rachel shook her head and wiped her eyes. "I just feel like someone is stalking me."

"Okay, okay," Katie said, her mind whirring back into police officer mode. "Let's think about this. Do you still have the letters?"

Rachel nodded. "They're in the top drawer of my desk."

"Let's take a look at those after this hearing is over. I can't leave now, but I'll come straight to the office when I've finished testifying."

"Okay."

"Do you still have the envelopes?"

"Yes."

"Were they sealed?"

"Yes."

"So, there's potential DNA evidence there."

"I didn't think about that." There was a hope in Rachel's eyes that nearly broke Katie's heart.

"Do you have any suspects?"

"Sorta."

"Tell me about them."

"Well, that attorney in there, the one that is working with Ashley and Noah."

"David?"

"I didn't know his name. At least I couldn't remember it, but that's what Ashley called him."

"Why do you suspect him?" Katie was surprised, but not *that* surprised. She'd gotten a bit of a creep vibe from him herself.

"Well, not him specifically, but maybe. He was my father's attorney."

"I think you might be mistaken."

Isaac Smithson, Rachel's legal father, was charged and convicted of sexually assaulting Rachel. He was also convicted of attempted murder after he poisoned Ashley. He was serving a life sentence. Katie had testified at his trial, and she spent several hours on the witness stand face-to-face with the defense attorney. That person was not David Dirkman.

"He didn't represent Isaac in the criminal case. David did all his civil work. Like wrote his will and whatever."

"Oh."

"He has the pens. I saw him writing on Ashley's notepad, so that note had to come from him. That color is the exact same color that's on the letters."

"It is an odd color, but it might not be rare. We'll have to look into that. I wonder how many of his clients use and keep the pens? Even if the color is extremely rare, that could potentially widen our net of potential suspects."

If Rachel wasn't so upset, Katie would have enjoyed this conversation. She felt like she was doing something again. Solving a puzzle, fixing a problem.

"That's what worries me. What if it is Isaac? He could be writing the letters and having David deliver them for him."

"That's possible," Katie said, but it wasn't probable. To be true, David would have to be driving back and forth from Anamosa Prison in Anamosa, Iowa, which was more than three hours away. Could it be done? Yes. Would it be profitable? Not likely. There was little chance a private practice attorney would waste his time like that.

"Then there's Jackson Weatherspoon."

"He's a client of yours," Katie said with surprise that was quickly followed by a pang of disappointment in herself. She used to carefully vet all of Rachel's clients to make sure she could handle them. But that was before they'd gotten really busy. They'd been swamped lately, with multiple new cases coming in each day, and she'd grown lazy, assigning cases in a pattern with everyone getting the same number of new clients.

"Yeah. I've been meeting with him, and he's just odd. He watches me far too closely and he makes sexual innuendos."

"There is a simple solution for that."

"There is?"

"I'll take his case. I can give you one of my female clients."

"Thank you," Rachel said, but she sounded more than thankful.

Exceedingly grateful, perhaps was a better phrase for her demeanor in that moment, and Katie knew that she didn't deserve it.

"Don't thank me. It's my job. I'm sorry this has all been happening. Are there any other clients that are bothering you?"

Rachel bit her lip.

"Out with it."

"You remember Trixie?"

"Yeah. She came in a couple days ago. Is she causing you problems?" She seemed like a good fit for Rachel. They were similar ages and both had traumatic childhoods.

"Not her. It's her neighbor. When I met her for the first time, she started talking about this neighbor who was creeping her out. And she also had letters that were written in that same curious blue ink in the same handwriting."

"What? Who is the neighbor?"

"Bryce."

"Your driver, Bryce?"

"Yeah," Rachel said, looking down at her feet.

"Damn." That was a harder problem to solve. "Well, I can't do anything about the driving situation, you'll have to talk to your aunt about that, but I'll take over Trixie's case, too. At least you won't be running into him during the day."

"You will?"

"Yes. In the meantime, we can arrange for someone else to drive you home. At least until we know who's stalking you."

"I can't accept that," Rachel said. "Aunt Stephanie lives really far out in the county, and I don't want to impose that much on anyone."

"Okay . . ." Katie pursed her lips, thinking. "Could you stay with someone else? Maybe Ashley?"

Rachel shook her head. "Aunt Stephanie would not be happy about me moving out. Even for a short period of time. Things have been going well with her, and I don't want to rock the boat."

"Alright." Katie didn't agree with Rachel's decision, but she had to respect it. "Any other potential letter writers?"

"I don't see any connection, but that Ivan guy gives me a bad feeling."

Katie understood why Rachel felt that way. She hadn't forgotten the way he'd been oddly obsessed with Rachel from the moment he showed up outside their office for his first appointment. All conversations were somehow steered back to Rachel, and his eyes were constantly seeking Rachel out.

"I've assigned Ivan to Tom's caseload. I'll tell Tom not to meet with Ivan at the office. He can do house calls instead. Anyone else?" The list was already pretty large, and it saddened Katie that Rachel had been bottling all these things up with no outlet for release.

"That's all for now."

"Have you discussed any of this with Ashley?"

"No. She's been busy with this stuff," Rachel nodded toward the closed courtroom doors. "I didn't want to bother her."

"Things will slow down for a bit once today's hearing is over, and it sounds like she wants to talk to you later today. I know you don't want to, but maybe you should consider staying with her for a little while."

"I'll consider it."

"In the meantime, you can go back to the office. Tom should be there, so there won't be any drop-ins that you'll have to handle alone. You can spend the afternoon preparing Trixie and Jackson's files for transfer to my caseload. I'll come back as soon as I'm done testifying. Does that sound like a plan?"

Rachel nodded and stood. "Good luck in the hearing."

Katie watched her assistant as she turned and disappeared down the stairs, leaving Katie alone in the hallway, her mind remaining on their conversation. Was the situation truly as bad as Rachel thought? Rachel's childhood had been traumatic, and that could lead to a hyperactive fight or flight reaction. She believed the letters existed. She'd been there when Ashley had handed two of them to Rachel. But was Rachel exaggerating, or was someone truly stalking her?

# 26

## ASHLEY

After what seemed like an eternity, the prosecutor finally finished questioning Deputy Pitch, reluctantly handing the baton to Ashley. Throughout direct examination, the deputy had grown bolder, his ego building with each softball question tossed his way. But it was time for cross, and Ashley was aiming to hit this batter so hard he spent the rest of his career on the injured list.

"Hello, Deputy Pitch," Ashley said, sifting through the stack of documents in front of her.

He tensed at the tenor of her voice, her unruffled air of confidence. Her tone was calm, conversational, completely devoid of emotion. It was when she was most effective. He was right to have his guard up. Danger lay ahead.

"Um, hello."

"Lake Goldenhead is in Brine County, yes?"

"Yeah. That's what I said earlier."

"And that's where Ms. . . ." she glanced down at her notepad. It was all for effect. She had already memorized the names of every potential witness and their expected testimony. "Stone, I believe that was her name."

"Yes. That's her name."

"Is Lake Goldenhead where Ms. Amanda Stone found Erica's body?"

"Again, I already said that."

"Bear with me deputy, I have a point. I promise." Here, she flashed a Cheshire grin.

"Okay."

"Now, that was where Erica was *found*."

"Yes. That's what I said."

"What you didn't say was where Erica *died*."

Charles Hanson was drinking from a cup of water, and he coughed, sputtering and spitting it all over his table. Ashley's gaze cut to him, then back to the deputy. She couldn't have asked for a better reaction from the prosecutor. He was surprised, and it drew attention to the point she was in the process of making.

That point was this: to bring charges in Brine County, the state had to prove that Erica's murder had occurred in Brine County. It was one of the technical nuances that most nonlawyers didn't realize, nor did they recognize its importance. Today, at least the citizens of Brine County would learn.

"She died in the toolbox. The toolbox was in the lake," Deputy Pitch said, his face flushing.

"You testified that she suffocated, right?"

"Yes."

"And the toolbox was airtight, yes?"

"Yes."

"Well, how do you know that Erica wasn't shut inside that toolbox in Greene County, then shuttled over the border and dumped in Brine County after she died?"

"Because it's not likely."

"Why not? Is there something that prevents Erica's killer from taking her body across county lines?"

"No, but they lived in Brine County. She was probably—"

"We're not in the business of *probably's* here, Deputy Pitch. You've accused my client of a very serious offense. You've arrested him and thrown him in jail. Nobody here cares about what you *think* happened. I'm asking what you *know* happened. And you don't *know* where Erica died, do you?"

"No." The word was barely above a mumble.

"What's that?" Ashley placed a hand behind her ear, "I didn't hear you."

"I said, no!"

"Wonderful. Let's move on, shall we?"

The deputy grunted.

"Now, there was a lot of discussion about DNA results earlier, wasn't there?"

"Yeah."

"You seem to think that the skin under Erica's fingernails is a smoking gun."

"I do think that. It proves that he killed her."

She tsked. "Now, now, deputy, you know it proves no such thing."

He narrowed his eyes.

"It proves that she scratched him, not that he killed her, am I right?"

"I guess, but—"

"But," she interrupted him, "you also testified that there was a bar fight the night Erica went missing, didn't you?"

"I don't know that I would characterize it as a bar fight."

"Well, you're a decent investigator, don't you think?"

"I'd say I'm better than decent."

"And a *decent* investigator would have contacted Mikey, the owner of Mikey's Tavern, and requested a copy of the video footage from that night, wouldn't you agree?"

"Maybe."

"Did you do that?"

"Not yet."

"Well, I did," Ashley said. "Would you like to see it?"

"Not right now."

"Well too bad," Ashley said, standing and striding over to the large, courtroom TV. She flipped it on and inserted the disk. "What I am about to play for you is labeled as Defendant's Exhibit A. I offer Exhibit A into evidence."

"Have you provided a copy of it to the state?" Magistrate Mirko said in a far kinder tone than she'd used with Charles Hanson.

"Yes, your honor. I sent it to him yesterday."

"Very well. Exhibit A is admitted. Go ahead and play the video."

Ashley pressed the play button and the screen burst to life with a lively bar. The camera was mounted near the ceiling at the back of the bar, facing toward the bartender, giving a full view of the entire establishment. Erica and Noah were at a table a few feet away from the camera. There was no sound, but they appeared to be engaging in a heated conversation. Erica had always been someone who talked with her hands, especially while angry. In the recording, she was waving her hands around like she was trying to guide a landing plane.

After a good five minutes of yelling, Erica got up and walked around the table so she could shout directly into Noah's face, standing toe-to-toe, nose-to-nose. Noah didn't respond. He merely sat there, taking the abuse. When Erica paused in her shouting tirade, Noah's mouth moved, indicating that he had responded with only a few words.

Then Erica grabbed her beer, threw it in Noah's face, then jumped on him, grabbing at his neck. Noah was at a high-top table, and the force of Erica's sudden attack knocked his chair over backward. They both went down together and were out of the picture for a good three minutes as they wrestled around on the floor. Then a group of men in biker gear separated them, pulling them both back up into view again. Erica was not deterred. She continued shouting and pointing, and a burly man in a Harley Davidson jacket led her to the door.

Ashley paused the video, turning back to Deputy Pitch.

"Now that you've seen Defendant's Exhibit A, would you agree that Erica and Noah's argument became physical?"

"Yes. Now that I see it, yes."

"And would you agree that scratching can occur during physical altercations like that?"

"Well, they aren't visible for a while, so I don't know."

"Please answer my question. I didn't ask you if you saw any scratching. I asked you if it was possible for Erica to have scratched Noah at that time."

"Is it possible, yes."

"And then she left."

"Yes."

"But Noah stayed."

"Yes."

"Erica was never seen alive after that moment, was she?"

"Not by anyone other than the killer."

"But that bar fight," Ashley pointed to the frozen TV screen. "That could explain why Noah's DNA was under Erica's fingernails."

"Possibly."

"You have no evidence to prove that Erica made it home that night, do you?"

"No, we don't."

Now that the state's case was going down the toilet, the deputy was using words like *we* instead of *I*. He was already trying to find a way to shift blame.

"Someone could have kidnapped Erica on her way home, killed her, and dumped her, and she would still have Noah's DNA under her fingernails, wouldn't she?"

"Possibly."

She would have liked a more definite answer, but that was the best she was going to get with a reluctant witness. It was time to move on. "I want to draw your attention to another individual in the video."

"Okay."

"Where is Ms. Amanda Stone during the bar fight?"

"She's standing near Noah and Erica."

Ashley was shooting from the hip with this line of questioning. It was risky because she had no idea how he would answer. She had only just found out that Amanda Stone had been present at Mikey's that night. But still, some risks were worth taking.

"This was the same person that found Erica's body, right?"

"Yes. She found her a week later while running."

"Did you ever question her about her presence at Mikey's Tavern that night?"

"What do you mean?"

"Did you question her about her whereabouts later that night or if she saw Erica again?"

"No. Why would I do that?"

"So, you're telling me that you *knew* the person who found the victim's body had been with her in the last moments she was ever seen alive, and you've never even *thought* to ask her, 'where were you later that night?'"

"No."

"I want to move on to a discussion about the toolbox."

"Okay."

"You testified that Noah bought a toolbox a month ago, but you didn't find it in a search of Noah's house, right?"

"That's right," a hint of his former haughtiness returning.

"Noah has a detached garage, doesn't he?"

"Um, yes."

"You didn't search Noah's garage, did you?"

"No."

"Wouldn't you agree that most people keep their toolboxes in sheds and garages?"

"I don't know what most people do."

Ashley shook her head, irritated, but she'd made her point. The toolbox could have been in the garage, but the deputies didn't bother to look.

"During your search of Erica and Noah's house, you found some letters, is that right?"

"Yes."

"Your subpoena ordered you to bring copies of those letters with you today. Did you do that?"

"Yes."

"Can I have them?"

Deputy Pitch's face reddened, and he looked to the prosecutor, pleading for some way to keep the letters to himself. Charles Hanson shook his head, and Deputy Pitch reluctantly stood and brought a small stack of documents to Ashley. Ashley flipped through them, scanning their contents.

"These appear to be love letters, is that right?"

"They appear to be, yes."

"And they are all addressed to Erica?"

"Yes."

"Where were they found?"

"Hidden in a notebook in Erica's nightstand."

"They appear to be recent."

"They are dated October and November, but there is no year."

"So, they could be from this year, right? Shortly before Erica died."

"They could be."

"Yet you've done nothing to track down the author of these letters?"

"No. They speak to Noah's motive, his jealousy, not a possible suspect."

"Now, you have no idea if Noah was jealous or not. You have no idea that Noah even knew about these letters, do you?"

"I guess not."

Ashley considered going a little further to try and coax the deputy into admitting that the letter writer could have been the jealous one. Especially if Erica refused to leave Noah for the author of the letters, but she knew she wouldn't get him to admit it. Some things were best left for closing argument. So, she ended her questioning of the deputy. The state conducted a brief cross-examination, attempting to save a floundering case, then rested.

Now, it was Ashley's turn to call witnesses.

# 27

## RACHEL

The walk back from the courthouse felt lighter now that Rachel had finally told someone her concerns about the letters. She wasn't trying to keep them a secret. She had been waiting and wanting to tell Ashley all along, but Ashley had been so busy lately. And David had been hanging around. But now that she'd shared some of her burden, she felt less alone, and a little closer to Katie.

"It's just me," Rachel called as she came through the front door of the office. She didn't want Tom to have to get up and walk all the way out there. They really needed to hire an office manager for the front desk.

"Thanks," Tom said as Rachel passed by his office. "How was the hearing?"

Rachel shrugged. "I wasn't there long. Ashley didn't need us both to testify, so she told me I could leave."

"How is Ashley?"

This was the question that Tom had wanted to ask all along. It had been years since their breakup, yet he still kept a candle burning for Ashley. He didn't care about the outcome of the hearing. Noah had been Katie's client, not his.

"She's fine."

"Is she working too hard?"

"I don't know. You'll have to ask her," Rachel said before continuing back to her office.

She didn't want to be the one he used to fish for information on his ex-girlfriend. He took any chance he could get to talk about Ashley. It infuriated Katie, and annoyed Rachel. It felt disloyal to Ashley to tell Tom anything, and he didn't seem to realize that he was putting them in the middle.

The letters in light blue ink were still in her drawer, but she didn't open it to look at them. She'd wait until Katie was back before she got them out. For now, she needed to start preparing Trixie and Jackson's files for transfer. Katie was doing Rachel a favor, so she needed to go through each file and carefully organize them so that all the information Katie would need would be right at her fingertips.

She opened her laptop and logged into the MEHR team's client software. Jackson's file was the one she wanted to get rid of most, so she started with him. She clicked on the client information link inside Jackson's file and landed on a nearly empty page. Rachel was never very good with organization.

"I need to find his address," Rachel mumbled.

It would be on the initial intake paperwork. That was where she'd originally found it when Katie assigned Jackson to her caseload. She was good with directions, so she hadn't needed to refer to the address after she'd been there once. She found the document and copied the address into Google Earth, saving the link in the address line on Jackson's identification page.

Before closing out of the Google Earth page, she studied the location. She wondered how far it was from Noah and Erica's house. If Jackson would have been somewhere along Erica's path home when she disappeared. Both Noah and Erica had worked with the MEHR team, so their addresses were available.

Katie's files were usually the most organized, so Rachel opened a new tab in the client management software and opened Noah's file. Sure enough, she found the Google Earth link right where it was supposed to be in the address line. She clicked on it and an image filled the screen. She split the computer screen so she could compare the two Google Earth images side by side. Noah and Erica lived only a few houses down from Jackson.

If Erica had been using the road instead of alleyways on her walk back on the night she disappeared, she would have had to walk right by Jackson's house to get to hers. There had been a good deal of crime in that area, so the city had added extra streetlamps, one of which was directly in front of Jackson's house, clearly illuminating the sidewalk. Rachel had witnessed Jackson's strange obsession with that peephole in his door. If Erica had been on his side of the street, he could have seen her pass while looking through the peephole. If it was late and she was drunk, it would have been easy for him to abduct her without any witnesses.

*Focus*, Rachel reminded herself. She was preparing her files for Katie, not conducting an investigation. Yet she also knew the information could help Ashley. If things didn't go Ashley's way during Noah's preliminary hearing, the information would probably help her with Noah's defense, so she jotted the addresses down on a notepad with a dash followed by the words, "Did Jackson know Erica?"

She turned back to Jackson's identification page, filling in his known conditions in the diagnosis portion with borderline personality disorder, bipolar disorder, conduct disorder as a child. Next, she moved on to the criminal history section. The sentencing order that brought him to the MEHR team's door named his most recent crime as possession of methamphetamine with the intent to deliver. Meaning Jackson was a drug dealer. But she had no idea about any prior convictions.

Curious, she opened a new web browser and maneuvered to the Iowa Courts Online Search engine. Iowa Courts Online Search was a public website that allowed anyone to input a defendant's name and it would generate their previous criminal case numbers and convictions free of charge. Rachel typed Weatherspoon, Jackson and pressed search. A moment later, several case numbers popped up.

Criminal cases in Iowa had four letters followed by numbers. The letters indicated the level of offense at the time of arrest. FECR case numbers were felonies. AGCRs were the most serious misdemeanors. SRCRs were the middle-of-the-road misdemeanors, and SMCRs were the lowest level of crimes aside from traffic citations. There were multiple

FECR case numbers in Jackson's past and some AGCRs. Rachel started clicking on the case numbers to learn the nature of the crimes, and as she did, her already astronomical level of stress started to climb.

Jackson had multiple weapons convictions—felon in possession of a firearm, assault with a dangerous weapon, carrying weapons—but those weren't the most concerning convictions. It was the stalking and indecent exposure convictions that had Rachel's hackles up. He was a sex offender; one who stalked his victims. Exactly the type of person who would send creepy letters that ended in abduction and possibly murder.

Rachel added the information to her notes of things to tell Ashley, then closed out of Jackson's criminal history. She'd have to discuss this information with Katie as well. Katie was a former police officer, and she could generally handle herself, but it wasn't safe for anyone to make house calls to Jackson, including Katie.

Before completely closing Jackson's file Rachel filled in his upcoming appointment dates, pharmacy name and location, and medication list. When that was finished, she clicked the x at the corner of Jackson's file's tab, and issued a heavy sigh of relief. She was done with him, and she already felt safer. It was time to move on to Trixie's file.

Trixie had multiple drug convictions, all for methamphetamine and marijuana. It made her a felon at the age of eighteen. Now, eight years later, she was a felon multiple times over. Rachel saved Trixie's address and the Google Earth link into her file, then started going through Trixie's other documents to pull out information. For Trixie's history and mental health, she opened the presentence investigation. A presentence investigation, or PSI for short, was a document prepared by the Department of Correctional Services for the judge to use at sentencing. It was always part of felony files, and it included a full workup of Trixie's social, emotional, medical, and work history.

As Rachel read through Trixie's PSI, she was surprised to find that Trixie had been a child sex abuse victim. Her abuser had been a stepfather, which was eerily similar to Rachel's background. Rachel wondered if she would be in the same place—a felon who was addicted to drugs—if she hadn't met Ashley. She'd definitely be a felon, because she'd been charged with murdering her baby, but she would also be in prison, so the drug addiction probably wasn't likely.

When she finished with Trixie's file, she closed it out and sat back in her chair, thinking. She needed to start spending more time reading through her client files. She'd learned something new about both of her former clients. It made her wonder who else she could or should learn about, and an image of Ivan Volkov staring at her popped into her head. What were his convictions? Was he, too, a violent stalking sex offender?

She brought up Ivan's file. She hesitated before clicking on the documents page. Ivan was assigned to Tom, and she had never gone through another member of the team's files without their permission, but she'd never been told that it was against the rules either. In this situation, she'd rather beg for forgiveness than ask permission, because she needed to know, so she clicked.

The first document she opened was his intake form. His address was within a quarter mile from Noah and Erica's, easy walking distance, but it also wasn't on the way back from Mikey's Tavern. Not that that meant he couldn't have abducted Erica. Nobody knew what had happened to Erica after she left, only that she had been in an altercation with Noah moments before. Maybe she'd gone for a walk to blow off some steam before returning home and facing Noah again.

Next, Rachel turned to Ivan's sentencing order. His conviction was for lottery fraud, which was not one that came through their office often. Gambling addictions could be one of the most difficult to break, but those clients usually came to them with burglary or theft convictions rather than lottery fraud. She didn't even know what someone had to do to commit lottery fraud.

Curious, she copied Ivan's case number into the court filing system, where all court documents were maintained. She added his last name, then clicked search. Nothing came up. Instead, in bright red lettering, the website said *case not found*.

"That can't be right," Rachel said. She verified that she'd typed the correct case number, and that she'd spelled his name correctly. "So why doesn't his case exist?"

Rachel deleted Ivan's last name out of the parties line and replaced it with State. In criminal cases, the State of Iowa was always a party to the action, so in a pinch, she could use it to complete a case search. When she clicked this time, the case came up, but it wasn't *State of Iowa v. Ivan Volkov*. The defendant's name was Michael Evers. Rachel opened the sentencing order in the Michael Evers case, placing it side by side with Ivan's sentencing order. They were exactly the same.

She scanned each one, line for line, and there were no differences other than the defendant's name in the caption and the section ordering Ivan to complete the MEHR team program. It could only mean one thing. Ivan's sentencing order was fake. He had no criminal history, so why was he making one up?

Rachel closed out the file, shaken, before writing a note about Ivan on her notepad. The information she'd learned about Jackson had been concerning, but this, this was disturbing on an entirely different level.

# 28

## KATIE

Katie was in the hallway, scrolling through Facebook in a failed attempt to stave off the boredom of waiting for her turn to testify. A steady stream of people had come through the hallway, some disappearing into the courtroom while others visited various other government offices housed inside the courthouse. But nobody was around anymore. The hallway had been empty for a good ten minutes by the time the courtroom doors opened and Ashley poked her head out.

"We're ready for you," she said, motioning for Katie to follow her.

Katie stood and tucked her phone into her pocket, walking a few steps behind Ashley as they entered the courtroom. The magistrate couldn't be more than a year or two older than Ashley, and she watched Katie with a curious yet guarded expression. Ashley motioned for Katie to take a seat in the witness box, and she did. The magistrate swore Katie in, and Ashley started with a few introductory questions about Katie's current job, her former job, and the nature of her work with the MEHR team.

"In your capacity as the leader of the MEHR team, have you come in contact with someone by the name of Noah Scott?"

"Yes."

"How do you know Noah?"

"He's a client."

Normally, HIPAA would prevent Katie from even identifying Noah as a client, but in order to work with the MEHR team—which almost always was the last-ditch effort to avoid a prison sentence—the clients had to sign a release of information for any and all court hearings. Both Noah and Erica had signed that agreement.

"How often do you meet with Noah?"

"In the beginning, it was daily. He was one of our first clients, so that would have been about six months ago. Our office uses a tiered process. The clients start with intensive supervision that slowly decreases over time, so long as they are maintaining their sobriety, addressing their mental health appropriately, and staying on the right track."

"Can that supervision increase again if issues arise with the client?"

"Yes."

"You said you were visiting Noah daily in the beginning, but what about more recently?" Ashley said. "How often had you been seeing him?"

"We were down to monthly appointments. He started out daily, transitioned to weekly after the first month. We had weekly appointments for two months before moving on to biweekly and then monthly. He's been doing really well, so he should graduate from the program soon."

"What is Noah's addiction?"

"Noah's drug of choice is methamphetamine. I say *is* and not *was* because although Noah is sober, he will always struggle with his addiction. It's not something to beat. Using any substances would lead him down a slippery slope and ultimately back in trouble."

"In the six months you have known him, have you seen any signs that Noah might be violent?"

"No."

"Your team also works with Erica Elsberry, right?"

"We did, yes. Tom Archie had Erica's case."

Katie couldn't be sure, but she thought she saw a reaction in Ashley when Katie stated Tom's name. A slight stiffening of the shoulders that nobody would notice aside from someone like Katie who knew Ashley so well.

"Did Erica graduate from the MEHR team program?"

"No. She was down to monthly appointments as well. I used the past tense when referring to Erica's involvement with the MEHR team because she isn't alive anymore, not because she graduated from the program."

"Did Noah and Erica show up for appointments together sometimes?"

"They were often together. At first, I didn't like that they were even dating. It's hard enough for one methamphetamine addict to get sober, but it's even more difficult when there are two of them. There's the risk of relapse, and when one goes off the rails, the other is usually quick to follow. Luckily, that hadn't happened with these two."

"How many times would you say you've seen them together?"

"I don't know. A lot."

"Have you ever seen Noah behave violently toward Erica?"

"No. She's the hot tempered one."

"Thank you," Ashley said, flashing Katie a quick smile. "I have no further questions."

The courtroom fell silent, and the magistrate turned her attention to Charles Hanson. He was quiet for a few moments, before launching into his own line of questioning, this time focusing on Erica instead of Noah.

"Was Erica involved with someone outside of Noah?"

"Involved? How so? I mean, she was involved in a lot of things."

"I mean romantically."

"Not that I know of, but she wasn't my client, and she didn't like me. We'd been on the wrong foot since my days as a police officer, so I rarely even spoke to her."

"Did Erica seem afraid of anyone?"

"Like I said, I wouldn't know. We weren't friendly. If she was afraid, she wouldn't have told me."

"Is that something she would tell Tom?"

Katie shrugged. "Maybe. Probably. People like Tom, so if she was going to say anything to anyone, it would probably be him."

"Did he ever tell you that Erica was frightened of anyone?"

"No."

"Was Erica and Noah's relationship tense?"

"They were both dealing with sobriety, ongoing legal issues, and a new relationship. Those factors are bound to make any relationship tense.

That's why I don't like clients dating each other. At least not until they've had more than a year of sobriety under their belts."

"You said Noah's appointments were monthly, but they could increase if you saw risk factors. Recently, have you seen anything that would cause you to increase his appointments?"

"Yes. I ran into Noah a few days ago. I was on my way to meet a friend at Mikey's Tavern. Noah had said he was on his way to the MEHR team office. I told him that it was already after hours, and I obviously wasn't there, but he could see if Tom was still there and schedule something."

"Did Noah talk to Tom?"

"No. He spoke to my other assistant, Rachel."

"Did he schedule an appointment with Rachel?"

"I don't know. I don't think so, because there wasn't a new appointment on the schedule when I checked my calendar."

"Was that Rachel's first time talking to Noah?"

"No. They'd met one other time. It was probably a month or so ago, maybe a little less than that. I had a conflict in my schedule, but I didn't want to cancel the appointment, so Rachel agreed to meet with Noah."

"Why did Noah recently request an extra appointment?"

"I don't know. He said that something had happened, and he was worried that he might fall off the wagon. Erica would have been gone a week by then, so that was probably it. The sudden disappearance of a long-term girlfriend can be stressful for anyone."

"Thank you. I have no further questions."

The magistrate excused her, and Katie stood, making her way toward the back of the courtroom, relieved that her testimony was done. This was not her first time testifying in court, not by a long shot, but she'd never been able to take the stand without her heart racing and her palms sweating.

She walked down the aisle between the prosecution and defense tables. As she passed the defense table, she noticed that both Noah and David were writing on legal pads. They were both using the curious blue ink that Rachel had mentioned earlier. Katie wondered if it meant anything, if that truly was the same ink that was used in Rachel's letters, or if it was simply a coincidence. Either way, she intended to find out.

# 29

## ASHLEY

"Does the defense rest?" Magistrate Mirko said, her gaze locked on Ashley. She hadn't looked at David once.

"Yes, your honor," Ashley said.

It had been a long morning, calling witness after witness. She'd subpoenaed every member of the Sheriff's Department, calling each one to the stand to fish for information about the case. Deputy Pitch was right that the discovery process wasn't underway, but this hearing was her opportunity to get witnesses under oath without taking depositions and before they prepared their testimony with the prosecutor.

It was an old tactic that law enforcement often used. Question someone enough times and they are bound to give conflicting information. Sometimes they remember more details, sometimes those details change. It was usually small things like the color of clothing or the height of an assailant. It didn't necessarily mean the witness was lying—the human mind worked in strange ways—but it sure made it easy for Ashley to make them look like liars to the jury.

Ashley was mentally planning her next steps—scheduling depositions —when the magistrate's voice cut through her thoughts.

"Any rebuttal?" The magistrate's gaze was focused on Charles Hanson.

"No."

"Very well," Magistrate Mirko said. "Since it is the state's burden to prove there is probable cause to continue with the prosecution, I'll hear argument from Mr. Hanson first."

"Thank you, your honor," Charles said as he struggled to his feet. "I'm going to keep this short and sweet, because the evidence is clear. There is probable cause to believe that the Defendant, Noah Scott, murdered his live-in girlfriend, Erica Elsberry. Erica's body was found inside a toolbox similar to one Noah bought right before Erica's disappearance. The defendant never reported that Erica was missing. The defendant's DNA was beneath Erica's fingernails, where she'd scratched him to defend herself from his vicious attack. She died a slow, horrible death, and it was that man," he paused and pointed at Noah, "who killed her." He paused again, then added, "Thank you," before lowering himself back into his seat.

"Ms. Montgomery," the Magistrate said.

This was the moment that Ashley lived for, when all eyes in the courtroom settled on her. When she was poised and ready to strike. She slowly stood, and walked around the defense table, turning to address everyone in the courtroom.

"I'm going to keep this even shorter and sweeter," she said, flashing a smile at Charles. "I could spend the next thirty minutes pointing out all the problems with the state's case, but I'm not going to waste your time. That's because the state can't prove one essential element and without it, there is no probable cause. They have no idea where Erica died. They know where she was found, but that was a dumping site, not the location of the murder. The state must prove that a crime occurred in Brine County. That is the only way Brine County has jurisdiction over the crime. The crime here is murder, and the state has presented no evidence as to where that murder occurred. As such, the defense requests that the Court dismiss the case against Noah Scott."

Ashley turned and walked back to her seat. As she passed Charles Hanson, she could see his hands, knuckles white from gripping the table in front of him. His nostrils were flaring. He was next-level furious. But how had he not seen that coming? Ashley had more than alluded to it in her questioning. And this wasn't Charles's first rodeo. He knew he had to prove jurisdiction, but he had made a rookie mistake. He'd focused on the facts of the case and disregarded the technicalities.

"I'm ready to rule," Magistrate Mirko said. She paused and looked down at a notepad that she'd been using. "I agree there are some gaping holes in the state's case. The DNA under the victim's fingernails doesn't mean anything, not unless the state can prove it occurred after the physical altercation at Mikey's Tavern."

"But—"

"Mr. Hanson," the magistrate snapped. "You had your chance to speak. Now it's mine. The toolbox could mean something, but the state didn't even search the defendant's garage. Why that didn't happen is beyond me, because I specifically remember signing that search warrant, and I permitted law enforcement to search every building on that property, including the garage. But that's not my problem, it's yours," she said glaring at Charles.

"If I may—"

"You may not," Magistrate Mirko said, cutting Charles off. "I don't know what this business is with the love letters, but it doesn't prove anything at this point. Maybe the victim was having an affair, maybe not, but it doesn't do anything to prove the defendant's potential guilt. True, the defendant didn't report the victim missing, but that hardly makes him guilty of murder. Then there is the most glaring issue of all. Ms. Montgomery is right. You failed to prove jurisdiction. This murder could have occurred in any one of Iowa's ninety-nine counties, or even another state. I have serious doubts as to the probable cause for many of the elements of this charge, but the prosecution presented absolutely no evidence of jurisdiction. I have no clue where this murder occurred. Therefore, I cannot allow you to continue with this prosecution at this time. I am dismissing the case."

Noah gasped, and David patted him on the back, but Ashley remained still. They had won the battle, but there were still plenty more left in this war. The magistrate was not finished speaking yet.

"As such, you will be released from jail today."

"Oh, thank you, thank you," Noah said to Magistrate Mirko.

"Don't thank me just yet. The rules of criminal procedure allow for the state to refile these charges. If they get their case together, you may be back behind bars in a matter of hours. Nice job, counsel," she said, directing her last statement to Ashley.

"Thank you," Ashley said quietly.

Then Magistrate Mirko stood and stepped off the bench, exiting the courtroom and going into her private chambers. Once the magistrate was gone, everyone else stood and started funneling out. Ashley had expected some excitement in the audience, but there was just a stunned silence. The two deputies that had brought Noah into the hearing hustled him back to the jail to be processed and released. Within ten minutes David and Ashley were the only two remaining in the courtroom.

"Well, I'm glad that's over," David said, standing and stretching.

"It isn't over."

"What do you mean?"

"They're going to charge him again. They aren't going to give up. They'll keep digging for evidence, and it's only a matter of time before we're right back here again."

"So, what do we do?"

Ashley gazed down at the stack of letters seized from Erica's nightstand. "We work." They needed to get the identity of the letter writer.

"How long until Noah's out?"

"It'll take at least an hour. The jail is always pretty slow, and there's a lot of paperwork."

"I think I'm going to wait for him."

"Okay," Ashley said, standing and shoving the notepads and pens she'd used for the hearing into her bag. "I'm going to pop over to the MEHR team offices."

"You are?" David had seemed almost bored with their conversation there at the end, but he perked up with the mention of the MEHR team.

"Yeah. Some of my friends work there, and I've been too busy to be much of a friend to any of them lately. It's about time I start making up for that."

"Do you want me to stop by?"

"No," Ashley said, furrowing her brow. It was an odd question. Did he think she needed an escort or something? "It's not the eighteen hundreds anymore, David. Women are allowed to go outdoors without a man."

"I didn't mean that. I just . . ." he shook his head. "Never mind."

*Never mind is right,* Ashley thought. "I'll call you tomorrow and we can discuss next steps."

Then she grabbed the stack of letters and hurried out of the courtroom, down the stairs, and toward the MEHR team's office. As she walked, her mind kept rolling over the result of the hearing and what it meant. She'd won, but she'd agitated Charles Hanson pretty good, and he was a connected political figure in Brine County. Today's results were wonderful for Noah, but a potential problem for Ashley's upcoming bid for the bench. If she kept up like this, she'd never be donning that coveted black robe.

# 30

## RACHEL

It was eleven thirty when Katie finally returned to the office. She looked weary, worn down from a combination of stress, sleep deprivation, and a heavy dose of constant worrying.

"How was the hearing?" Rachel asked.

Katie jumped. She had just walked through the door, and she hadn't seen Rachel standing there, waiting for her. She immediately relaxed when her gaze settled on Rachel. "You scared me. It was fine. I'm not sure if I helped or hurt Ashley's case, but it's always hard to tell what tricks she has up her sleeve. Her mind works differently than mine."

"Yeah."

Katie's gaze landed on the flowers still sitting on the unoccupied reception desk. "Let's throw those out, huh?"

Rachel nodded, a sudden rush of relief filling her body.

"Do you want to do the honors, or shall I?"

"I can do it," Rachel said.

Rachel hated the flowers and the creepiness that they represented; she couldn't wait to throw them in the garbage. The action wouldn't make her feel safer, but it was symbolic, a declaration that her stalker was not getting to her. That he should back the fuck off.

Rachel grabbed the flowers and headed out the front door. It was the middle of the day, and the sun was shining warm against her skin. She hadn't seen the sun in days, and this, too, felt like a good omen. But as she made her way down the alleyway and toward the back dumpster, her optimism began to fade. The two-story buildings blocked out the sun, casting cold shadows over her body, and she once again felt as though someone was watching her.

She picked up her speed, clutching the flowers tighter. One side of the trash bin was already open. Trash day had been the day before, so it was nearly empty. Rachel took the flowers, lifted them high above her head, gathering all her frustration, all her fury at her stalker, then threw them as hard as she could into the dumpster. The vase hit the bottom with a loud *crash* and the flowers scattered in every direction.

That done, she turned and ran to the back door of the MEHR team office, suddenly feeling exposed. Was someone truly watching her, or was it all in her head? Removing her office keys from her pocket, she unlocked the back door and rushed inside, closing it behind her and breathing heavily. When she looked up, she saw that Katie was making her way down the hallway toward Rachel's office, but she wasn't alone. Ashley was with her. A burst of relief bloomed inside Rachel's chest.

"You're done already?" Rachel said.

"Yeah."

"What happened?"

"Case dismissed," Ashley said. Her voice was so devoid of excitement that Rachel almost wondered if she was joking. But Ashley had always taken her job seriously. She wouldn't joke about something like that.

"Shouldn't you be happy about that?"

Ashley shrugged. "It's definitely a positive way to start the case, but Charles Hanson will charge him again. At least there was a local reporter in the audience. He'll report on it and get the gossip mill down at Genie's Diner going. I'm not sure if they'll see it as a guilty man who got off, or as an innocent man who was wrongly accused. Obviously, I hope it's the latter, but you never can quite tell with the locals."

"Now that you're here, we've got some stuff we need to talk to you about, right Rachel?" Katie said.

"You do?" Ashley looked from Katie to Rachel, taking stock of their grave expressions. "What happened?"

"Let's go into my office," Rachel said with a heavy sigh. "I've found some new information, even since the last time I spoke to Katie."

All three women funneled into Rachel's spacious, tastefully decorated office. Everything was light colored. A glass writing desk, a large fluffy white rug over beige hardwood, white bookcases. It was all designed and paid for by Rachel's aunt, Stephanie, who felt to Rachel like a Disney dad. Stephanie was rarely physically around, but her money was everywhere.

Once everyone was situated, Rachel at her desk and Ashley and Katie in the chairs across from it, Katie said, "Should I start by filling Ashley in on what I know?"

Rachel nodded, and Katie told Ashley about the letters before giving background on Jackson, Ivan, Bryce, and David, explaining each of their behaviors and what ties they had to Rachel. Ashley's expression grew darker and stormier with each detail. When Katie had finished, Rachel pulled the two letters and the card from the flowers out of her desk drawer and set them on the table.

Ashley stared at the letters. Without looking away, she reached into her laptop bag and pulled out another stack of letters, setting them next to Rachel's with shaking hands.

"Where did you get those?" Rachel asked. "They aren't addressed to me, are they?"

Ashley shook her head. "No. It's worse. These are copies of the letters seized from Erica Elsberry's house. The ones written by the person I think could be her killer."

Rachel leaned forward, comparing the letters. They were written in the same ink color. The handwriting was the same, all caps with each sentence starting with a slightly larger capital letter. The slant and careful script looked the same. She was no handwriting expert, but she didn't need to be to know that these letters were written by the same person.

"I think we can safely rule out Isaac Smithson as the letter writer," Katie said. "He's in prison. He couldn't have committed any murders, and although it seemed possible that David might deliver the letters for his former client, it's doubtful that he'd kill Erica on Isaac's behalf."

"That, and I don't see how Isaac would have known Erica," Ashley added. "Isaac was from Waukee, a Des Moines suburb. He hired David, but David does a lot of work in that area and has a second office out there. Their connection makes sense. There's no reason to believe that Isaac has ever even set foot in Brine County."

Rachel released a breath she hadn't realized she'd been holding. While this bit of information solved nothing, it was still a relief to know that her childhood tormenter was not continuing to harass her.

"There was a fourth letter, too," Ashley said, reaching into her bag and pulling out an envelope that said FOR RACHEL. "Someone left it on the back step of the Public Defender's Office. It was the evening after I gave you those first two letters," she nodded at Rachel, "shortly after we ran into each other at Mikey's Tavern," she nodded at Katie.

"That would have been the day before the flowers," Katie said.

"The fourth letter wasn't there when I left for Mikey's. I always check both doors to make sure there are no packages. UPS and USPS leave them at the front door, but Amazon, for some unknown reason, sets them out back. Anyway, I checked for packages before I left, and there was no letter there. But when I walked back to my car after leaving Mikey's, I saw it sitting there, wedged beneath the door."

They all looked down at the letter.

Rachel didn't want to touch it. She silently wished it didn't exist.

"We have to open it," Katie said. "At least so we know what it says."

"Okay," Rachel said, reaching into her desk and grabbing a letter opener. She held it out in front of her, allowing Ashley and Katie to choose who accepted it.

Ashley hesitated, so Katie took it. She slid on a pair of winter gloves that she'd had in her coat pocket before sliding the letter opener along the top of the envelope. "Fingerprints," she said, by way of explanation. "Any gloves are better than none." She pulled out the letter and lay it flat on the desk so everyone could read it. There were four simple words, written in the same blue ink with the same handwriting. YOU WILL BE MINE.

"Ashley sat back in her chair, her face heating with anger. "That's fucked up."

And it was, but they all knew that while this felt like a threat, there was nothing criminal about it. Whoever was writing these letters understood the criminal justice system and was able to walk a thin line, careful to get his point across while still remaining firmly within the bounds of the law.

"I've had enough of this," Ashley said, shooting to her feet. She started to pace along the back wall of Rachel's office. "We have to find out who this motherfucker is."

"Agreed," Katie said. "You said you found some more information," Katie said, turning to Rachel. "What did you find?"

"When I was going through Jackson Weatherspoon's file, I realized that his criminal history is, well, it's bad."

"Like how bad?" Katie asked.

Rachel looked down at her notepad, although she didn't need to. She was using it more as a prop, a safety net to keep her hands from shaking. Jackson's background was now seared into her brain. "Indecent exposure, stalking, felon in possession of a firearm, carrying weapons."

"Is that possible?" Katie said, turning to Ashley. "Did you represent him in any of those cases?"

Ashley shook her head.

"None of them are from Brine County," Rachel added. She'd been wondering the same thing—if Ashley had sent him over to them knowing that he could be dangerous—but she quickly discovered that wasn't the case. Ashley had never represented him. She would have no reason to know him or anything about his past.

"All those charges fit with what we are seeing in these letters," Ashley said, gesturing toward the desk. "I wish I still had a private investigator to follow up on it. We could be solving two problems here, Rachel's harassment and finding Erica's true killer, but I don't have anyone to send out on these kinds of errands anymore. And I'm far too busy to do it all myself. I could ask David to hire an investigator, but he's a possible suspect, too, right?"

Rachel and Katie nodded.

"The ink is the same, and it is an uncommon color," Katie said. "It seems unlikely that he would be helping Isaac, but he would have seen her from afar for years. He could have developed an obsession with her and started writing these letters."

"He certainly didn't tell me he knew Rachel, and anyone who knows anything in this town knows that Rachel and I have a history."

"But that isn't limited to Brine alone. Your representation of Rachel made national news. David could have lived anywhere and still known that you had ties to Rachel."

"That piece of shit," Ashley said, balling her hands into tight fists. "If that's true, I'm going to knock every one of his perfect little teeth out."

"Alright, let's try to avoid committing any felonies," Katie said. "Is there any other information you learned?"

All eyes turned back to Rachel. She told Katie and Ashley about Ivan's sentencing order. They were both shocked and wanted to see the comparison. Rachel pulled both court orders up on her computer and laid them side by side.

"That's one of my clients," Ashley said, pointing at the name Michael Evers. "See there, see the first few lines. They all began to read.

*We are convened on today's date for sentencing in the*
*above-captioned case. The State of Iowa is present and*
*represented by Charles Hanson, the Brine County Attorney.*
*The Defendant, Michael Evers, is present and represented*
*by his counsel, Ashley Montgomery, the Brine Public Defender.*

"Now look at Ivan's sentencing order," Ashley said, pointing to the first line. It read exactly the same except the name *Michael Evers* was replaced with *Ivan Volkov*. "I didn't represent that guy, though. I remember all my clients, and Ivan Volkov is not one of them."

"Well, now, that's odd," Katie said, breaking the silence. "Why would someone fake a sentencing order just so they could work with our office?"

Ashley and Katie turned to look at Rachel.

"He creeped me out from the second I saw him," Rachel said. The way he had looked at her, and how his gaze had lingered, she'd never forget it.

"He wanted to work with Rachel, demanded it, actually. So much so that he even gave me the creeps. I assigned him to Tom's case load."

"Okay, so I've got to look into David, Jackson, and Ivan. Anyone else?" Ashley asked.

"Bryce," Katie said. "And we'll help you. We have a common interest here."

"Bryce, as in Rachel's driver?" Ashley said, shocked. "What does he have to do with this?"

"He gives me the creeps and he lives across the hall from one of my clients, Trixie. Right downtown here."

"How would he get a hold of one of those pens, though?" Ashley asked. "Ivan and Jackson could have ties to David. It is possible that he has represented them in some capacity, but Bryce has never been in trouble. Queen Stephanie would never hire him if he had a criminal history." Ashley had recently taken to calling Rachel's aunt Stephanie a queen because Ashley claimed that Stephanie acted like one.

"Maybe he hired David to do the same kind of work that Rachel's father had. Estate planning kind of stuff," Katie suggested.

"Maybe," Ashley said.

"Bryce also used to date Erica Elsberry," Rachel added. "And I know they were talking before Erica died, because Bryce said so one time when he was driving me home."

"Oh yeah, I forgot about that," Ashley said, snapping her fingers. "It was back before Erica even started using. That feels like decades ago."

"Okay, so we've got our list of people. Bryce seems the least dangerous, so, Rachel, why don't you focus on him," Katie suggested.

Rachel nodded, relieved she wasn't getting stuck with Ivan or Jackson.

"I'll talk to George and arrange a time we can go visit Ivan. At the very least, he doctored a legal document and passed it off as an original. It's very likely that he's going to end up charged for that."

"I don't relish the idea of bringing Sir George into the mix, but he's better than the other assholes down there at the Sheriff's Department, and Ivan could be dangerous, so I'm fine with it," Ashley said.

"That leaves David and Jackson," Katie continued. "With Jackson's criminal history, George and I should probably handle him, too. He lives over by Ivan, so we can pop from one meeting to the next. Can you handle David?"

"Can I handle David?" Ashley said crossing her arms, a flash of excitement in her eyes. "Oh, I'll handle him."

"Don't break any laws."

"I'll try not to. But if he is using me to get to Rachel, I can't make any promises."

Katie sighed and rubbed her temples. "I guess that's the best we're going to get with you."

Rachel watched her two mentors discussing and dissecting a problem that had plagued her for nearly a week. Rachel had come up with no conclusions, no answers on her own, but these two had broken the problem apart and divvied it up into manageable pieces. For the first time since she started receiving those letters, she was finally starting to feel safe, but part of her wondered just how long that feeling would last.

# 31

## ASHLEY

It was thirty minutes past noon when Ashley left the MEHR team office. Her stomach was growling, but she hadn't packed a lunch to bring with her when she left the house that morning. Noah's preliminary hearing had been occupying all parts of her mind, leaving no space for normal, daily tasks like meal planning.

She paused on the sidewalk, looking around. Genie's Diner was just down the street, but it would be packed this time of day. She'd probably have to wait for a table, which she didn't have time for, and then she'd have to eat alone, which was humiliating in a small town.

*No*, she thought, shaking her head and turning away from the diner, *not a good option*. Then she saw the corner gas station and convenience store at the end of the street. It was called Frankie's Corner. It wouldn't be good food, but it would be quick. She headed toward it.

Once she walked inside, she immediately regretted her decision. She remembered a moment too late that Frankie's Corner was owned by Deputy Frankie Pitch's parents and the man behind the counter, Frankie's father, was glaring at her like he'd caught her drowning a bunch of kittens.

She froze, paralyzed with indecision. Should she turn around and walk out, or should she go about business as usual? Leaving now felt an awful lot like cowering and running with her tail between her legs. That was fine when she was in the wrong—which was always difficult to admit—but she hadn't done anything wrong this time. It was Frankie Pitch who had screwed up the investigation, not her. All she'd done was point out his mistakes, which was her job.

Straightening her back and lifting her chin, she strode into the small convenience store. She could feel Frankie's father's eyes continuing to bore into her, as well as the curious gazes of the few other onlookers fortunate— or perhaps unfortunate—enough to witness the encounter. Ashley walked back to one of the refrigerators, selecting a sorry-looking hoagie sandwich, carrying it with her to the front and setting it on the counter in front of Frankie's father. He was the only person working and he didn't make any move to scan the item.

"That's not for sale," he said around a large clump of dip in his cheek.

"That's odd," Ashley said, feigning surprise. "I could have sworn it said $4.49 there on the side." She picked the sandwich up, flipped it over, then pointed to the yellow sticker. "See, there. $4.49. I was right."

"It's $4.49 for other people, but not for trash like you."

"We're really going to do this?" Ashley said, placing a hand on her hip.

"Do what?"

"You're going to deny me service, and then I'm going to complain to anyone who will listen, including Genie down at Genie's Diner, and you know how her gums flap. It'll be no time before people in town start choosing sides. Some will be with you, while others will remember what happened the last time that I was persecuted for doing my job, and they'll feel sorry for me or angry at you, honestly it truly doesn't matter which, because the outcome is still the same. You will lose half your business. Now, judging by the looks of this place," she paused and made a show of looking around, "you need all the money you can get. I'd guess you're barely making ends meet as things sit today. Sure, the storm will eventually blow over, but can your little shop here withstand some rain, or is it exactly how it looks—barely afloat?"

Frankie's father grabbed the sandwich, squeezing it in his palm while he scanned the barcode. "That'll be five dollars and fifteen cents," he said through gritted teeth.

Ashley handed it to him in exact cash, trading it for the hoagie like it was a ransom drop. When goods and money finally exchanged hands, he pointed the red light of the scanner at her forehead like it was a gun, and said, "Now, you'd better get out of here little girlie, before I go changing my mind."

"Fine," Ashley said, turning her back and marching toward the door. Before she left, she called over her shoulder, "Pleasure doing business with you." She was certain he had a response, but she was gone before she heard it.

She unwrapped the sandwich as she walked back toward her office and took a bite. It was bologna and the bread was soggy from a thick layer of mayonnaise. *All that for a shitty sandwich*, Ashley thought irritably, but she was hungry so she kept eating. It was gone by the time she reached her office. She stepped inside, the bell above the door jangling merrily. She was still in her own head, thinking about Frankie's corner, paying little attention to her surroundings. She ran straight into David, who was standing with his back to the door.

"What the hell, man," Ashley said. "Get out of the doorway."

"Sorry," he said, taking a large step to the right. "I was waiting for you."

"Why? I told you we didn't need to talk until tomorrow. You know, I do have other cases that need my attention. I can't devote every second of every day to Noah. And Jesus Christ, he should be doing a happy dance right now. Both of you should. I saved your asses. It might not be for long, but at least for today you should consider your asses saved and be happy for it."

"Woah. Calm down."

"You do realize that telling a woman to 'calm down' is the worst possible thing to say when she's angry. It's a backhanded way of saying that I'm overreacting."

"Okay." He drew the word out long and slow in a way that made Ashley think that was exactly what he was trying to say—she was overreacting.

She was about to launch into him, but then she reminded herself to keep her cool, that she wasn't really mad at him. She was mad at Frankie's Corner and that idiot harassing Rachel. *Rachel*. In that moment, she remembered that she needed to talk to David for another reason completely unrelated to Noah, and she forced herself to do the one thing she hated to do. Apologize.

"I'm sorry. I've had a long day. Why were you looking for me?"

"I need to talk to you."

"Okay." *Need and want are not the same thing*, Ashley thought. "Let's go back to my office."

They walked in silence, Ashley leading the way.

"I'm worried about Noah," David said the moment Ashley closed her door.

*No shit*, Ashley thought. "Why?"

"Because he's teetering on a knife's edge of sobriety. He was struggling with Erica's disappearance, and then he finds out she's dead, and in a very gruesome and horrible way. He was charged and jailed, which kept him from using, but now that he's out and waiting for the other shoe to drop, well, this is rock bottom for him."

"I don't understand," Ashley said, dropping into her old but comfortable chair. "Are you complaining about Noah's release? Because we are defense attorneys. Well, you aren't, but you are pretending to be one in Noah's case, so you better start acting like you are. Defense attorneys try to get their clients released. Call it a goal. Like a high cash settlement for your personal injury clients." She had been trying to play nice, but he was being a complete and utter jackass, and acting had never been her thing anyway.

"You're missing the point."

"And that is . . ."

"That we need to find a way to keep him from falling off the wagon."

Ashley almost responded, *Honey, if that were possible, if clients actually listened to me, I'd have a very short case list and quickly be out a job*, but she held her tongue because it was an opening to steer the conversation in the direction that she wanted.

"We could encourage him to start meeting with the MEHR team more regularly. Katie did testify that Noah had wanted to increase the number of meetings."

"Oh, yeah," he said, snapping his fingers in an exaggerated *I can't believe I forgot* manner that made Ashley think that there was no way he did actually forget.

"Did you know Katie before meeting her today?"

David shook his head. "I didn't know her. I mean, I've crossed paths with her a time or two during the few criminal cases that I've done in the past. Same thing goes for the guy. He was a jailer years ago, wasn't he?"

"Yeah," Ashley said. Her heartbeat quickened at the thought of Tom back then. When things were so simple between them. Two people who enjoyed one another's company without all the emotional baggage that came with betrayal and breakups.

"But that other girl, she's a mystery. What's her name?"

"Rachel Arkman."

"Oh," David's eyes widened. "As in the super-rich Arkmans or is the name just a coincidence?"

"It's no coincidence. Stephanie Arkman is her aunt."

David whistled long and low. "A loaded pretty girl like that. It's a wonder she's not married."

Ashley bristled at his characterization of Rachel. She was more than a face and cash. She was a complicated, loving young woman, and to consider her anything other than that was akin to objectifying her.

"Yeah, well, she had a tough childhood, but maybe you'd know a little about that."

"Why would I know?"

Ashley was tiring of his little ignorance routine. Everyone in Iowa knew about Rachel's past. It was on all the news stations and in all the papers, and it wasn't that long ago. It was possible that he hadn't recognized her face—it had been years since he'd last seen her in person—but her name, that should have given it away. The Arkman family was very public about Isaac Smithson's conviction and incarceration. Of course, that wasn't until after Rachel's acquittal, but still.

"She changed her name. It used to be Rachel Smithson."

David's eyebrows shot up at the mention of the name Smithson.

*Bingo*, Ashley thought. "You knew him, didn't you? Isaac Smithson."

"Yes," David said slowly, cautiously. "I did some work for him. Estate planning type work."

"Do you still keep in touch with him?"

"From what I've heard, he doesn't have much of an estate left to plan anymore. It sounds like his daughter cleaned him out."

"Yeah, well, he deserved it after raping her throughout most of her childhood."

David put his hands up in a gesture of surrender. "I didn't mean anything by it. But the answer is no. I don't speak with Isaac Smithson. I swear I didn't even realize that the girl working for the MEHR team was the same girl. It's been so many years and I barely saw her in passing back then."

Ashley studied him for a long moment, looking for a tell, but she saw nothing. Maybe he was telling the truth. "You haven't visited Isaac in prison?"

"No. Why would I do that?"

"Delivered any letters for him?"

"Absolutely not. What is this all about?"

"Nothing," Ashley said, satisfied that he was telling the truth.

"Have you ever represented a guy named Jackson Weatherspoon?"

"Yes. Fairly recently. It was a drug charge and he ended up on probation and working with the MEHR team."

"Why did you represent him? He has no money."

"I've got to get my pro bono hours in somehow."

It wasn't a requirement that attorneys provide pro bono work. At least not to maintain their license. Yet many attorneys in private practice logged some hours of free or reduced-fee work to make themselves look good to the bar association. It absolved them of any guilt for the outrageous prices they charged regular clients.

"Is he violent?" Ashley asked.

"Not that I've seen."

"Did he take any of your pens?"

"Is this an interrogation?"

"Just answer the question."

"I don't know. A lot of my clients take the blue pens. They aren't cheap —I have to order them from a specialty shop in Des Moines—but I've learned to build the price into my retainers, so it doesn't bother me. Really, what's this all about?"

"Nothing."

"Nothing," David repeated, looking skeptical. "You must really think I'm an idiot."

"It's not anything you should worry about. So, are you going to schedule an appointment for Noah with the MEHR team?"

David narrowed his eyes in a way that said, *I know you're changing the subject but I'm not going to call you out on it.* "I am probably going to wait until tomorrow. Do you want to meet me at Noah's house tomorrow morning?"

"Yeah. Let's meet there at eight o'clock. I have a hearing at nine o'clock in front of Judge Ahrenson and I need to talk to the Judge about an unrelated matter."

"An unrelated matter, huh? Could it be the upcoming judicial vacancy?"

"Yeah. I'm considering applying, but I'm a little concerned that today's antics could hurt my chances."

"I know several people on the judicial nominating committee," David said, rising to his feet. "Let me know if you need me to put in a good word for you."

Ashley smiled in the sweetest possible way she could muster, which wasn't very sweet considering she still didn't know David's level of involvement in Rachel's letters. She believed him when he said that he wasn't in contact with Isaac Smithson, but he'd played too dumb for too long for her to truly believe that he didn't know Rachel's identity. So, why was he feigning ignorance? Ashley didn't know, but she was hell-bent on finding out, and she would have another opportunity the very next morning.

# 32

## RACHEL

"I just got off the phone with George," Katie said, popping her head back into Rachel's office.

Rachel startled at the sudden appearance of her boss.

"He's going to go with me to Ivan's house," Katie continued, "but he's tied up with something else. He says he'll be ready in thirty minutes. Do you want to pop over to Genie's for a bite of lunch?"

"Um, sure," Rachel said.

"Let's bag up those letters before we go," Katie said. She held a box of Ziploc plastic sandwich baggies in her hand. "Do you mind if I give them to George when I meet him later? He wants to send them to the lab for evaluation and comparison to Erica's letters."

"Do what you want with them." Rachel pushed her chair back from her desk and stood, pulling on her coat. "I don't want to look at them again."

Katie pulled on her winter gloves and picked up the letters, putting each one in its own baggie, then she stuffed them in her laptop bag. The moment they were out of sight, a sense of freedom washed over Rachel. The letters weren't her problem anymore. Katie was taking that weight off her shoulders. It didn't make Rachel any safer physically, but it was a small chip out of the wall of stress surrounding her.

"Let's go," Katie said.

As always, Genie's Diner was packed for the lunch hour and buzzing with chatter, but there was an excitement in the air that wasn't always present.

"Hey, y'all," Genie said, greeting Rachel and Katie at the door. "I have a table reserved for you."

Rachel and Katie exchanged a knowing look. Genie had always been a big supporter of Ashley even when most others had hated her, but she was also the town gossip. There was a reason she was reserving a table for them. They only came to the diner once or twice a week, and at different times. Genie had no way of knowing that they were coming, but she probably hoped that they would.

Genie led them to a corner table and gestured for them to sit. "The usual?"

Rachel nodded, and so did Katie. It would be a water for Rachel and a coffee for Katie. Rachel didn't ingest any stimulants, not even coffee. She saw a lot of addiction in her line of work, and with her past, she worried that using any substance could lead her down a slippery slope.

"I'll grab those for y'all. By the way, have you seen Miss Ashley this mornin'?

There it was. The reason for the reserved table. Genie wanted payment in news.

"We have, but we don't know much," Katie said. "Only that the magistrate dismissed the charge against Noah."

"But why? That's not normal, is it?"

Katie shook her head. "It doesn't sound like there's anything normal about this case."

Genie nodded, returning within a few minutes with their drinks. They ordered and their food came out almost as quickly. Katie's gaze followed Genie and she kept the conversation light until the diner owner was busy with another patron. Then she leaned in, motioning for Rachel to do the same.

"What are you planning to do after this?" Her voice was barely above a whisper.

"Well, I'm supposed to be looking into Bryce. That was my assignment.

He's been living in one of the apartments above here. So, I thought I would start by walking around and taking a second look at the setup of the apartments."

"Why?"

"I think the window placement and the balcony would give him a clear view of our office, but I'm not completely sure. It's possible that he could see both doors of our building and into the alleyway from up there."

"You think that's where he's been watching you?"

Rachel shrugged. "Maybe. And Trixie was also getting letters. His proximity to me and Trixie makes him even more suspicious."

"But he wouldn't be able to see Erica's house, would he?"

"I don't know what he can see from the second floor. That's another reason I want to check it out. Honestly, I don't know that his proximity to Erica's house matters. They dated and he admitted they kept in contact. His connection to her is pretty solid."

"True, true."

Genie stopped by, bringing the check, and Katie paid with the office card. They parted ways with Katie heading toward the Law Enforcement Center to meet George, and Rachel around the back of the building.

While the diner was bustling with energy and patrons, it was surprisingly quiet in the alleyway behind it. The brick walls of the building created an isolation that made Rachel feel exposed. She wanted to leave immediately, let someone else do this part of the investigation, but she forced herself to move forward. This was the easiest task. The others were busy with other things. If she didn't do this, it would only take more time to discover the letter writer and Erica's true killer.

When she was directly behind Bryce's apartment, she took several steps back, moving across the alley and into another abutting alleyway so that she could see all the windows. She was counting them and trying to determine what could be seen by looking through them when the energy around her shifted. A sense of heavy foreboding settled into her chest followed by that familiar weight of eyes upon her. She froze, the hairs on the back of her neck standing on end.

*It's in your head*, she told herself. *Nothing is going to happen to you.* There were literally dozens of people inside the diner. They'd hear if something happened to her, wouldn't they? But it was so quiet, so isolated, that she was starting to question her safety. Just as she was about to turn and leave, to run back to her office, something struck her in the back of the head.

It was something blunt and hard, and it hit her with a *whomp*. She felt her legs buckle beneath her before the world around her went dark.

# 33

## KATIE

Katie walked down the street and into the front door of the Sheriff's Department. She hadn't wanted Rachel to investigate Bryce's home on her own, but she rationalized that it was the middle of the day and there were plenty of people around. It didn't make the situation completely safe, but nothing was 100 percent in this life, and it would be far less safe for Rachel to come along with George and Katie. There was no telling what Ivan would do once he was confronted with his lies.

"I'm here to meet George," Katie said to the woman at the front desk of the Sheriff's Office.

"There you are," George said, coming out of the back. "I've been waiting on you."

"Bullshit," Katie said, glancing down at her watch. "You said 'a half hour.' That was at noon. It is twelve thirty now. I'm exactly on time."

"Sure, sure," George said, coming through the locked door that separated the visitors from the deputies.

"Still unable to admit when you're wrong, huh?"

"Still unable to let it go, huh?"

"Touché."

"I'll be back in an hour," George called over his shoulder to the woman at the front desk. "Drive or walk?" George said once he was out in the hallway.

"Drive. I don't know what Ivan is going to do. If things go south, I want to be able to get out of there fast."

"Okay." George pulled out a pair of keys and whistled as he led the way out a side door and to a row of vehicles with Brine County Sheriff written in yellow along the sides. He pressed his key fob and the lights of a nearby Ford Explorer flashed. "Like my new ride?"

"Yeah," Katie said, getting into the passenger seat. The inside was familiar yet foreign to her. She had been a police officer, not a sheriff's deputy. Most of the equipment was the same, but there were some differences in brands between the two departments.

"It's the only thing in this job that's better than the old one." He placed the key in the ignition and the vehicle thrummed to life.

"You miss the police department?"

"Like a phantom limb." He put the car into gear and began driving. "How about you?"

"I miss it sometimes, but it's more of a fleeting thing. Not quite so visceral as what you seem to be experiencing. I mostly miss the investigation part, not the place itself."

Katie had centered her life around her job as a police officer, and it had seemed like the end of the world when she'd been laid off, but she'd gotten over the loss pretty quickly. That was when she started working with Ashley, and she'd found that she enjoyed that job even more. If the funds had been there, she would have gone on working with Ashley for the rest of her career. It didn't sound like George had been quite so lucky.

"Before I forget," Katie said, reaching into her bag and removing the letters from Rachel. "I want you to send these off to the criminalistics laboratory for testing."

George pulled up in front of Ivan's house, putting the SUV into park. "What are they?"

Katie launched into the lengthy background of the letters, explaining the potential connection to Erica.

"So, you think if we track down the person who wrote these letters, we also might have Erica's killer?"

"At least you'll have a legitimate suspect other than Noah."

He looked down at them for a long moment, then back up at her, a smile spreading over his lips. "Thank you for this," he said, accepting the letters and tucking them into his jacket. He caught her gaze and held it. "Seriously, you don't know how much it means to me."

But she did. He would have never come to her asking for help unless he truly needed it. George had been through some tough stuff over the past few years. His wife had left the state, taking their son with her. He'd lost the only job he'd ever loved. He'd even lost his friendship with Katie for a while. He wasn't broken, but he was bending. Seeing a cousin take the fall for a serious crime that he potentially didn't commit could be the last straw.

"Don't mention it," Katie said, breaking away from his gaze and swallowing hard. There had always been an easiness between them, a sibling-like closeness, but something felt different about their relationship in that moment. A shift was taking place, and she wasn't quite sure where it would lead. "You're helping me out now. We're even," she said as she got out of the SUV, closing the door behind her.

George followed suit, turning to look at the house that Ivan had identified as his home. "This place is a real shithole."

"Yeah," Katie said.

The two-story house had probably been a nice home at one time, but there was little evidence of that anymore. The paint was chipping, the shutters were cockeyed or missing, and the front porch was so bowed that it made Katie wonder if it was actually meant to be a trap.

"Do you have your gun?"

"Yeah." She didn't always carry her gun, but she had been lately. She had a conceal and carry permit, and she'd been a police officer for so long that it felt like an extra appendage that she was all too happy to reattach. Leaving it behind while meeting with clients like Ivan and Jackson was not an option. "But let's hope I don't need to use it."

George nodded and started making his way up the stairs. Katie followed close behind. He stepped gingerly onto the deck, careful to avoid the worst-looking boards, and picked his way up to the front door. He waited for Katie to take her position a little behind him, then he knocked, three sharp raps.

"Ivan Volkov," he shouted. "Open up. It's the Sheriff's Department."

Silence followed. Katie strained her ears, listening for movement inside the house. All was quiet for several beats, then she heard the telltale creak of old wooden flooring as footsteps drew near.

"Who's there?" The voice was raspy, as though thick with sleep, but Katie recognized it as Ivan.

"George Thomanson with the Brine County Sheriff's Department." The door opened a crack and Ivan poked his head out. "Can I have a word with you?"

"Um, yeah, I guess," Ivan opened the door wide to allow George to enter. It was in that moment that he noticed Katie's presence and he froze, his eyes growing wide before narrowing. "What's this all about?"

"We need to talk, Ivan," George said, nodding to the door.

Ivan issued a heavy sigh, then stepped aside to allow them to enter. The inside of his residence was in worse condition than the outside. A few moments earlier Katie wouldn't have thought it possible, but a quick scan of the room changed her mind. Battered furniture showed holes consistent with rodent teeth. Cigarette butts littered the floor. Something tiny skuttled around in the darkest corners of the room. *Cockroaches*, she thought with a shudder.

"Alright, you're in," Ivan said, looking at Katie suspiciously. "Now, what do you want?"

Katie could have eased into the conversation, but she decided against it. They had the element of surprise, might as well use it to her advantage.

"I know you doctored your sentencing order," Katie said. She paused, waiting for a reaction, but all she saw was a slight twitch of his thin lips, so she continued. "I spoke to Ashley Montgomery. She never represented you. That sentencing order was from someone else. You just replaced your name and added a paragraph about working with the MEHR team."

Ivan remained still, silent.

"There's no use denying it," George said. "We have hard proof."

"So, what," Ivan said, crossing his arms. A defensive gesture. "It's not a crime."

"Maybe, maybe not," George said.

It was a crime. Ivan had forged a legal document, but this was how George often behaved around suspects. He acted as though he was their buddy, made them feel comfortable so they would talk, and he'd remain that way right up until he slapped the handcuffs around their wrists.

"I don't know what you mean."

"Your intent matters."

"Intent?"

"Your reasoning for changing a legal document," George said. "Why did you do it?"

Ivan's gaze cut to Katie, then shifted back to George, before dropping to the ground. "I had to," he said in a voice just barely above a whisper.

Katie and George waited in silence. They'd interviewed countless suspects in the past, and they had a good understanding of those that needed prompting and those that would continue but needed to do so in their own time.

"I gamble. At this casino up the road," Ivan nodded in the direction of the casino.

The casino was built five years earlier. It brought a lot of money into their community, but it had been controversial with the locals. Crime often followed gambling. People won, but most of the time they didn't. Those that won were robbed. Those that lost too much did the robbing. It wasn't always other gamblers either. Sometimes it was the convenience store down the street or a quiet house tucked into a cul-de-sac.

"It started as bets here and there. I won some and lost some. Then I started losing more than I was winning. I chased the losses, and the few wins that came then felt even sweeter." He sighed heavily. "At some point, I realized I was out of money, but I couldn't stop. That's when things really went downhill. I cleaned out the bank accounts, including my wife's. I got a second mortgage on the house. I even pilfered and sold my wife's engagement ring."

"You're married?" It was the one fact that seemed completely off kilter with what Katie knew about this man. He was dirty, unkempt, and smelled like the inside of a litter box. She couldn't imagine a woman that could tolerate such a man.

"Not anymore. She left me. Not that I'm surprised. I went from a nice house and family, to this," he gestured around him, "virtually overnight."

"This is a sad story," George said, "but I'm not sure what it has to do with altering court documents."

"I need help," Ivan said. "I can't stop. Even now when I've barely got a pot to piss in, I'll go running up to that casino the moment I have two dimes to rub together."

"So, go to a therapist," George suggested, but Katie already saw the gaping hole in George's logic.

"I have no money to pay for it. Like I said, I blow every penny I earn. It's part of my disease," he tapped his head. "I knew about the MEHR team. Heard about the program on the news. They were my only option, but I'd have to commit a crime to get their help. It seemed backward. I needed help. They could provide it. Why should I have to break the law to get it?"

"Fair enough," George said. His gaze cut over to meet Katie's.

There was a question there. It hung between them in the familiar way it used to, back in the days that they'd been partners at the police department. He wanted her to make the decision. But she didn't know enough to decide. At least not yet.

"Why did you ask to have Rachel assigned to your case?" Katie said.

Ivan smiled a crooked, loose-toothed grin. "I'm old and I don't take care of myself. I'd guess I have less than ten good years left in my life. If I can spend them looking at a girlie like that, well, I don't see the harm in it."

"What about the letters?" George asked. "Why did you send them to her?"

"Letters?" He seemed genuinely perplexed. "I didn't meet that little girlie until the day I met you," he nodded at Katie.

"Have you ever worked with an attorney named David Dirkman?"

Ivan gestured to his tattered clothing. "Do I look like someone who can afford a lawyer?"

He had a point. If his gambling addiction was as bad as he claimed—and she saw no reason to doubt that fact considering the squalor surrounding him—he would never be able to afford even the cheapest of lawyers, let alone David.

George gave Katie another questioning look. He believed Ivan, and she did, too. There was no reason to take any more of his time. George could arrest him—he had altered a legal document, after all—but arrest wasn't mandatory.

"Okay," Katie said. "When is your next appointment with Tom?"

"Tomorrow morning."

"Is he helping?"

Ivan shrugged. "Too early to tell."

"Alright, well, we'll get out of your hair now," George said, moving toward the door. "Thanks for chatting with us."

"Anytime." Ivan's tone was genial now. It was almost as though the truth coming out had relieved a burden on him.

George and Katie exited the way they came, walking in silence until they were both inside George's vehicle. He started it up and turned to her before putting it into gear, raising his eyebrows.

"It's not him," Katie said.

"I don't think so either. I snagged a cigarette butt just in case." He held up a plastic baggie with a half-smoked Camel red inside it.

"How did you get that? I didn't even notice you crouch down."

"I tied my shoe during his story. He's long-winded, that one. We'll send this puppy off with the letters. Have the experts over at the lab compare the DNA. It's probably not a match, but it's worth a try."

"Sometimes, George, you are a genius."

"Only sometimes?" He cocked a playful eyebrow.

Katie shook her head and laughed. "Let's get going. We've got one more stop."

George put the SUV into gear and turned toward the road. It was a short drive—a minute at most—to Jackson's residence. But her anxiety grew with every passing millisecond. To her, Jackson felt like the most likely culprit. He had the criminal history to match. Violent, stalking behavior. She only hoped that Jackson's reaction to them wasn't going to create a need to use her firearm.

# 34

## KATIE

George had just pulled up outside Jackson's house when Katie's cell phone started ringing. She fished it out of her pocket and looked at the screen.

"It's Ashley," Katie said, her tone apologetic. "I have to take it."

George nodded and made a gesture of zipping his lips. He knew Ashley hated him. She hadn't kept her feelings a secret, especially when she started calling him names like *Georgie*, *Sir George*, and *King George*. She definitely wasn't using them as terms of endearment. But George had never treated Ashley with disdain. At least not in Katie's presence.

"Hello?"

"Have you talked to Rachel?"

"Um, no," Katie admitted. "The last time I saw her was after lunch."

"I've been calling her for the last thirty minutes, and she's not picking up."

Katie's heartbeat quickened. Rachel always kept her phone in hand, and she rarely missed calls, especially those from Ashley. Something was wrong. "Have you tried calling the office?"

"Yes. Tom said she went to lunch with you, but she hasn't returned."

"Shit," Katie hissed.

"Was she on her way back to the office when you parted ways?"

"No," Katie said. "Bryce and Trixie live in the apartments above Genie's Diner. That's where we ate, so she said she wanted to walk around the building to see where his windows were and gauge what he could see from them."

"By herself?" It was an accusation more than a question.

Katie bristled. Partly from Ashley's tone, but mostly because she knew Ashley was right. She should not have allowed Rachel to do it on her own. It would have taken ten minutes at most. She could have asked George to wait that long, but she'd prioritized George over Rachel and now Rachel was missing.

"I shouldn't have let her. I'm sorry."

"Don't apologize. We don't have time for that. We have to find her. Where are you now?"

"I'm with George. We are getting ready to go into Jackson's house and talk to him."

"George is with you?"

"Yeah," Katie said, bracing herself for a tongue lashing.

"Good. Bring him to my office when you are done with Jackson."

*Good? That's a change*, Katie thought. "Okay. I'll do that."

"I'll keep trying to track her down in the meantime."

"We'll make it quick," Katie said, glancing over at George. He was watching her with an intensity that made her cheeks flush.

"It's a plan," Ashley said, and they both hung up.

"What's going on?" George asked as Katie lowered the phone from her ear.

"Rachel is missing. We need to stop by Ashley's office after we're done here." She nodded toward Jackson's run-down house.

"I guess we ought to get in there and get out, then."

They got out of the vehicle and approached Jackson's house in the same way they had approached Ivan's, George in front and Katie slightly behind. She was jumpier than before. With Jackson's criminal history, this house call had already been dangerous, but if Jackson had kidnapped Rachel, the threat to Katie, George, and even Rachel would increase tenfold.

When they reached the front door, George looked back at Katie, who nodded. Then he knocked on the door, several sharp raps with his knuckles. "Open up, Jackson. It's the Sheriff's Department." He paused, and silence descended all around them. There was no response. No sound. No movement. George knocked again with the same result.

Katie's mind began to whir. What were they going to do if he didn't answer? As a client of the MEHR team, his weekly calendar was kept in their client files. He didn't have any appointments at this time, and he didn't have a job yet. He didn't have any family or friends. He was free all day until six o'clock when he was due to appear at an alcoholics anonymous meeting a block away. So where was he now? Was he in there with Rachel doing God knows what? If that was the case, Ashley would never forgive Katie. She would never forgive herself.

Then the door opened a crack. "Jackson Weatherspoon?" George said.

"Yes."

A rush of relief washed over Katie. He was there, and he sounded like he was alone. But then she remembered how long it took him to come to the door. Long enough to tie someone up in the basement and warn them to keep quiet.

"I'm George Thomanson with the Brine County Sheriff's Department. Do you mind if I come in to ask you a few questions?"

"Yeah, I mind."

"Okay," George said with a self-deprecating chuckle. "Will you allow us to come in and ask a few questions?" He gestured toward Katie.

Jackson looked at her, then took a few steps backward. "I have to let her in or they're going to yank my probation."

"I get it," George said, stepping inside the residence. Katie followed.

The house was messy, but not quite as bad as Ivan's. At least there were no signs of bug or rodent life, which was a low bar, she knew, but that was often how her clients lived.

"What have you been doing all day?" Katie asked.

"I've been here."

"What about the last hour? Did you leave for any reason?"

"I went to pick up some lunch at Frankie's Corner, but that was it."

Frankie's Corner was not far from Genie's Diner. If Rachel was indeed missing, Jackson could be involved. It was an admission that he was in the area where she was last seen.

"Have you had any visitors?" Katie asked, scanning the room. There was no evidence of company—no extra dishes or shoes by the door—but then again, he wouldn't be treating Rachel as a guest.

"No," he said, shifting his weight in a way that made Katie think he was lying.

She looked around the room, wondering what to ask next. Should she try to get into the basement, or would he refuse and kick them out? They didn't have enough for a search warrant, and despite Jackson's original statement about allowing her inside, he didn't *have* to permit her to search. Working with the MEHR team did not completely negate his right to privacy.

The walls of Jackson's home were completely bare aside from one small picture hanging in the living room. Jackson wasn't much of an interior decorator, so its place of prominence likely had more to do with sentimental value rather than ambience. Katie walked over to it, stopping a few feet away. There were five people in the picture, one of which was Jackson. The picture was grainy, but it appeared to have been taken in some kind of facility.

"What's this?" Katie asked, nodding at the picture. It struck her as odd because despite the dreary background, all five people were smiling with their arms around one another's shoulders.

Jackson looked down at his feet. "Graduation from in-patient treatment."

"When was it?"

"Six months ago."

"So, why do you need to work with the MEHR team at all?"

"You know addiction," Jackson said, nudging some trash on the floor with his toe. "It's hard to stay on the wagon."

"Have you kept in contact with all these people?" Katie nodded at the picture. Two of the faces were notable. One belonged to Erica Elsberry, the other belonged to Trixie. Two women who received letters from the mysterious letter-writer. One of which ended up dead inside a toolbox.

"No," but he'd answered a little too quickly for it to be believable.

While Katie and Jackson talked, George had been wandering around the place. He'd stopped in front of a heavy wooden door. It was firmly shut and locked. An exterior door on the interior of the house.

"Where does this go?" He asked.

"Nowhere."

"Nowhere? That doesn't seem possible. Doors in the middle of a living area like this usually go to a basement or a bedroom or something."

"It's the basement." Jackson was looking at his shoes again.

"Mind if we take a look down there?"

"Yes, I mind," Jackson said, his head snapping up. There was heat in his eyes and his words that hadn't been there before.

"Why?" George was keeping his tone genial, but Katie knew him well enough to recognize the irritation creeping in at the edges.

"Because nobody goes down there."

"You realize that could be a problem with your probation, right?" George asked.

Jackson narrowed his eyes. "Some things are worth the risk."

"What kind of things?"

"Are we done here? With this meeting? I've answered your questions, and now I'd like you to leave."

Katie and George exchanged a look.

"We can be done," George said, pulling a card out of his pocket and handing it to Jackson. "If you have anything you'd like to tell me, you can give me a call. Any time, any hour. I'll answer."

Jackson looked down at the card. "Why would I need to call you?"

George shrugged. "Maybe there's something you want to get off your chest. Something weighing on your conscience. A burden that you just need to unload."

"Not likely. You two are all the burden I see right now."

"Fair enough," George said, flashing his characteristic smile.

Katie kept quiet. She didn't know how George could remain so calm. Rachel could be down there in that very basement, tied up and gagged. All they had to do was find a way to her, but they couldn't. They didn't have a warrant. They didn't have probable cause. All they had was a hunch, and that would never be enough.

With no other reason to remain, Katie and George left. As Katie descended the rickety stairs on the front porch, she couldn't help wondering what kinds of burdens Jackson was hiding within that twisted mind of his. Did they involve Erica's murder? Would they lead to Rachel? Or were George and Katie already too late?

# 35

## ASHLEY

Ashley had spent the remainder of the afternoon on her phone, calling anyone and everyone who could possibly shed light on what had happened to Rachel. She spoke to Genie down at Genie's Diner, who hadn't been able to give her any more information than what she'd already learned from Katie. She'd called Rachel's aunt, who hadn't answered and was yet to return Ashley's call. Not that Ashley was surprised. She and Stephanie had always been at odds.

She hadn't wanted to, but she'd called Tom, her ex-boyfriend. It was an awkward conversation to say the least. She'd even called a few former clients who lived near the diner. But she'd learned nothing. Absolutely nothing. Zip. Zilch. And she was starting to grow despondent.

It was nearing five o'clock when Katie and George walked through the front door. Elena had stayed late helping Ashley with the search. Elena and Rachel were close in age, and they'd become friends. Ashley and Elena had been at the front of the office in the reception area just in case Rachel stopped by. They both looked up, hopeful, when they heard the front door open. But those hopes were dashed when they saw it wasn't Rachel.

"Did you find anything?" Ashley said, a new sort of optimism surging within her.

Katie shook her head. She had walked in first, and George had followed behind her. He remained slightly back even as Katie approached the counter, like he was afraid Ashley might bite him.

"Maybe we should try calling Stephanie," Katie suggested.

"Knock yourself out," Ashley said, flopping down into one of the flimsy office chairs haphazardly placed around the front of the office. "I tried earlier. Left her a voicemail. But, of course, the princess didn't call me back."

Katie took out her cell phone and dialed Stephanie's number, turning it on speaker phone. Stephanie picked up after two rings.

*That bitch is screening my calls*, Ashley thought irritably. She'd understand if she was calling Stephanie all the time trying to reach Rachel, but this was the first time Ashley had ever called her.

"Stephanie Arkman's phone."

"Hi, Stephanie, it's Katie Mickey."

"I know that. All phones have caller ID now, and I can read."

"Right," Katie said, her face flushing crimson. "You're on speakerphone, and I'm here with Ashley Montgomery and George Thomanson."

"Hello, George." Naturally, she didn't acknowledge Ashley.

"We were wondering if you have heard from Rachel. She's been missing all afternoon."

"What do you mean by 'missing?'"

"I mean we can't find her."

"And this has been going on since . . . when?"

"Around one o'clock."

"So, you haven't talked to her for four hours."

"That's right."

"And why are you calling me?"

Ashley fought the urge to snatch Katie's phone and shout, *because this isn't normal behavior for your emotionally fragile niece, and you'd know that if you weren't such an arrogant asshole who only focuses on herself*. She wanted to give Stephanie a piece of her mind, tell her just how shitty of an aunt she turned out to be, but she kept her restraint. Yelling wouldn't help them find Rachel and that was the only priority for the moment. But she'd be ripping Stephanie a new asshole just as soon as this mess was cleared up.

"Rachel had some concerns about the man you had driving her

around," Katie said after a short pause. "She was outside his apartment downtown when she disappeared."

"Who, Bryce? Don't be ridiculous. He doesn't live in Brine. He lives out here." Stephanie lived on a gated compound on the north side of the county.

"We have reason to believe that isn't true, Ms. Arkman." Katie had used Stephanie's last name, which meant that she was trying to remind herself to stay businesslike and to keep her cool. She was nearly as furious as Ashley.

"Well, I have every reason to believe that it is. Give me a minute. I'll call for him. I've got a Bryce buzzer. I press it and he's here in a few minutes. Just like that," Ashley could hear Stephanie snapping her fingers. "There. I pressed the button. You'll see he's right here with me if you only wait a few moments."

"Fine," Katie said, crossing her arms.

They waited in silence, Ashley watching the second hand tick tick tick around the face of the clock. One minute. Two minutes. Three.

After five long, heavy, minutes, Stephanie spoke. "He should have been here by now. I don't know where he is."

This was where Ashley would have loved to shout, *told you so, you stupid wench*, but she again restrained herself.

"I'll look into it, but I'm not worried. Bryce has worked for me for years, and he's never given me cause to doubt him. Rachel will turn up. She probably forgot to charge her phone or something."

That was highly doubtful. Rachel never let her phone's power get below 50 percent. It was rarely below 75, because Rachel knew how cell phones could ping off towers and potentially provide her location if something truly horrible happened, but it only worked when the phone was on. Rachel would never allow herself to be caught with a dead phone, unless she, too, was dead. Ashley shook her head, trying to force the horrible thought out of her mind.

"Well, that wasn't helpful," Katie said, ending the call.

"It was a little helpful," George said. "At least we know that Bryce has been lying to his employer about his whereabouts."

"So, what now?" Ashley asked, looking to George for guidance. It was the first time she had ever allowed herself to look at him with anything other than hate.

"I'll draft a report about the letters and include Rachel's disappearance. I know it's early to open a missing person's case since it's only been a few hours, but I think we can all agree this is out of the ordinary for Rachel."

"Yeah," Katie and Ashley said in unison.

"Then I'll send off all the evidence to the criminalistics laboratory, including the letters sent to Rachel, those seized from Erica's house, and the cigarette butt I took from Ivan's place. I'll look around behind Genie's Diner and see if there's any evidence indicating foul play. There probably won't be, but it's worth a shot. Didn't you say that someone else over there was receiving similar letters?"

"Yeah," Katie said. "Trixie. She's Bryce's neighbor. He's in apartment 2A and she's in 2B."

"I'll stop by there and see if she'll let me have her letters. If I can, I'll send hers off with the other bunch. It'll take some time to get results back, so it's better to get the ball rolling. Besides, it could help with the investigation into Erica's murder. Does that sound good?" George was looking straight at Ashley, waiting for a response.

"Yeah," she said after a long silence. "I feel helpless. I wish I could do more."

"You're doing all you can. You're not used to being in this position," George said.

His tone was so genial, his demeanor so kind. Ashley wondered why he was being this way to her. She didn't deserve it. If anything, she deserved his scorn. Perhaps she'd misjudged some parts of his personality. Maybe he wasn't all bad.

"Thank you," she said.

"Anytime. Now, you lot should go home and get some rest. I'll let you know what I find in the morning."

Ashley stood and stretched. She wouldn't be able to sleep, she knew that already, but she did need to go home and feed her dogs. It wouldn't hurt to try to get some rest either. She was due to meet David and Noah in the morning, and she wanted to be prepared to question David. He'd left her office, which was right down the street from Genie's Diner, right around the time Rachel had gone missing. She had suspected him before, but now he seemed like a much more likely candidate.

# 36

## RACHEL

Thursday, December 12

Rachel came to in the dark. A pitch-black inkiness so thick that she couldn't even make out the outlines of her surroundings. Was the room truly this dark, or had something in her brain been dislodged when she was attacked?

She was lying on something hard, but not cold. A wood floor. She tried to push herself up but realized that her hands were bound. She twisted her hands in front of her but didn't feel any pain. It was some kind of fabric wound around her wrists, not as rough as rope or firm as twine. She twisted her body and used her hands to push off the floor, rising painfully into a sitting position.

Her head pounded, keeping time with her heartbeats. She could hear the blood rushing through her ears. A roaring *whoosh* that ebbed and flowed with the thumping in her chest. What had happened to her? Someone had struck her from behind—that she knew—but who? A familiar sense of panic fluttered its way into her chest. This scene was all too recognizable. She was a captive. Again.

It brought back flashes of her childhood. That man cornering her, forcing her to do things that made her stomach turn. That constant hunted feeling. She was the prey and there was no escape. A hare caged in with a wolf. One that would never kill her. He'd just tortured her—a little at a time —for his own sick pleasure.

*Stop thinking about him*, she scolded herself.

Her childhood tormenter was locked away in Anamosa Prison. Whatever was happening now was different. A different perpetrator, and a different time in her life. She wasn't a child. She wasn't helpless. She'd been behaving that way lately—like she had no control over her surroundings— but she'd been wrong. She could see that now that she was in a situation in which she truly lacked control. At least in the traditional sense.

What she could do was try to garner as much information as she could. Her eyes were no help, but her other senses seemed to be working fine. She began scooting along the floor on her bottom, moving around the room. She didn't dare stand for the unsteadiness in her head. The last thing she needed was to lose balance and hit her head a second time. She used her feet to propel her backward, counting each time she pushed her body. Five scoots until her back bumped into a wall. She turned. Ten scoots until she ran into a second wall. She continued methodically counting and moving around the room until she'd discovered all four walls.

It was a small room, but decent sized for a small house. There were two doors, one she suspected was a closet and the other likely the exit. A bedroom. There was no furniture, and it was small enough that only a twin-sized bed could comfortably fit in the space. It reminded her of older houses. The ones found in towns that had a couple of large rooms and then one child-sized one.

Now that she'd discovered her surroundings, she was starting to feel a little better. This small act of defiance—the refusal to lie there waiting for her captor—gave her strength. So, she turned to her other senses. She froze, listening hard, but she didn't hear anything. Only a heavy silence, weighted by darkness and captivity. But then there was a sharp clang. It was distant, but it had been there. Several more bangs and clangs followed that first one. A ringing that sounded almost like pans in a kitchen.

A few moments later, she smelled it, the familiar aroma of bacon. Someone was making breakfast somewhere nearby. That meant people. But was her captor cooking, or someone else? Was her makeshift prison cell part of an apartment or a townhome? If so, then maybe she could bang on one of the walls and call out for help. But which wall?

She was in the process of scooting toward another wall so she could press her ear against it and listen for the common sounds of other people, but then she heard something that made her freeze. A rhythmic *clunk clunk clunk*. Heavy boots coming down a hallway. A doorknob creaked, turning against the wood of the door, and her heart stilled. Whether she was ready or not, she was about to discover her kidnapper's identity.

# 37

## KATIE

Katie spent the night tossing and turning. Her mind wouldn't shut off. Scenarios of *what if's* and *where is she now* plagued her thoughts. Each one was quickly followed with the same personal condemnation. *It's all my fault. Ashley will never forgive me.*

Before separating for the night, Ashley had been a complete mess. Katie had never seen her like that. She was jittery and jumpy, apologetic and even kind to George. She'd actually thanked him. If hell froze over to subzero temperatures, Katie still wouldn't believe that Ashley would thank George. But maybe this would end up becoming an opening for the two of them to form an unlikely friendship. Much like Katie and Ashley had all those years ago. Then again, she was probably getting a little ahead of herself. That would only happen if George *found* Rachel.

When her bedside clock read four o'clock, Katie gave up on sleep and got up for the day. She showered and dressed, all while checking her emails and texts every few minutes, hoping for a response from Rachel or George. Still nothing. It wasn't a good sign, but she was trying not to dwell on the negatives.

Katie had purchased her house earlier that year. It was less than a mile from downtown, so once she was in her car, she was on the courthouse square within moments. As she drove by Ashley's office, she noticed the lights were on. She pulled off to the side of the road in one of the two-hour courthouse parking spots, then got out and approached the front door.

"Ashley," Katie called, as she softly knocked on the front door. "It's me, Katie."

Ashley was at the door within seconds, unlocking it and pulling it open with wide, hopeful eyes that quickly deflated when she realized Katie was alone. While she had been a mess the night before, Ashley looked far worse today. Heavy, purple bags hung beneath her eyes, her clothes disheveled, and her hair greasy.

"Have you heard from Rachel?" Ashley said, stepping aside to allow Katie inside.

"No."

"I haven't either. I talked to George a little while ago."

Katie took notice of Ashley's use of his actual name. No cutesy "ie" at the end or royal titles. "Oh. What did he say?"

"Not a lot. There was a tiny bit of blood in the snow behind Genie's Diner, and he said it looks like someone was dragged. He thinks someone hit Rachel, possibly knocking her out and then dragged her off."

*Oh shit,* Katie's heart pounded wildly. "That's so bad. And it's all my fault. I shouldn't have—"

"Stop," Ashley said, surprising Katie. "Rachel is an adult. She chose to go back there. And honestly, I walked by there not long before that. People were everywhere. It should have been a safe place. But someone was stalking Rachel. He was either going to get to her, or we were going to get to him. He had a head start. That's all."

Katie nodded, tears springing to her eyes. She was so worried about Rachel, but she had also been afraid of Ashley's reaction. She didn't want this to drive a wedge between them. She couldn't bear the shame of something horrible happening under her watch while also losing Ashley at the same time.

"I think we should call Stephanie," Ashley said after a long pause.

Katie glanced at the clock on the wall. It was only five o'clock. "I'm not sure that's a good idea."

"Rachel is her niece. Stephanie should be as concerned if not more concerned than we are. If she isn't awake, then she should be. Don't be delicate with her. She's a self-centered stuck-up bitch."

Katie nodded. She hadn't had the same experience with Stephanie as Ashley had. Stephanie had funded their team, paid for the renovation of their building. She'd thrown gobs and gobs of money at them. It had all seemed so generous, but now she was starting to wonder if that generosity was only because she had more money than she could spend in four lifetimes. What was a million here and there when you had hundreds of millions.

She dialed Stephanie's number and turned her phone on speaker. The phone rang and rang until it went to voicemail. Katie ended the call.

"I don't know why I'm surprised," Ashley said bitterly.

"Yeah. Me neither. But I can't sit around anymore doing nothing. Outside Bryce's place was the last place we know Rachel had been, so I'm going to go over there and talk to him. Even if he had nothing to do with it, he may have seen something."

"Okay. Do you want me to go with you?"

"No. You keep trying to get through to Rachel. Maybe she'll pick up eventually?"

"I think her phone's dead. It's still going straight to voicemail, but I'm going to keep sending text messages. Just in case . . ."

Katie left Ashley's office and walked down the street toward the diner and the apartments above. Once she neared, the familiar scent of bacon, eggs, and freshly brewed coffee had her stomach rumbling. She hadn't eaten since lunch the day before when she and Rachel had been at that very same diner. She walked around the building and up the rickety stairs leading to the second floor and headed to the left, to the apartment Rachel had said belonged to Bryce.

She took two steadying breaths before banging her fist against the door. It was cold and dark while she waited, and she was glad she had her handgun. Bryce was not a big man, and she was in good shape, but he could easily overpower her in hand-to-hand combat. When nobody answered, she raised her fist to strike the door again, but it opened before she could.

Bryce stood there, backlit by the soft glow of the few lights on inside the residence. He was in his traditional suit, but it was rumpled, and he was unshaven. His eyes were bloodshot and there were scratches on his cheek that looked like they could have come from a set of nails.

Katie had so many questions to ask him, but she couldn't think of where to start. In the end, she blurted out the first one that came to mind. "What are you doing here?"

"What?" He gave her a bewildered look. "Lady, you knocked on my door."

"Don't call me 'lady' like you don't know who I am. I'm Rachel's boss. And you're supposed to be living out in the country with *your* boss. Not here."

He looked at her again, this time harder before recognition blossomed in his eyes.

"Answer my question."

"Where I stay the night is none of your business."

Fair enough. He was right. She had no control over what he did or where he slept. "Fine. Then where is Rachel?"

"I don't know. I haven't seen her since yesterday morning." The words came out so quick, so smooth, that they sounded rehearsed.

Katie wondered just how much practice he had at lying. After all, he'd been lying to his employer about where he'd been living. What else was he hiding? "I don't believe you."

"Too bad," Bryce said, then he slammed the door in her face.

Katie stood there, stunned. She'd never been treated like that before, and certainly not by someone who claimed to be as polished as Stephanie Arkman's driver. He looked as though he was unraveling. But what was causing it? Had Stephanie confronted him about lying to her, or was it something worse?

# 38

## RACHEL

The door to Rachel's makeshift cell slowly creaked open. A bright light filtered in through the opening, assaulting her eyes. Rachel brought up a hand, shielding her eyes, sensitive from the dark. She blinked hard, willing them to adjust to the light. Her heart raced, pounding inside her chest as adrenaline flooded her system. Part of her mind felt as though it was shutting down, while another part—a more feral part—kicked into high gear.

"Hello, Rachel."

She could not see the man, backlit as he was in the doorway, and she could not place his voice. He was doing something to disguise it, speaking in a lower octave. Still, she thought she recognized something about it. She couldn't discern anything based on the man's build. It was average. Not too tall or too short. Not fat or thin. Just regular. Nondescript.

"You haven't responded to my letters."

A surge of anger ran through her. Partially because she was once again a victim—the damsel in distress—after promising herself she'd never play that role again. But also because she'd spent enough time with Ashley to know how Ashley would react, and in this situation, Ashley would have responded with righteous fury. Rachel decided in that moment that she would channel her mentor. Emulate Ashley the best that she could. She didn't have Ashley's strength—at least not yet—but she could pretend that she did.

Rachel lowered her hand, staring directly at the shadowed man. "Yeah, well, you didn't exactly identify yourself. It's not like I had anyone to write to."

"You wouldn't have written if you'd known."

"Probably not."

"Why not?"

Rachel thought for a moment, pondering what Ashley would say if posed the same asinine question. And somehow, she knew, and she responded with the appropriate amount of sarcasm. "Because your weird love letters weren't exactly what I would call wooing. I mean, creepy, yes. Off-putting, yes. Disturbing, yes . . ." She paused, cocking her head to the side. "Shall I go on?"

"No. That won't be—"

"And then there's the fact that you knocked me over the head and kidnapped me. That, on its face, is a serious dating no-no. Did you really believe I was going to be interested in you after all this?"

"No. Not now, but in time you will see."

*In time.* Those two words stuck to her, rattling around in her brain. He meant to keep her. But for how long? Whether it was an hour or a month, she didn't care. Any amount of time was too much for her.

"When you hear the full story, I think you'll understand."

"Okay," Rachel said, shifting forward so her legs were crossed and her hands were in her lap.

"I have been watching you for a long time. Ever since your arrest and your acquittal. We have something in common, me and you."

"What's that?"

"Ashley Montgomery."

"Ashley has lived in Brine all her life. She's got something in common with everyone in town, including me and you. So, I'm not sure what that's supposed to tell me."

"It tells you—" He paused. "What's that?" He paused again. "I think someone is at the door. I'll be right back. You stay quiet now like a good little girl. If not, I'll kill you and whoever is at my door. Okay?"

"Okay," Rachel said, trying to keep the quiver out of her voice.

He had said those words, *kill you and whoever is at my door*, in such a nonchalant way that it sounded like something he did every day. A routine task like brushing his teeth or getting the mail. When said like that, she had no doubt that he would carry out the promise. She had plenty of experience with violent men, and the detached way this man was talking meant that he had no qualms about carrying out his threat.

Then the door shut, and she was once again greeted by darkness. But this time she didn't entertain any hopes of escape. Instead, she positioned herself by the door, pressing her ear against the wood, trying to hear the voice of the unfortunate soul who had interrupted her kidnapper. Hoping against hope that it wasn't someone that she knew. Brine was a small town, after all.

# 39

## ASHLEY

When they arrived at Noah's house, Ashley hung back, allowing David to knock on the door. He rapped his knuckles against the wood several times, then waited. Nobody appeared. He tried a second time, turning halfway around and shrugging.

"I called earlier this morning. He said he'd be here," David said.

Ashley glared at him for a long moment, wondering if she could believe him. She didn't know who or what to believe anymore, and the lack of sleep wasn't helping. Her mind simply wasn't firing on all cylinders.

"What?" David asked. "You're looking at me like I've grown a second head."

Ashley wanted to ask where he had been the afternoon before, if he'd abducted Rachel, but the timing wasn't right. She had no evidence to support her accusation, so he'd simply deny it, and that would potentially put Rachel in a more dangerous situation. Instead, she decided to play along.

"Maybe he *is* here but he's not answering the door."

"It is early," David glanced at his watch. "He might not be awake yet."

David didn't seem to notice that this statement was contradictory to his earlier statement that he'd called, and that Noah had answered the phone. Still, she played along. "Yeah," Ashley said. "Try knocking one more time."

David knocked again, and this time they were greeted with the familiar click of a dead bolt shifting and the door swung open.

"David," Noah said with what seemed like a genuine smile, "and Ashley," he added when his gaze swung to meet hers. There was a note of trepidation, a slight tremor, around his pronunciation of her name.

"Can we come in?" David said, shifting from one foot to the other. "It's freezing out here."

"Yeah, yeah," Noah said, stepping aside. His hands were trembling.

Ashley followed David inside and was struck with the familiar scent of bacon. "Cooking breakfast?"

"Something like that," Noah said.

The kitchen was open to the rest of the house and Ashley could see two plates sitting on the counter. One was plastic and the other ceramic. Bacon sizzled in a pan atop one of the burners on the old electric stove. The pan was large and full. Either Noah was saving some for later or he was expecting company.

"Why did you want to meet?" Noah said. There was a slight quiver at the end of his sentence.

"I wanted to see how you are holding up. I also need a signature on a few documents," David said. "And Ashley decided to tag along."

Noah looked up, catching Ashley's eye. There was a flash of something there. She couldn't tell if it was rage or fear or a mixture of both. "I'm fine. Living the good life, thanks to Ashley," Noah said. "I'll sign whatever."

David produced a stack of documents and they moved over to the kitchen table. As they walked, Ashley heard a loud *thump* coming from somewhere else in the house. It was a split level with one bedroom on the main floor and Ashley guessed that there was at least one other bedroom up the small flight of stairs. It sounded like the noise had come from up there.

"What was that?" David asked, cocking his head.

"The um, cat."

Ashley knew for a fact that Noah didn't have a cat. He was allergic to cats. He'd told her that years earlier when she had represented him in another case. That had actually been their defense. An alibi. He couldn't have been present, because the place was full of cats, and he was allergic.

She didn't remember all her past arguments, but the cat defense was one that had stuck in her mind.

"Okay," David said, tapping his finger on the documents and holding out a pen. "I just need you to sign here, here, and here."

When Noah focused back on the documents, Ashley discreetly reached into her pocket and pulled out her phone. She opened her text chain with Katie and typed, "At Noah's. Things are off. Come now." She sent the message and then pocketed the phone before Noah finished reading and signing the documents.

"Is that all?" Noah asked, straightening and looking from David to Ashley.

There was a long silence as both David and Noah looked at Ashley. But it wasn't Ashley's voice that cut through the silence. It was her name—"Ashley"—in an unmistakably familiar voice. Instinctively, Ashley followed the sound, heading toward the stairway.

"Rachel?" Ashley called, but there was no answer. The only response came from behind her.

"Stop," Noah said, his tone suddenly dark.

Ashley turned and saw to her horror that Noah was pointing a gun at her. Fleetingly she thought, *but he can't have a gun, he's a felon*, then she dismissed it as foolish. How many people had she represented over the years for that same crime? Felon in possession of a firearm. She didn't know the exact answer, but it was lots. Guns were readily available in Iowa and throughout the entire Midwest. Anyone who had ever been to a gun show knew that.

"Don't move or I will shoot you," Noah said, and he sounded as though he meant it.

# 40

## KATIE

Katie stood outside Bryce's apartment, staring at the door. She couldn't believe he'd slammed it in her face. She had to find a way to get inside. Rachel could be in there, desperate for help while she stood out there, twiddling her thumbs. Then her phone started buzzing. She picked it up, looking at the screen before answering.

"I'm sorry I called so early, Stephanie," Katie said by way of greeting.

"Have you seen her?" Stephanie sounded breathless, panicked. It was completely out of character for the smooth, rich woman who had always maintained a calm superiority.

"Rachel? No. That's why I was calling you. We've been trying to get in touch with her all night. I thought you'd know."

"Well, I don't. She didn't come home last night."

"I suspected as much. That's why I'm standing outside your driver's apartment, trying to get some answers."

"You're wasting your time," Stephanie said. "I've been on the phone with Bryce on and off all night. He had nothing to do with her disappearance. It's impossible."

"I'm not sure that it's impossible—"

"I have a tracker on his phone," Stephanie said, cutting Katie off.

"But I thought you didn't even know he was living downtown."

"I didn't. I admit I haven't been keeping close tabs on him lately. I've had no reason to invade his privacy like that."

Katie felt like the mere presence of the tracker without his knowledge was plenty of an invasion, whether Stephanie was checking it or not, but she kept that thought to herself.

"After our conversation last night, I decided to review his movements. You were right. He's been staying overnight in an apartment downtown. I confronted him about it—that's part of the reason we've been in contact overnight. He admits he's been living there, but it has nothing to do with Rachel. That is where his mother lives, and she broke her foot. She needs some extra assistance, so he's been staying there."

"Oh," Katie said.

"Bryce would never do anything to jeopardize his job. I pay him well and he needs the money."

"What for?"

"His mom has osteoporosis. Which was how she ended up breaking her foot. It isn't her first injury, and she doesn't have insurance or an income. He's stuck paying her medical bills."

Katie could hear the slamming of a car door on the other end of the line. "I'm going to the Sheriff's Department now to make a report."

"Don't bother," Katie said. "We already did."

"Then I am going to follow up on your report."

"Okay," Katie said. Stephanie didn't need to file another report or follow up on the one that was filed the night before—it was a waste of time—but Stephanie always did think she could do things a little better than everyone else.

"Leave Bryce alone," Stephanie said. "He's been up all night looking for Rachel. He needs to get some sleep if he's going to be any help to me later."

"Alright. Let me know if you find her," Katie said with a heavy sigh. Then they said their goodbyes and hung up.

Katie wondered what she was supposed to do now. She couldn't do *nothing*. That wasn't in her nature. She was a doer, and something needed to be done. She just didn't know what, exactly, it was. Until she heard more from Stephanie or George, she'd be left twiddling her thumbs.

Then her phone buzzed with a text message. She looked down at the small screen where Ashley's message was displayed. It said, *At Noah's. Things are off. Come now.* Katie immediately started down the rickety staircase that led up to Bryce's apartment and back toward her office where her car was parked. Ashley was not one to exaggerate. If she thought something was off, then she was right.

She jogged down the street while dialing her phone.

"Hello?"

"George. Where are you?"

"I'm at home, trying to catch a shower and a few hours of sleep before I go back to work."

"Well don't."

"Why?"

"Meet me at Noah's house. Something is going on over there."

"Okay," George said, concern etched its way into his voice. "I'll be there in five minutes. Don't do anything dumb. Wait for me to get there."

"Sure," Katie said, but it was an empty promise. If Ashley was in trouble, she couldn't stand by idly and do nothing. After all, she was a doer.

# 41

## ASHLEY

Noah kept his gun trained on Ashley. It was the right choice. Between the two attorneys, Ashley was the risk taker. The one who cared for Rachel. The one most likely to fling herself at him and slam her fists into his face until his bones were broken and his skin was swollen, bloodied, and unrecognizable. Because honestly, how could he do this to her? She'd been the one to get him out of jail. Without her assistance at his preliminary hearing, he'd still be sitting in a cell and none of this would have happened.

"Don't give me that look, Ashley," Noah said. There was a slight tremor in his voice. It was the only sign that this wasn't a casual, everyday conversation for him. "You didn't have to get involved in this. You didn't have to come over here."

"You have Rachel. Why?"

Ashley was furious and she didn't want to chat it up with him, but she also knew that he wasn't going to let her and David walk away even if they promised not to talk. No matter what they said now, they were going to report this to law enforcement, and Noah knew that. What Noah didn't know was that Ashley had already sent a message to Katie asking for help. Hopefully, Katie was on her way. But until she got there, Ashley needed to stall. She needed to get Noah talking.

"Because I love her." Noah was so matter of fact, so unemotional and blunt, that nobody in their right mind could honestly believe that he even knew the meaning of the word *love*. "That's why I was sending her those letters. She was supposed to find them exciting and appreciate them. That's how it had worked with Erica. She'd been excited about the letters. She would leave little responses on her doorstep."

"That's how your relationship with Erica started?" Ashley said.

"Yes. And she kept her notes in her nightstand all this time. I thought she'd thrown them away a long time ago. Right up until the search warrant."

They were dated, but the year wasn't included. Ashley had assumed those letters were from this year, but she'd been wrong. And that had led her down a different path, believing that the letter writer was someone other than Noah and that person had been Erica's killer.

"Where did you get the pen?" Ashley asked. "David didn't start representing you until recently."

"David didn't start representing *me* until a few weeks ago, but he did represent Erica's friend Amanda Stone much earlier than that. You remember her, right?"

"Yeah," Ashley said. Amanda had been the one to find Erica's body. She was also the little sister of Erica's friend and neighbor, Amy von Reich. A woman murdered by her husband years earlier.

"You represented Amy's husband, Arnold von Reich. Remember?"

"I remember," Ashley said. She'd won that trial, and Arnold had gone free. But within a year, someone had murdered him.

"David represented Amanda in the wrongful death suit against Arnold von Reich's estate. Amanda kept some of his pens. One day I was over there, and I snagged one. That was right around the time that I met Erica. Amanda introduced us."

"What really happened to Erica?" Ashley asked.

Noah sighed heavily. Ashley thought for a moment that he wouldn't answer, but he did. "I'd been wanting to break up with Erica for a while. We were in a rut, and I was bored. For a while, I was into that Trixie girl, you know her, you represented her, but then I crossed paths with Rachel again. I remembered her from her trial, that beautiful broken face, and I wanted her. I needed her. I tried to do everything right. I was in the process of breaking things off with Erica, I just hadn't found the right time. Then we were at Mikey's Tavern that night and she was drunk, spouting off about something. I just snapped and I told her that it was over. She flipped her shit and scratched me. You were right about that one, by the way. She did scratch me at the bar."

*Right about one thing, wrong about everything else*, Ashley thought.

"I wanted Erica to move out that night. I thought she'd start packing her stuff and be ready to leave by the time I got home. That's why I stayed at the bar. To give her time to get out of my way. But when I got back, she was sitting on the couch drinking wine. She hadn't packed a thing. That led to another fight, and I started throwing her shit in a bag myself. Then she grabbed my arm, ripping my shirt. I turned on instinct. I had a TV remote in my hand at the time. I hit her in the head with it and it knocked her out."

"So, how'd she get into the tool chest?"

"I put her in there," Noah said. There was a note of distress in his voice, so raw that if he hadn't been pointing a gun at her, Ashley would have felt sorry for him. "I wanted to scare her. That's all. She's claustrophobic. So, I thought that if she woke up in a tiny, dark space, it would be the last straw. She'd realize she hated me, and she would move out." He paused for a moment, and a sob escaped his lips. "I didn't realize it was airtight. I didn't know she'd suffocate. She was already dead when I went back to check on her."

Ashley thought about Erica in that toolbox and how long it would take for her to run out of air. She was no expert, but she knew it wouldn't have been minutes. It would have had to be hours. Even if she hadn't died, it would have been extremely cruel to lock her inside like that, especially for someone who had such an extreme fear of small spaces.

Ashley considered calling him out on his cruelty but decided to keep her thoughts to herself. He was starting to get emotional, and the only thing worse than a man with a gun was an emotional man with a gun.

"How'd the toolbox get into the lake?"

"I drove her there and threw it into the lake. I thought it would sink, and it did. I don't know how it ended up on that bank. It should still be at the bottom of the lake."

It was the gasses that emitted from Erica's body during the decomposition process. They were trapped inside the airtight container, causing it to rise back to the surface. It was ironic that the thing that had killed her also led to her discovery.

"Nobody was supposed to find her. Everyone was supposed to think she went on a bender and disappeared on the streets like so many junkies do. And I would be free to pursue a relationship with Rachel."

"But Rachel didn't reciprocate your feelings, did she?"

"Not yet," Noah said, his eyes flashing with a momentary beat of fury. "But she will. That's why she's here. She's going to learn to love me."

Ashley shook her head. It wasn't unheard of for kidnapping victims to sympathize with their captors. Stockholm syndrome. But that would never work with Rachel.

"Is that why you were making breakfast for two? You were going to dine with her. Give her the plastic plate so she couldn't use it as a weapon."

"Something like that."

Ashley could tell that Noah was tired of talking. It was in his stance. He was shifting his weight from one foot to the other. A sign of impatience. He wouldn't be enticed into talking much longer, and she shuddered to think of what would happen to her and David next. Not that David had done anything to improve their situation. He'd been standing in the corner, shaking like a Chihuahua.

Then, just as Ashley was starting to lose hope, there was a knock at the door. A civilized knock. A scream in frustration bloomed within Ashley's head. *Just come in!* She wanted to shout, but she didn't know who it was. Maybe it was a pack of girl scouts selling cookies. But then Katie came barreling through the door, gun drawn, screaming, "Drop the gun! Drop the gun! Drop the gun now, Noah!"

## 42

## KATIE

Katie was parking when she saw George turn down the street. He was in his marked SUV. Katie's car was a couple houses down from Noah's. As George neared, she got out of her car and motioned for him to park behind her, then she stood there and waited for him to get out. He was in full uniform.

"Hey, George," Katie said.

"Why aren't we parking in the driveway?"

"David's car is there. And I don't know what's going on, but it sounded like Ashley was scared," she paused, "of Noah."

"Noah?"

"You didn't tell him you were on your way, did you?" They were cousins, George had mentioned that a few days ago, but she knew they weren't close. That conversation was the first time she had learned that they were of any relation at all, and she'd known George for years.

"No. We don't talk like that. I mean, I don't want him going down for killing his girlfriend, especially on flimsy evidence. But if he did kill her, that's a different story."

"You're not *help him bury the body* close, then."

"Um, no," he gave her a sidelong look. "Are you that close with anyone?"

Katie shrugged. "Probably Ashley."

"I'll remember that," he said, giving her a playful jab in the ribs.

"Now that we've got that out of the way, can we go make sure my friend isn't being tortured in there?"

"Tortured? Aren't you being a little dramatic?"

"I've sent five text messages and she hasn't responded to any of them."

Katie hadn't heard anything from Ashley after the text saying, *At Noah's. Things are off. Come now.* It was just like Rachel, how she'd gone suddenly silent. Katie had sent text after text, trying to get Ashley to respond, all the while growing more and more alarmed. Then she stopped sending texts altogether, because she didn't want Noah to realize that Katie and George were on their way.

George's smile dropped and they walked up to Noah's house in silence. When they reached the front, they split up. George went to the door and Katie to the large picture window at the front of the house. She crouched down and peered through the window, hiding as much of herself as possible. What she saw had her blood running cold.

Noah was inside, pointing a gun at Ashley. David was near the dining room table, hanging back, watching Ashley and Noah with wide, frightened eyes. He was taller than Noah, but Katie doubted the man had the courage to stand up to someone with a gun. He was one of those fancy lawyers. The ones who didn't get their hands dirty. Which was probably why Noah wasn't even paying attention to him.

Katie turned and jogged back toward George. As she did, she pulled out her handgun.

George wasn't paying attention to her. He had his hand up, ready to knock. She wanted to scream at him to stop, that they had the upper hand because Noah didn't know they were there, but that, too, would give up the element of surprise. Instead, she picked up her pace, making it back to the front door just as George's knuckles cracked against the door.

"Stop," she hissed, her voice just above a whisper. "He has a gun."

"A what?"

Katie grabbed the doorknob with her left hand while she maintained her grip on her gun with her right. The knob turned easily. It was unlocked. She burst through it, leaving George behind her. She barreled into the room shouting, "Drop the gun! Drop the gun! Drop the gun now, Noah!"

Noah looked up at her in surprise, but he didn't lower his weapon.

A deafening, earsplitting shot rang out. It wasn't Katie's gun. She hadn't squeezed the trigger and she didn't feel its kick.

# 43

## ASHLEY

There was so much shouting. The room went from near silent to Katie screaming, "Put the gun down!" Simultaneous feelings of relief and anxiety warred within Ashley, pushing her adrenaline level to an all-time high. Then the gun fired. An earsplitting sound that Ashley could feel inside her chest and all around her.

Her ears were ringing, her vision clouded, and time seemed to slow. She didn't feel any pain, but she hadn't expected it. At least not yet. A client who had been shot before had once told her that there were a few beats of nothing before the brain registered the searing agony surging through the body. Ashley assumed he was right. That shock and adrenaline were shielding her, and the pain was soon to follow. She waited for the inevitable, but the gut-wrenching torturous pain never came.

A few moments later, the ringing in her ears subsided and time sped up. Her mind cleared and she began to register the room around her. There was so much shouting. George Thomanson came rushing past her.

"Put your hands behind your back or I'll shoot again!" George shouted on repeat as he ran toward Noah.

Katie was right behind George. They worked in tandem, moving forward as one. A team. It looked as though they had it all planned out, trained together for this very scenario, even though Ashley knew there had been no time for that. When they were both past her, George continued toward Noah and Katie broke off, grabbing Noah's gun and stepping away.

Noah was screaming too. "Oh my God! Oh my God!" His words were twisted in agony as blood gushed from his right arm where George had shot him.

Ashley stood rooted to the spot, watching the scene as it unfolded around her. It was a surreal experience, like she wasn't a participant. She saw David cowering in the corner, unharmed and frozen with fear. He was certainly not the image of bravery. Every ounce of the polished attorney was now gone, replaced by a giant, sniveling child. The change was almost comical, and she would have laughed if not for everything else going on around her.

Noah screamed. A sharp piercing noise, more animalistic than human. Ashley whirled to see George pulling Noah's hands behind his back for handcuffing. Ashley's initial instinct was to tell George to stop, that he was hurting Noah, but that sentiment was fleeting. He kidnapped Rachel, killed Erica, and was planning to shoot Ashley. He could fuck off for all she cared. And that's when she remembered Rachel. She was still somewhere upstairs.

Ashley started moving toward the stairs, giving George and Noah a wide berth. George was speaking into his radio, calling for backup and an ambulance. Katie stood beside him, and she looked up, noticing Ashley making her way to the stairway. Like George, Katie had been focused on Noah, but now that he was no longer a threat, she was considering the rest of the room.

"Are you okay?" Katie asked, falling in step beside Ashley. Her voice sounded muffled, like it couldn't completely permeate the daze surrounding Ashley.

"Yes," Ashley said, starting up the small flight of stairs.

"Where are you going?"

"Rachel," Ashley said. She knew it wouldn't make any sense to Katie. Katie didn't know Ashley had heard Rachel calling for help moments before Noah produced the gun. She would explain it all. Once she found Rachel.

"What about Rachel?"

"She's here."

"Here?" Katie said in disbelief.

"Yes," Ashley said, pressing a finger to her lips in the universal sign for quiet as she rushed up the remaining stairs with Katie close behind her. The house was silent now. The ambulance and backup deputies had arrived, whisking Noah off to the hospital before taking him to jail.

There was an L-shaped hallway at the top of the stairs with four closed doors. Ashley guessed one would be a bathroom and the other three bedrooms. Rachel would be in one of them. But which one? Ashley froze, listening intently, and as she did, she could hear the faint sounds of muffled cries coming from the second door. Ashley went straight for the door. She twisted the knob, her heart pounding. She didn't know what she'd find behind it. If Rachel had been hurt. If she'd been abused again . . .

As the door swung open, Rachel came into view. She was sitting in the middle of the room, curled up into a ball with her knees tucked up to her chest. It was completely dark aside from the light filtering in from the hallway. Rachel looked up, squinting at Ashley, and her beautiful, full lips twisted into a sneer.

"You shot her." Rachel spat. "You fucking shot her. I'm going to kill you. I don't know how. I don't know when. But I will. Consider that a promise."

"Rachel," Ashley said softly. "It's me."

"Ashley?" Rachel said, a sob catching in her throat. "I thought you were him."

"No. He's going to jail," Ashley said as she rushed toward Rachel, pulling her into her arms. They both began to cry then, hugging one another tightly.

"I thought you were dead," Rachel sobbed.

"I thought you were gone," Ashley replied.

They sat like that, crying and clinging to one another for several moments before their tears started to subside and Ashley pulled back. The words Rachel had said when she'd entered the room popped into her mind.

"You threatened to kill him," Ashley said. "While he held you captive."

Rachel shrugged. "I was trying to be strong. More like you. I didn't want to be scared anymore. Not after so many years of abuse."

Ashley hugged her tighter. "You were very brave. And anyone would be scared. I know I would be. Strength isn't about being fearless. It's about standing up for yourself in spite of that fear. That's what you did today."

Rachel nodded slowly.

Ashley noticed a bundle of fabric clutched tightly in Rachel's left hand. "What's that?"

"He used it to bind my wrists. I was going to try to strangle him with it."

Ashley looked at Rachel's wrists, they were a bright, angry red. Rubbed raw from twisting them against her restraints. "There should be an ambulance outside. Let's have them look at those burns, huh?"

Rachel glanced at her wrists. "I didn't realize I did that."

"Adrenaline," Ashley said as she helped Rachel to her feet.

Katie stood awkwardly in the doorway. She was Rachel's boss, and they were friends, but they'd never been particularly close. Not in the way that Ashley and Rachel were close or even in the way Ashley and Katie were close.

Ashley guided Rachel past Katie, keeping a hold of her arm in case she needed someone to lean on. Katie followed closely behind. They were all silent as they descended the steps and into the living area of the house. There was no need for words in that moment. There were splatters of Noah's blood in the living room, and they swerved past them to get to the front door. Once outside, they were met with a burst of activity. Noah was nowhere to be seen, but Brine County sheriff's deputies were everywhere. Some were hanging up crime scene tape, others were knocking on neighbors' doors looking for witnesses, and there was another cluster circled around George Thomanson right outside the entry.

"There they are," George said as he caught sight of Ashley and Katie. A bright smile lit up his features, but it quickly dropped when he saw Rachel. "What the—"

Katie put a hand up in a gesture for silence. "We will fill you in later. For now, let's get Rachel to a doctor." She sounded tired. Ashley felt the same way, now that the adrenaline was wearing off.

A few moments later, a second ambulance arrived, and they loaded Rachel up. She resisted, claiming that she wasn't hurt, but Ashley wasn't taking any chances. She loved Rachel like the daughter she never had, and she'd almost lost her.

"We'll meet you at the hospital," Ashley said, shortly before the ambulance doors slammed shut.

"Want to take my car?" Katie asked after a beat of silence.

"Yeah," Ashley said, watching the ambulance pull away. "My car is still at the office. I walked here to meet David."

"Where is he, by the way?" Katie said, glancing over her shoulder. "His car isn't here anymore."

"Don't know. Don't care," Ashley said with a sigh. He hadn't done anything to help Ashley when she needed it the most. Yes, he was frightened. She understood that. But she had been, too. And still, she'd had the wherewithal to keep Noah talking. If it wasn't for her—and Katie—she and David would both be dead.

"Let's get going, shall we?" Katie said.

They walked down the street and got into Katie's vehicle. Ashley's mind whirred during the short drive to the hospital, dissecting all that had happened over the past few days. No matter how she looked at it, she felt as though Rachel's kidnapping was her fault. If she hadn't helped represent Noah, if she hadn't been so effective at the preliminary hearing, he would have been sitting in jail. Instead, she'd gotten angry and wanted to prove a point to that jerk, Deputy Frankie Pitch. She'd proven her point, but also endangered Rachel. For the first time, she was starting to wonder if it was all worth it; the pride that came with winning.

"What's on your mind," Katie said as she pulled into the hospital parking spot and shut off her engine.

Ashley sighed heavily. "I just can't help feeling like this is my fault. What happened to Rachel. If I had refused to help David, then Noah would be in custody right now."

"Yes, that's true," Katie said slowly. "But we also wouldn't have the details of Erica's murder. They would have tried that case and likely lost, and then Noah would have been able to go free. Now the county attorney has the evidence he needs for Erica's murder and Rachel's kidnapping. Noah will be in prison for the rest of his life."

"At the expense of Rachel's mental health, which you and I both know was precarious before any of this happened."

"That will be a consequence of what happened, yes, but it's not your fault. Noah stalked her. His contact with her was unsolicited. You didn't ask for it, she didn't either. You're an attorney, not a psychic. Nobody can predict the future."

Ashley sighed. Katie was right, of course, but it didn't make her feel a whole lot better. Through her years of defense work, she'd been confronted with so many unintended consequences. From the murders of Arnold von Reich and Victor Petrovsky, Ashley's poisoning at Rachel's stepfather's hands, and now Rachel's kidnapping. It made her wonder if it was time to take Judge Ahrenson's advice and apply for a judgeship. Maybe it was time to move out of the world of criminal defense and let a younger attorney take the reins.

# EPILOGUE
## ASHLEY

Tuesday, December 24

The doorbell rang, and Ashley rushed to it, swinging it open. "Katie, George, thanks for coming."

"Smells good in here," George said, lifting his nose up into the air.

If someone had told Ashley a month ago that George Thomanson would be a Christmas guest, she would have thought they were insane. Yet, here he was.

"It's ham."

"Ham for Christmas?" Katie said, feigning disgust. "That's an abomination. Everyone knows turkey is for Christmas."

"Everyone? Really? Every single person on this earth other than me serves turkey for Christmas?"

"Basically," Katie said with a shrug. "Are you going to invite us in or leave us standing out in the cold?"

Ashley took a step back, motioning for them to enter. "Wine is in the kitchen, help yourself."

Katie's gaze turned toward the couch, where Rachel sat, cuddling with Ashley's two dogs. Since the kidnapping, Rachel had been staying with

Ashley. She would eventually go back to her aunt's house, Ashley knew that, but she was enjoying it while it lasted.

"How are you holding up, Rachel?"

"I'm fine. Actually, I have some news for you all."

"News?" Ashley said, cocking her head to the side. "Good or bad? I don't know that I can take any more bad news."

"Good . . . I think."

"Better get some booze for this one," George said, disappearing into the kitchen and returning with two very full glasses of red wine. He handed one to Katie and kept the other for himself.

Ashley grabbed her glass off the side table where she'd set it down to answer the door. "Okay, we're ready."

"I'm not going back to Aunt Stephanie's house."

Nobody said anything for a long moment, then Ashley said, "You aren't?"

"No. I'm going to stay here until the start of the next school semester."

Ashley blinked several times. She was happy to hear that Rachel planned to stay longer, but she didn't understand what school had to do with any of it. Rachel had been taking online classes ever since she'd graduated from high school. She was only a year and a half shy of obtaining her undergraduate degree. Ashley had assumed Rachel would continue taking classes as she always had.

"I need to get out of here. I mean, after everything that happened, I just, well, I need to leave for a bit. I'm going to move to Des Moines, finish out the semester in person. I plan to take the LSAT."

"The LSAT," Ashley repeated. "Like, as in law school LSAT?"

"Is there any other LSAT?"

"Good point," Ashley said. "Where do you want to go to school?"

"Drake. They have that 3+3 Program. Where the last year of undergrad counts as the first year of law school. I've taken all my online classes through Drake. So long as I do well enough on my LSAT, I should be a perfect fit for the program."

"You've done your research," Katie said, sitting in the chair across from Rachel. "I take it this means that you'll be resigning from your job with the MEHR team."

"Yes, sorry," Rachel said, shaking her head. "I can't go back there. Not after all this stuff with Noah."

Noah had been arrested and, shockingly, immediately pled guilty. There would be no trial, which was a relief to everyone. Another violent man locked away for life. Even though Noah wouldn't be around to cause problems, Ashley understood why Rachel would want to get away. It was time.

"Well, I think you'll make an excellent lawyer," Ashley said.

"And you'll make an excellent judge," George said from behind her.

Ashley whirled around to face him. "How did you know I was considering applying for Judge Ahrenson's position?"

He tapped his head. "I know everything. I have eyes and ears everywhere. I am King George, after all."

"You always have been a bit of an ass," Ashley said, but she was smiling.

It had been a rough couple of months, but they'd gotten through it. All of them. They had come out at the other end arguably better than before. Rachel was ready to spread her wings, going out to make her own way in the world. Katie and George were spending time together, and this time there was a spark that hadn't been there before. And Ashley, maybe Ashley would turn in that judge's application after all. If King George—of all people—thought she deserved it, then maybe she did.

# UNEXPECTED DEFENSE
## ASHLEY MONTGOMERY LEGAL THRILLER #5

As a prime location for wind energy, the locals in the small town of Brine, Iowa find themselves locked in a vicious battle with a wealthy oil company who is buying struggling farm properties to put up windmills. Half the town is for the windmill projects, the other half will stop at nothing to keep the iron giants out of their skyline. When the conflict turns violent, a murder shakes the town and leaves expert public defender Ashley Montgomery with a trial on her hands that is both criminal and political.

Meanwhile, Ashley is in the process of applying for a judgeship, a political position, while tasked with building a rock solid defense for her client who is charged with murdering a neighbor that had leased property for the construction of windmills. The more Ashley digs, the more ties she finds between her client, his alleged victim, and the Texas Oil company, forcing her to make a decision between her ethics as an attorney and her dreams of becoming a judge.

Desperate to find a balance between her ambitions and her client's needs, Ashley is faced with a near impossible task with conflicts of interest that run far deeper than she ever imagined.

Can Ashley navigate this turbulent case and come out on top? Or will she need to burn some bridges in the name of justice?

# ACKNOWLEDGMENTS

Writing is solitary work. It requires grit, imagination, and a commitment to do the work. It is an everyday grind to get the stories that form inside my head onto the page. It demands long hours in front of a blinking cursor, working through thoughts and words. Bringing a book all the way through trough the publication process takes a village. It requires the hearts, minds, and creativity of many. In that regard, I have so very many people to thank.

First, I must thank my family. My husband, Chris, and our children, H.S, M.S, W.S, for their ever-present love and support. You make every day an adventure. I am fortunate to have all of you in my life. My parents, Madonna, Dennis, Alan, and Tammy, and siblings, Stephanie, Anne, David, Rachel, Megan, Kristen, for your constant affection and unrelenting belief in me. You are all integral parts of my life. You have shaped who I am today. You created the early stories, some of which have bled their way into my characters and their lives.

A special thanks to my agent, Stephanie Hansen, of Metamorphosis Literary Agency. Her constant determination and encouragement created the gateway for my books to see publication. Without her, this book would not exist. She literally makes dreams come true.

Thank you to all members of the Severn River Publishing Team. You saw potential in my books and in me. Your professionalism, organization, and attention to detail transformed a good book into a fantastic series. You continue to put time and effort into the success of each and every one of my novels. You have made the publication process, a sometimes frightening and overwhelming procedure, a truly enjoyable experience.

Finally, I want to thank all the public defenders out there. This book is my wholehearted thank you for the work that you do every day. I am not one of you anymore, but I will always remember the days I spent fighting alongside you. You deserve applause. You deserve recognition. You deserve respect.

# ABOUT THE AUTHOR

Laura Snider is a practicing lawyer in Iowa. She graduated from Drake Law School in 2009 and spent most of her career as a Public Defender. Throughout her legal career she has been involved in all levels of crimes from petty thefts to murders. These days she is working part-time as a prosecutor and spends the remainder of her time writing stories and creating characters.

Laura lives in Iowa with her husband, three children, two dogs, and two very mischievous cats.

Sign up for Laura Snider's newsletter at
severnriverbooks.com/authors/laura-snider